Praise for the previous works of
SUSAN R. MATTHEWS

"An extremely talented writer."
Martha Wells, author of *The Death of the Necromancer*

"Powerful . . . compelling."
Locus for *Prisoner of Conscience*

"Powerful, insidious, and insightful—
a singular achievement."
Melanie Rawn, author of the *Exiles* series for
An Exchange of Hostages

"Clarity, consistency, and readability . . .
one of the best SF books of the year."
Starlog for *Prisoner of Conscience*

"An intelligently written book full of
unexpected moments of beauty."
Sherwood Smith, author of *Crown Duel* for
An Exchange of Hostages

"Susan Matthews is a writer to watch—and to
keep away from explosives and sharp objects."
Debra Doyle, co-author of the *Mageworld* series

AVALANCHE SOLDIER

SUSAN R. MATTHEWS

AVON · EOS

This is a work of fiction. Names, characters, places, and incidents either are the product of the author's imagination or are used fictitiously. Any resemblance to actual events, locales, organizations, or persons, living or dead, is entirely coincidental and beyond the intent of either the author or the publisher.

AVON BOOKS, INC.
1350 Avenue of the Americas
New York, New York 10019

Copyright © 1999 by Susan R. Matthews
Excerpt from *Signal to Noise* copyright © 1998 by Eric S. Nylund
Excerpt from *The Death of the Necromancer* copyright © 1998 by Martha Wells
Excerpt from *Scent of Magic* copyright © 1998 by Andre Norton
Excerpt from *The Gilded Chain* copyright © 1998 by Dave Duncan
Excerpt from *Krondor the Betrayal* copyright © 1998 by Raymond E. Feist
Excerpt from *Mission Child* copyright © 1998 by Maureen F. McHugh
Excerpt from *Avalanche Soldier* copyright © 1999 by Susan R. Matthews
Cover art by Chris Moore
Published by arrangement with the author
Library of Congress Catalog Card Number: 99-94996
ISBN: 0-380-80315-1
www.avonbooks.com/eos

First Avon Eos Printing: December 1999

AVON EOS TRADEMARK REG. U.S. PAT. OFF. AND IN OTHER COUNTRIES, MARCA REGISTRADA, HECHO EN U.S.A.

Printed in the U.S.A.

WCD   10 9 8 7 6 5 4 3 2 1

This book is respectfully dedicated to citizen soldiers and to the police: the people we expect to make the "right" decision with no time to consider, and never enough information, in full knowledge of the inescapable fact that there's no going back on a decision with a bullet behind it.

To the "real" Avalanche Soldiers, ski patrols and mountain disaster rescue teams, the people who dedicate their lives to responding to day trips or mountain climbs gone wrong.

And especially to my father, who taught us from the beginning that there is no refuge or absolution in the illusion of certainty where other people's lives are concerned; and who raised us up warriors.

One

From where she stood poised and tense at the end of the line of the avalanche soldiers in her squad, Salli Rangarold—tall and sleekly muscled, her long brown hair tied up in a heavy braid at the nape of her neck—could see across the narrow valley to the shrine that was to be consecrated today.

It was the Day of Deliverance, the annual remembrance of the arrival of the first of the Prodigal ships from the dying colonies in space. The shrine that stood waiting for consecration housed what was left of the last of the Prodigal ships to return to Creation before the great silence had fallen across the interstellar lanes, and the colonies were given up as lost.

That had been more than three hundred years ago; and no one had risked the loving rebuke of an offended God by taking to the air since the ship christened *Forlorn Hope* had crashed here. It had been snowing on that fateful day, and the ship had escaped more severe damage partially because the snow was winter-deep and had compacted beneath the transport as it staggered to get to ground.

Its power plant unstable, its air contaminated, no potable water left on board, and no proper clothing either on bodies long grown used to the easeful warmth of the tropical alien environment of the colonies—the refugees

1

had walked out into the snow, across the valley, through Needle's-Eye Pass and down the mountainside to the cities of the great prairie beyond, carrying with them such tales of horror . . .

It was a beautiful day for a consecration; Salli scanned the snowy mountainous horizon, smiling in pure pleasure at the glories of Creation despite the tense state of her nerves. Late winter; the sun shone on a brilliant pristine field of new-fallen snow. There was just enough of a breeze to be pleasant against one's face without reminding one of the actual ambient temperature.

She took a deep breath, drinking the air like cold water on a warm summer's day. The air smelled crisp and clean, newly washed after several days of light but constant powder-snow precipitation scrubbing the inevitable atmospheric pollutants that the great and invisible currents of the wind carried over the prairies and toward the holy state of Shadene east of the mountains.

"Who-all is coming a' this event?" Sharka asked suddenly, from the middle of the line. Halfway up the slope of the sides of the Needle's-Eye Pass, there was no danger of his being overheard; and the event was not yet formally under way.

Squad Leader Morrissey—one of the shorter run of Pilgrim people, with a good deal of red in his moustache for which no one would dream of faulting him—shifted his weight fractionally on his skis before he answered. At least Salli expected that he did. Morrissey was at the other end of the line, two teams—one squad—bracketed between the two of them, squad leader and second team leader.

"Reps from most of Creation, things being quiet. Speaker Tarish from the Prairie States. Peraille of the Islands. Mother Aire from the Long Coast, Nesfiter from the Ice. Even the Parliamentarian from the Grand Convention."

The Orthodox states of Creation had come together to regulate church affairs and manage political concerns alike, and the Parliamentarian was that Grand Convention's single most influential officer. There was only one non-Orthodox state in Creation: and that was an irony of sorts, because the single non-Orthodox state in Creation was the secular authority that governed the holy land of Shadene itself.

From whose mountains, these mountains, the Revelation had come, over two thousand years ago.

In whose mountains, these mountains, the holiest of all Orthodox shrines still remained—shrines holy to Orthodox and Shadene heterodox alike.

"No representative from our own government? Come on."

Shadene was ruled by a secular government, elected by a franchise extended equally to Orthodox citizens in residence there and the heterodox Wayfarers that formed a scant majority of aboriginal people. In Shadene alone Orthodox were required to suffer living and working with people of a debased and degraded theology, political penance for an act of petty discrimination that dated back eight hundred years.

When the Prodigals had first set out to establish colonies in space, they left the Wayfarers behind—and during the five hundred years between the establishment of the first colonies and the catastrophic collapse of the same, the Wayfarers, left to themselves on Creation, had swallowed Shadene whole; and convinced themselves that they had been there all along.

"There'll be Teacher Sheylune from the Church," Salli corrected. If she was remembering her briefing correctly, at least . . ."Sadrilla from the Secular Authority. No heterodox."

Good taste on their part to stay away, too. Heterodox

and Orthodox were still learning to live with each other.
Even after so long a time.

"Your people were on this ship, weren't they, Salli?"
Allyx asked, with respect. "How does it feel to be here?"

Yes, her lineage had returned to Creation on the *Forlorn Hope*; convention assigned her that status on the basis of four ancestors, four ancestors only, out of how
many after three hundred years? But before she could
answer, Morrissey kicked one of his ski sticks out to the
side—a gesture small enough to be glossed over as
meaningless if anyone noticed it, but one that his squad
knew meant that they were to pay attention.

"Mark on your fields for observation, and report.
Salli."

Time to work. Salli felt a little thrill of excitement; suppressed it. She was an avalanche soldier. This was what
she did. It was just that she wasn't quite senior enough
not to get keyed up when the action started—

"From between Vennor and Hopkins, second squad,
to between Ellan and Phibs. Third squad. To the cordon."

Second and third squads were downslope, and their
assigned fields extended all the way to the pilgrim path
itself. Solt stood next to Salli, and his field overlapped—

"Between Ellan and Phibs, to between Eagen and Mollony. To the cordon, Squad Leader."

No confusion. No blind areas. Salli stamped her foot
as far as the ski's bindings would give. She didn't know
if she was scared: she never did. It didn't matter. It only
mattered if fear interfered.

"We're on, squad. Let's do it. Remember your briefing,
now."

Right.

The access to their shrine of assignment was to be controlled from the other side of the pass, the Eye of the
Needle, a cleft so deep between two towering scarps of

solid rock that the sun never reached the ground for
more than a few moments out of any given day.

Through the Eye of the Needle the refugees of the *Forlorn Hope* had staggered in the snow toward salvation,
toward rebirth of a sort. Through the Eye of the Needle
the pilgrims would come, approaching the shrine on foot
in respect for the Prodigals who had gone before.

There were always faithful first in line where a shrine
was to be consecrated, people whose lives revolved
around collecting as many shrine-stamps as possible.
They would be through first.

It only took twenty minutes to clear the Eye of the
Needle on foot, what with the ground scraped and
leveled and paved; and a crowd in attendance as the
dignitaries arrived—humbly on foot, like everybody
else—was good window dressing for the newscasts.

The first of the pilgrims were coming through now,
channeled by Security to stand behind the cordon that
lined the pilgrim track to wait for the church leaders
who would perform the consecration ceremony. Second
and third squads spaced themselves downslope according to the predetermined interval, and Salli marked her
field of observation.

Pilgrims in this weather were hard to tell one from
another, because everyone wore coats and hats or hoods
or cloaks to keep warm. Only a very few fanatics were
there without winter garments, determined to walk the
distance like the Prodigals of the *Forlorn Hope* itself,
dressed only for the tropical paradise-turned-hell from
which they'd fled and functionally naked in the snow.

She had been trained, and trained, and trained in iden-
tifying what a person looked like from behind as they
drew a weapon or armed a grenade.

More than one of the pilgrims she watched wrapped
their arms around their torsos for warmth, or folded
their arms; she had to watch carefully. The first run of

pilgrims was clear of the Eye of the Needle now, the newscasts all focused on the empty pilgrim path that led out of the darkness into the brilliant sunlight. The pilgrims were drably dressed, by and large, and Salli appreciated the utility of the dark colors for cutting the glare of the snow.

She scanned her field.

Pilgrims with their arms wrapped around themselves for warmth, yes; but why would a man be cold in a thermal greatcoat?

It was a Shadene greatcoat. A Wayfarer greatcoat.

Salli focused on one man, reminding herself not to jump to conclusions. There was more than one pilgrim wearing Shadene—even Wayfarer—clothing; she herself wore Wayfarer-style winter clothing in the mountains of Shadene when not in uniform. The Shadene Wayfarers were the people who had adapted to life in these cold environs, after all. Plenty of Prodigal blood had settled in Shadene, and she was as good an example of that as anyone. There was no reason to be suspicious of the man simply because he wore a Wayfarer coat, which heterodox also wore. If anything, any terrorist would naturally disguise himself so as not to give Security a second thought—unless wearing a Wayfarer coat was a complicated double bluff.

One way or the other, the man that Salli watched would have no reason to be cold; so why did he hug himself?

What did he hug to himself?

The pilgrims behind the cordon to either side of the pilgrim track downslope were getting restless, excited, watching the Eye of the Needle. So the priests and heads of state would be clearing the shadows soon, and coming out into the light.

Salli watched her man raise his right arm, as if to shield his eyes from the sun.

But the sun was to his left.

And there was a bulge at the back of his shoulder.

He had a mortar up his sleeve, or an avalanche gun, a rocket-propelled grenade launcher; and as Salli watched, he tilted his arm until his elbow pointed at the sidewall of the Eye of the Needle.

He meant to bring down the pass itself upon the heads of the consecration party, and bury them all in the rock-fall.

How could she be sure?

She had no time to ask for a second opinion.

She broke the safety on her own avalanche gun and brought it to her shoulder, aiming, focusing.

"Down in front!"

Second squad, third squad dropped so that she could fire over them; her own squad, her teammates, snapped to crouched attentiveness. Waiting for her shot to set out in chase. They didn't know what she was looking at, they couldn't see that man, his head turned toward her—as if he'd heard, as if he knew that she had noticed him. As soon as his head turned toward her, though, it snapped back with renewed concentration on the un-natural angle of his right arm.

Perhaps the others had seen it, too, by now.

Salli couldn't afford to rely on that.

She fired her avalanche gun; and the crowd-control round struck the pilgrim she suspected at the bulging point in the back of his right shoulder, knocking him to the ground.

The cordon closed across the entrance to the Eye of the Needle; Security would move everyone back out to the other side, but Salli had no time to appreciate the precision and efficiency of well-drilled troops as they re-sponded to the situation. Salli pushed off on her skis as soon as she had fired, and headed downslope past squads two and three, homing in on her target.

Pilgrims scattered right and left, scrambling in the trampled snow. The man Salli wanted struggled to his feet and sprinted desperately into the nearest clump of pilgrims to hide himself in their numbers. He was wounded; there was blood on the snow.

He couldn't move fast enough. The crowd of pilgrims drew away from him, and would not give him shelter.

Salli had the speed, she was on skis. She had her bolo. Discarding one of her ski poles, steering by the more primitive single-stick method, Salli set her bolo whirling overhead and unleashed it as she sped past her prey struggling in the snow.

The terrorist staggered drunkenly under the impact of the bolo's kinetic energy, trying to keep his feet; then went down, and lay there, and there were three squads of avalanche soldiers to make sure that he didn't make any sudden moves. Salli cut her turn sharply to stop herself and stood for a moment, staring into the crowd.

The crowd stared back.

All right, she'd done it, but what had she done?

Had she stopped a terrorist attack on the assembled dignitaries?

Or had she given some harmless soul the surprise of his life?

She ratcheted her feet free from her skis, and walked back upslope to see.

The man she'd shot was sitting on the ground, sitting in the snow, and second squad had laid his armament out to one side—rocket-propelled grenade launcher; air-burst grenades. The kind used for heavy-duty demolition. The round that Salli had fired had impacted against the man's shoulder but didn't seem to have done too much harm. He looked up at Salli with frustrated hatred in his cold clear Wayfarer eyes, and spat.

Terrorist, then.

Shadene Wayfarer terrorist, blue eyes the color of the

thin ice coat over the rim of an anchor on a cold winter's morning; blond.

She should have trusted her instinct. There was no reason for her to have hesitated for a single moment.

She turned away to collect her skis and find her discarded pole. She was responsible for her equipment. There would be a debriefing.

She had done her duty, and been vindicated. She had been privileged to protect the people from the fearful consequences of a terrorist attack.

It was good to be an avalanche soldier on days like today.

Three days later, and Salli Rangarold sat at ease in Colonel Janelric's office. There was a stack of message prints on the cover of the colonel's desk and a wonderful view of the shrine through the glassy apertures in the wall behind the desk. Colonel Janelric herself was in an expansive mood, leaning well back in the worn chair she'd brought with her from their previous duty station, her feet up on the desk.

"The review board's report has come in, Salli. I'm not supposed to let you see it, of course."

Of course. The review board's members were strictly anonymous as far as Salli was concerned. All she knew was that one would be from her squad and one from the more senior officers in her unit, as well as representation from both Heterodox and Orthodox churches and the Shadene secular authority.

The role of the avalanche soldier was much less controversial than that of the pilgrim police. Avalanche soldiers protected not just Orthodox shrines, but also kept recreational mountain facilities technically open to all free from terrorist attack.

The pilgrim police, on the other hand, had the unenviable task of protecting the Pilgrim enclaves from increasingly violent attempts on the part of mostly inner-city Wayfarers to forcibly reduce their boundaries. Not exactly the same thing as terrorism, and Salli was proud of her brother for doing the harder—if less glamorous, less elite—job. Meeka was a policeman.

So even the avalanche soldiers were reviewed by heterodox and Orthodox alike whenever a terrorist was apprehended, to satisfy any potential heterodox mutterings about trigger-happy, prejudiced Pilgrims in positions of power. Salli wasn't worried. This one had come out as cleanly as any poor soldier could hope.

"So I won't let you see it." Colonel Janelric waved the folder around in the air, casually. "But I can let you know. The score is 'fully justifiable.' As good as it gets. Oh, all right, there is one. Technical. Reservation on the record, for information only," Colonel Janelric admitted, taking her feet down and squaring herself to her desk. "This part I'm supposed to tell you." Leaning on her forearms, with her hands clasped in front of her.

Salli felt a twinge of concern: a reservation clause? Someone found fault with an aspect of her performance?

What could she have done differently?

But the look on the colonel's genial face was relaxed and good-humored, her dark eyes glittering with a secret joke. Colonel Janelric's eyes tended to disappear when she smiled. It was a function of her perfect Pilgrim cheekbones.

"A 'technical reservation without criticism implied' has been placed in the record and is to be duly communicated to you. Under the provisions of . . . so, so, so . . . this information is for your information only and does not constitute a critical or derogatory entry to your service record."

Yes, they both knew the language. For all of Colonel Janelric's informality Salli felt herself becoming tense. Wasn't it a bit warm in here?

"All right, then. You ready?—You should have shot him in the elbow, not the shoulder, to minimize the possibility of the gun going off. Failing that, you should have aimed for the buttocks in order to knock him backwards so that the round if fired would go straight up in the air. I'm not saying whose idea that is, of course. Name three hypercritical Shadene secular authority— oops, I didn't say that, did I?"

Salli relaxed.

And then got irritated.

As a technical reservation it was in truth technical in the extreme; and she could think of only one person in the cadre of Shadene secular authority officers charged with training and oversight of avalanche soldiers who could possibly have put something so petty-minded on record with a straight face.

"Colonel Travers. Son of a bitch. With respect, ma'am."

Colonel Janelric only smiled, confirming Salli's guess. What was it that Colonel Travers had against her? He was one of the single most unfathomable men in cadre, too, Wayfarer half-breed, eyes in the back of his head, no sense of humor—at least no sense of humor that ever fell out to the benefit of a poor inoffensive avalanche soldier cadet. No allowing for mere standards, and that was what he had against her, now that she thought about it.

The fact that she had passed all of her marksmanship tests meant nothing to Colonel Travers. He had decided that she could shoot better than the standards required. And here he was, months after her graduation, still demanding that she shoot better than anybody else to gain the same scores—not because the standards required it, but simply because he thought she could.

She'd forgotten how much she resented that, till now.

And Colonel Janelric had sobered up.

"Well, Salli. Just one more thing before I let you go. This is not going to be good news, I'm afraid." Passing a message print across the desk, Colonel Janelric met Salli's eyes with a frown of concerned sympathy.

For what?

"Here's news from the chief of police at the Pannath Enclave. Take a moment to read it, please."

Pannath Enclave was where Meeka worked—

It is with reluctance that I inform you, Salli read.

After a moment the meaning of the phrase clarified in Salli's mind: it wasn't "Sad duty compels me to report" or "It is my melancholy responsibility to tell you"—so Meeka wasn't dead.

But the inquest hearing wasn't scheduled for weeks yet, so Meeka could not have been convicted by some bizarre and disastrous turn of injustice of having killed the man rioting in the street that day on purpose, rather than by tragic and bitterly regretted mischance in the proper and lawful performance of his assigned duties.

So what could be wrong?

Salli shook her head to clear it of the buzzing confusion of wonder and speculation that all but addled her. Concentrate. All she had to do was concentrate, and she'd know soon enough.

Again.

Focusing on the message print, Salli started over.

. . . having failed to report for duty on three consecutive shifts we went to Meeka Rangarold's residence and found there evidence of intent to depart his place of duty without leave. Subsequent research efforts have been nonproductive. It is my painful duty to report your brother absent without leave under suspicious circumstances. I will be glad to personally meet with you at your earliest convenience to discuss any aspect of this most regrettable situation.

Salli set the message print down and stared at Colonel Janelric's concerned face, unseeing.

Meeka had run away.

Rather than face the inquest hearing into the accidental death of that wretched Wayfarer rioter, Meeka had run away, deserted his unit, abandoned his sworn duty—Meeka, her brother, her role model, her idol—

"Three weeks' leave," Colonel Janelric said finally, standing up from her desk to let Salli know that she should get up and go away now. "Keep us posted, Salli, let us know if there's anything we can do to help. The details don't have to go any farther than this office unless you choose. See you in three weeks."

Meeka, absent without leave.

When every evidence of slippage in the normal administrative processes of the Shadene secular state could be used by the Orthodox nations that surrounded them as yet one more reason why Orthodox should intervene—oh, out of pure benevolence, of course—and install a more stable government than one based on the elected representatives of heterodox as well as Orthodox citizens of Shadene . . .

She could not fathom it.

Numb with shock, Salli nodded in appreciation of the grant of leave, remembering almost as an afterthought that she ought to salute.

Meeka had run away.

This had to be a mistake of some sort: and she had better get to Pannath Enclave right away, to find out what it was and make it right.

Salli stood in the center of the darkened room, staring at nothing in particular.

This was her brother's small apartment in Pannath Enclave. Meeka lived here. Meeka used to live here. She

had been living here for three weeks now, three weeks
that felt like so many years. Three weeks.

Three weeks in which her world had fallen into sense-
less chaos, three weeks in which everything that had
given meaning and order to her life had failed her.

Three weeks ago—

Three weeks ago she had been Salli Rangarold, an avalanche soldier, recently distinguished in action. Three
weeks ago she had been the loyal daughter of the Orthodox church, a world citizen of Prodigal stock residing
in the holy land of Shadene and serving all faithful souls
by providing protection against terrorism to those who
came to worship at the shrines in Shadene's holy Revelation Mountains.

And now.

Within the space of three weeks.

Meeka was away without leave, and through careful
investigation aided by the Shadene secular authority's
undercover agents Salli—as well as Meeka's chain of
command—knew where Meeka had gone to, at least in
a general sense. Meeka had run away to the Heterodox.
Meeka had hidden himself in the closed community of
the Shadene Wayfarer population.

Meeka had turned tail, turned apostate, renounced his
religion and run to some Wayfarer teacher-without-
portfolio or another, one of the number of so-called religious teachers outside the pale of authorized teaching
that kept the Wayfarer heterodox in such a constant fer-
ment of discontent and rage.

Meeka Rangarold, the child of Prodigals, had forsaken
the austere purity of awaiting the one true Orthodox
Teacher in favor of plunging into the heterodox promiscuity of teacher after teacher after teacher. Each with a
piece of the truth. Each in turn Awakening the world in
some small incremental way.

She could hardly believe it.

And she wouldn't stand for it.

How could such shameful behavior be countenanced? It was intolerable.

The only solution was to make it right, to wake Meeka from whatever altered state of consciousness made his madness possible, to bring Meeka back to be reconciled to the true faith of the Prodigal. To stand the judgment that was owing for the accidental death of a Shadene Wayfarer rioting in the streets—and quiet the vocal condemnation of the ethnic Shadene press that chose to interpret Meeka's disappearance as a cover-up.

She had to find her brother, and bring him back.

It was something that she had to do alone; and that meant accepting dishonor and opprobrium for desertion on her own part, because if the tenuous connections she had made with the Wayfarer religious underground believed her to be acting in any official capacity she would lose credibility.

Meeka had deserted; she would be a deserter. Meeka had fled to some unauthorized Wayfarer cult that offered him absolution for a crime that had not been a crime, the accidental death of the rioter. She would not do that. She would seek her brother. It was a value that Wayfarers and Pilgrims had in common, the importance of family; it would be enough to justify her quest, and even win her some small degree of sympathetic cooperation.

Three weeks.

The police in Pannath knew she had to report back to her duty station at the *Forlorn Hope* shrine. Colonel Janelric knew that she was in transit from Pannath. It would be a few days before anyone really wondered where she was, for Colonel Janelric could reasonably assume that she might be delayed at Pannath for last-minute business, and Pannath wouldn't think twice about her leaving until they got the inquiry that would come from the *Forlorn Hope* shrine.

One last look around.

Her trekking gear was cached at the trailhead to the Fernifax Park. The Wayfarer pilgrimage season was beginning; Wayfarers by the hundreds would pass through Fernifax and thence into the forbidden zones, the sacred precincts of the Revelation Mountains.

The avalanche soldiers and the Shadene secular authority did not prosecute such pilgrimages.

Wayfarers went on foot for tradition's sake and to do the least amount of ecological damage, and the foot pilgrimages were an ancient and honorable part of their religion.

It was only to recreational or other development that the forbidden zone was forbidden; in practice, forbidden to Orthodox but permitted to Wayfarers, so long as they went in small groups and did not call attention to themselves.

She would go to Fernifax Park and make herself useful and wait. It would be the single best place to listen for news of Meeka, and once she had news she would know what to do with it.

Salli let her eyes travel full sweep across the small apartment, marking for remembrance all that she meant to turn her back on.

Meeka's pictures, Meeka's things, but things that spoke as well to who she was and the privileged position she had enjoyed.

Her graduation from her cadet class, a picture taken by a friend, Salli looking all-knowing and serene in the first flush of qualification and Meeka grinning ear to ear with his arms wrapped around her in a bear hug.

The standard shrine-frame with their genealogy back to the time of Return, and the Sacred Promise at its foot:

That insofar as God has brought us safely out of the colonies of death and back to the sacred ground of Creation once again, we will not take to the air by any means from this time forward; and trust in this way to preserve our children from the evil fate that has befallen the once-proud colonies of Creation.

Their parents, mother and father in opposing frames to leave space for the little floral wreath and its tag that decorated their mother's picture. *Blessed martyr in memory, Promise-keeper.* Their mother had been buried in an avalanche at the ski resort of Barift Lake; dug out alive, but died before evacuation, of injuries that would not have been life-threatening had aerial evacuation been available to move her to a hospital in time.

The incident had occurred during one of the periodic demands that the Promise be qualified to allow air transport for humanitarian purposes; Salli could remember that much, but little else about her mother. Their father had raised them, with their aunt Ishan. And Aunt Ishan would die of rage and shame if she ever found out about Meeka's apostasy.

Father was dead.

There was no danger there.

Finally, a card that Salli had added to Meeka's small display. Congratulations on the award of a medal, in connection with her good work at the opening day of the *Forlorn Hope* shrine. Signed by her platoon, with ribald comments from her own squad and team members.

It was a lot to turn her back on: her ancestry, her position in the elite ranks of the avalanche soldiers, her duty and her honor.

But the only way to redeem her family honor—to reawaken Meeka to his duty, to bring him back to face that wretched but all-important hearing—was to turn away and accept the contemptible name of a deserter until such time as she could atone for her act by restoring Meeka to his true position.

Salli stared at the pictures of their parents for long moments, trying to make the faces change. Trying to see some evidence of approval or disapproval there, and finding nothing.

No help there, then.

Lights off, heat off, power off, no perishables left to rot in the cooler, no dirty laundry. No unmade bed. No loose cash: she needed all she could lay hands on, to minimize the dangers of being tracked by the audit trail when she was forced to pull a cash packet on account by voice-authorize.

No pets to be fed.

Turning around, finally, Salli stepped across the threshold into the hall, closing the door behind her. Pulling it to with a decisive snap of the latch as it engaged.

An end to a whole era in her life.

With God's help, the beginning of Meeka's rescue.

Looking neither to the left nor right, Salli hurried down the stairs out to the street, to make her way to the trailhead at Fernifax Park.

Two

It lacked several minutes yet before actual sunbreak, given that it was early fall already. Salli eased the front of her right shoulder into a braced position against the papery bark of the highpalm tree that sheltered her and tapped the focus on the field glasses that she wore, frowning down in concentration at the small Wayfarers' camp below.

They would have to come out of the dormitory to reach the washhouse, and they'd have to do it soon. Morning prayers was one of the things that heterodox and Orthodox—Wayfarers and Pilgrims—had in common, and no faithful child of Revelation would think of "opening the mouth to praise the Awakening" with the taint of sleep still upon him.

The door to the long low sleeping house swung open. Salli tensed. *Come on, Meeka*, she whispered to herself, her breath so still it didn't so much as stir the layered mat of fallen palm fronds on which she lay stretched out behind the tree trunk. *I know you're in there. Come out. I have things I want to say to you.*

The camp below was an artifact from olden days, four hundred years old by the thatching of the steeply sloped roofs with their overhanging eaves. Not a Pilgrim camp by any means. No, this was a Wayfarer camp, built by the interlopers who had occupied the holy land in the years after the Pilgrims had left for their colonies in the sky—centuries ago.

A leftover, an anachronism, part of the heritage of Shadene and its long history of pilgrimage to the Revelation Mountains, where the Awakening had first been prophesied. Shadene, where the heterodoxy that had stolen Meeka away from her flourished.

And before the Awakened One she had a thing or two to tell him about that—just as soon as she could find him by himself, and get him away from these people. . . .

Older people first. Three men and two women, heading off in different directions. The men's washhouse was little more than an open shed, though there wasn't anything for her to see from her vantage point halfway up the slope to the hillcrest. The women's washroom was more fully enclosed. That was where the hot springs would be, then.

Where was Meeka?

The sun would clear the east ridge within moments, and yet no man of Meeka's size or shape had left the sleeping house. In fact the younger people were already hurrying out to wash, and no adults whatever between old folks and the young, so what was going on here?

Then even as Salli realized that she knew the answer, she heard the little friction of fabric moving against fabric behind her. Felt rather than heard the footfall in the heavy mat of fallen palm fronds that cushioned her prone body like a feather bed. Well, of course she didn't see any able-bodied men in camp below. They were all out here, on the hillside.

Looking for her.

"Good morning, pilgrim, and it's a beautiful morning. Even if it is only a Dream."

She heard the voice behind her: careful and wary. But a little amused. Yes, they had her, no question about it. She could have kicked the cushioning greenfall into a flurry in frustration. But she was at the disadvantage; she had to be circumspect.

"How much more beautiful the Day we Wake." And what did she have to worry about, really? Nothing. These were Wayfarer heterodox, true, or if they weren't she was very much mistaken. But there were rules of civility. She had meant to get Meeka by himself, without betraying her presence; but she had every right to have come here on her errand. "Say, I imagine you're wondering what this is all about."

Now that she was discovered she had no further need to huddle behind the trunk of the great tree. Salli put her hands out to either side of her, carefully, moving slowly to avoid startling anybody. She didn't have any tricks up her sleeve. She wasn't going to try to pretend otherwise.

"That would actually seem, pardon the language, obvious." The tone of voice was utterly grave, but there was no missing the buried good-natured joke in it. Jelock city accent. Jelock city natives put a lot more music into their cadence than people from more barren places in Shadene. "We're accustomed to being watched. No Wayfarer's allowed into these mountains without leave, after all, even though they are our mountains."

That was a little overstated, but true enough. And gave Salli her cue. Salli rolled over onto her back and hiked herself up into a seated position so that she could lean up against the trunk of the forest giant in which she'd spent the night, thinking all the while.

"And yet what is ever what it seems, in the land of the living illusion?"

She was angry at herself for having been found out, and her voice sounded harsh and hostile in her own ears. She had to be careful. There was no sense in provoking a confrontation.

Unstrapping her field glasses with an irritated tug at

the catch at the back of her head, Salli rubbed her eyes,
squinting up at the man who confronted her. Men. There
was more than one of them, moving so quietly in the
early dawn that Salli had heard no sound to announce
their presence. "What's next?"

"Carib, it's the pilgrim police," someone called out;
Salli knew he didn't mean it literally. The pilgrim police
were nowhere near this camp, or her name wasn't Salli
Rangarold, which it was. Wayfarers frequently lumped
the avalanche soldiers together with the pilgrim police,
out of hostility for both organizations. "She's probably
called the dogs. Let's neutralize her and be away from
here, while we still can."

But instead of responding immediately, the man who
had been talking hunkered down on his heels to lock
eyes with Salli. He had a square and somewhat fleshy
face, with a mouth gone wrong years ago and soured
there since. Clear blue eyes like so many of the Shadene.
Blue eyes were cold and heartless. Salli suppressed a
shudder. She'd done nothing wrong, even if she was one
of the enemy. She only wanted to see Meeka, and convince him to come home.

"If she'd called any dogs we'd have heard them by
now, Farlu. No. Let's all go down to the meeting house
where we can talk about this. Then we'll find out—"

Someone was coming down the slope toward her as
Carib spoke, though, and Salli's heart turned over in her
chest. Made her sick to her stomach with longing and
short of breath at one and the same time.

"No need."

Carib paused, clearly a little surprised to be interrupted. Salli knew the voice, if the face itself was strange
with a beard and half-wild about the eyes with the horror that had taken him. He came up beside her, reaching
down to raise her to her feet, steadying her as she rose;
she knew his hands and his strength, and the smell of

his clothing. Meeka. Meeka, but so strange.

"And I can't let you make any threats, Farlu, not even just talk. If she'd wanted to bring the police they'd be on us already. I can explain this, Carib, there's no problem here."

By the look on his face Carib half believed that he knew Meeka's explanation already. Salli flushed a fierce crimson. All right, maybe it did look that way. They'd always been close. But only so close as they should be, and no closer.

"No, it's not what you think," she said firmly, before Carib could answer. She was cold and she was hungry, she was tired, and she'd been walking for days to find her Meeka. To find out what had happened to him. To shake him loose of whatever baleful Shadene influence had poisoned his mind, and make him come back. Passion and fatigue made her reckless; she shook off Meeka's steadying hand and turned down the slope to descend toward the camp, flinging one final taunt over her shoulder.

"Meeka is my brother."

Then Salli shut everything else in the world out of her mind, to focus on walking—not falling—down to the camp, where the enemy lay in wait for her.

Wayfarer heterodox.

And they had taken her brother away.

Once a person no longer had to be concerned about concealing a person's presence, a person could move much more quickly through the trees and down into the camp. Salli trod her path through the thick springy mats of greenfall with deliberation and due care, mindful of the people coming up around her. Her disgust with the entire situation did not quite swamp her sense of self-preservation. She was angry and frustrated; but she was also in a distinct minority, here, whether or not anyone had threatened her with any actual violence.

It would be better all around if she refrained from doing anything that might shift her status from that of an uninvited, unexpected, and mostly unwilling guest to that of an official representative of a mistrusted authority alone in a hostile camp well removed from any immediate source of aid.

Meeka came up on her left side to walk with her and shelter her brother-wise as they moved down into the camp. The sun was rising; they would miss prayers if they didn't hurry. Why should she be concerned about it? They were the enemy. They had stolen Meeka away from her.

Halfway down the hillside, and the sun broke through the lower branches of the forest canopy, clearing the eastern ridge. Salli heard a voice.

"Behold she rises, like the Awakening."

A deep voice, behind her, above her on the slope. Passionate and powerful; and then voices spoke in response, tenor, bass, and baritone in a sort of minor chord that made harmony out of dissonance.

"Like the Awakening. Holy One, let us also see the light of the truth of the waking world."

She should have known better. These were Wayfarers. Prayer was not an option: it was as necessary as breathing, and as natural.

"The waking world rises, opening its eyes to the light of truth. Behold, she rises."

Let us also wake.

The entire camp was in full voice, now, around her, behind her, before her in the camp itself. The music raised the small hairs at the back of Salli's neck. *Let us also wake.* She knew the prayer; and it was an effort not to raise her own voice, to pray with her enemies as one congregation.

That would be presumptuous of her, though. She did

not belong there and had no intention of staying longer than to bring Meeka to his senses. It wasn't so much arrogance or disliked heterodoxy as delicacy of feeling, Salli told herself.

As the sun rises on the mountain, let us also wake. Behold, she rises. Let us also wake.

Then there was a silence that reverberated through the camp like a species of noise in itself. Salli could almost reach out and touch that great stillness, void of noise in the absence of noise. She shook herself. It had been a long night; she was tired and cold. And hungry.

Meeka took her by the elbow and walked her to the common hall, holding the slat door open from behind as she climbed the steps. Salli smelled breakfast and stopped abruptly, feeling awkward, thinking fast. She was alone here. They had her outnumbered. She hadn't ever meant to get into such a situation, but here she was. Much as she wanted to cling to some symbolic armor she could not bring herself to cross the threshold carrying weapons, not if she was to be offered food.

Grimacing as much at her own too-strict sense of propriety as at the stiffness of her back and shoulders, Salli stripped her gear and piled it by the doorway. Flares. Game traps. Small arms, for self-protection. Climbing axe and hatchet. The slim black two-cubit length of the rocket-propelled grenade launcher that every avalanche soldier carried any time she went into the woods.

Meeka was staring, but Salli didn't care. The words she had to say to him were weapon enough against these Wayfarer heteros, or she was no longer his sister.

She went in.

Places were set on the long tables. Meeka pointed to a seat and Salli went, pausing just long enough to rinse her hands and kiss the hearthspoon that hung by the door. Breakfast was served and eaten in silence—bread and meat, fruit and hot black tea. Salli was hungry. The food was good. She cleared her plate three times, eyes stubbornly lowered, refusing to look up at Meeka seated across from her.

The room emptied by degrees as people finished their meals until there was no one left but the three of them—Salli, and Meeka, and the patient cook waiting to be sure that Salli had had all that she wanted to eat. Salli surrendered her dish at last, with a heartfelt smile of gratitude; then the cook went away as well, and they were alone.

Looking past Meeka, over his shoulder, Salli scanned the room restlessly. Just another Shadene hill-camp, really, built generations gone past to accommodate pilgrims on their way through the hills to the high holy ground that Wayfarers took for sacred, maintained by the Shadene secular authority ever since the Prodigals had returned to Creation.

Low thatched roof braced against massive support posts, steep-pitched to shed the winter snows.

Open rafters for coolness in the summertime, supporting openwork osier grids that caught debris falling from the roof thatch and served as the foundation for the resultant gauzy layer of dust overhead.

Windows screened with wooden louvers and shuttered with wood so old it had weathered to soft silver-gray; and trestle-benches, worn soft and rounded by the backsides of countless pilgrims before them.

Nothing to betray it for a terrorist camp, except that honest Wayfarers had no business being there—and they knew it. It was true that ethnic Shadene and Pilgrims went guarded against each other in the city; but out here? Decent law-abiding citizens went where permitted when permitted. Citizens who violated that easy guide placed themselves under suspicion of disloyalty to the civil government, whether it was expressed through passive or active means.

The moments chimed softly one against the other, and finally Salli spoke to the empty hall.

Meeka.

"So." Her voice sounded shrill and almost hateful in her own ears; but she hurt so badly for him that she saw no help for it. He should be hurt. He had disgraced them all. He should understand how unfairly he had treated her, and make appropriate restitution. Starting with return. "What's this all about, Mik?"

She dropped her gaze back from the far wall to fix on Meeka's face as she spoke. He was so pale. He'd always been as fair-skinned as any Shadene. Even his hair was but three shades short of blond, but looking like a Shadene hetero was no excuse for behaving like one.

"I should ask you, Selly. What are you doing here?"

The exchange of childish pet names seemed distasteful, suddenly. "I came to bring you to your senses. It's no good running away from it, Meeka. Sooner or later you've got to face up to what you did."

He frowned. "What I did's for me to deal with, sister. You don't know. You can't even guess what it's been like. But it's over now. I'll pay the price, but it'll be of my own choosing, do you understand me? And I'm never going back."

Meeka had been a policeman on the rolls at Pannath, where their deceased parents had raised them. Pannath was a Pilgrim enclave, and there were civil disturbances each year, especially in the summer when the heat got bad and the rains were weeks away. There had been a riot. The police were armed with crowd quieters, meant to merely knock down and discourage the rioters; but there had been an accident. A round from Meeka's crowd quieter had struck a rioter in the head. The man had died.

"You couldn't be more wrong." Shaking her head in disbelief, Salli reached for words. "It's not just you. And it's not over. And you're coming back. You're not afraid, surely."

Taking human life was a monstrous burden for any man to have to bear, even when it was an accident. That Shadene rioter had had no business being in the streets of a Pilgrim enclave with a brick in his hands in the first place. Who was to say he hadn't been a Wayfarer terrorist?

For a moment Meeka stared, mute, and the fathomless misery in his eyes nearly overwhelmed Salli with feelings of tenderness. Her own brother. She could only guess how awful it was for poor Meeka. Had she been to blame for this rash act? She only wanted to help him return to his family and friends again—but then Meeka spoke, and Salli hardened her heart against him.

"Not afraid. Not anymore. Salli, I've met—someone."

He had no right to run away like a thief in the night and join up with a group of Wayfarer heteros. She knew what he was saying; she'd heard he'd fallen under the influence of an unlicensed Teacher. This was Meeka she was looking at, though. There was liable to be something more—or less—to it than that.

The very idea of the grandson of a Pilgrim pioneer being seen at prayer in the company of Wayfarers made Salli's blood boil. It was indecent. "Oh, please. You're not going to sing me 'blue-eyed Shadene maiden.' Meeka. Talk sense."

She knew that expression on his face, patient and understanding, but full of love. It made her want to cry and infuriated her at the same time. This was Meeka. This was her brother. She had adored him from the moment she'd been born. She had joined the avalanche soldiers because Meeka was a policeman.

"It's not what you think, Salli. But you can't begin to understand unless you open your heart. I can't describe it. The compassion."

What was he talking about?

She was tired. It had taken her weeks to find where Meeka had gone, and more weeks yet to find this one group of Wayfarers, following them into the woods, waiting for her chance to get Meeka alone. She was angry at herself for having been caught. Most of all she was desperately desolate for her brother's sake. Meeka had run away from his duty.

"I'll tell you what I think. You've run away, Meeka. That's a coward's way out. And the only way you can fix it is by going back for the inquest hearing. What are you afraid of?"

She thought she knew what he was afraid of; it was the way people looked at policemen. Especially when there had been a killing. It was a tragedy for both of them, for Meeka and for the Shadene man he'd killed, but it was a hundred times worse for Meeka. The pilgrim police were chartered by law to secure the enclaves against squatters. Meeka had done nothing wrong, not even if killing had come of it.

And there was more to it than that. The Wayfarers were waiting for a hearing, waiting for their day in court. There were powerful pressures from outside the state of Shadene itself to surrender its secular identity and join the other nations of Creation as Pilgrim states.

As a Pilgrim it didn't so much matter to Salli if the Wayfarers lost their voice in the government of Shadene; but as an avalanche soldier Salli was fiercely devoted to the historical continuation of the state of Shadene as secular and representative. So there was so much more riding on Meeka's attendance at the inquest than might seem obvious.

"I'm not coming to the inquest hearing," Meeka said quietly, with a certainty that collapsed any hope Salli might have had into a small solid burning lump of betrayed anguish in her bosom. For a moment Salli did not quite hear what Meeka said next.

"I'm going before the Jarrod court. I'll answer for it there. I'm not a coward, Salli, but there are things that have changed in my life. You must understand."

The Jarrod court?

The ecclesiastical court of Wayfarer heterodoxy?

Had Meeka lost his mind?

Nobody went before the Jarrod court—unless—unless he had embraced Wayfarer heterodoxy and imagined himself bound by Wayfarer canon law—

"You're hallucinating!"

Apostate. Heretic. Seduced by an alien creed away from the true scripture to a Wayfarer hallucination. This went far beyond professing a false creed out of persistent desire to make some young lady's acquaintance. Faithless and foresworn. Her brother.

How could he do this to her?

Meeka sat up. "You're upset, Salli. We can talk about this later. Maybe you'd better have a nap."

Not all the comforting familiarity of Meeka's fraternal condescension could make it right, if Meeka had forsaken Orthodoxy.

She'd be a laughingstock amongst her peers, and she was in enough trouble already, because she had gone looking for Meeka without taking steps to clear her absence.

Hiding her head in the crook of her elbow, forehead flat to the table, Salli wept; with frustration, with grief, with fury, but above all with anguish born of betrayal.

Meeka.

Her brother.

How could it be that he had forgotten the true Dream?

Someone came into the meal hall. Salli awoke with a start, but stayed where she was with her head down; she had the advantage, if they didn't know she was awake. Who was it? Not Meeka, by the sound of the footfall. She only heard one person, walking slowly and deliberately around the banks of benches to approach her from the front. Polite.

She was stiff and sore. Sleeping sitting up with her head on the table had stretched her lower back muscles all out of true. It hurt. Slowly, Salli raised her head, put her arms out, stretched; and the man who had come in to see her sat down in Meeka's place across from her. Wayfarer, ethnic Shadene. The man called Carib.

"What time is it?" Salli asked, to make it clear that she'd been asleep. "Must have dozed off. You'll be needing the table, I imagine."

It was the first thing that came into her head, and she almost wished she hadn't said it. It made no sense. But Carib just smiled at her.

"No need of that, Salli. May I call you Salli? I came to intervene with you, on your brother's behalf."

Well, she didn't know what else Carib would call her if it wasn't her name. "My brother is a good man, of upright conduct."

This was establishing ground rules for negotiation, stipulation of starting points. It was traditional amongst Shadene to appoint someone to intervene when trouble arose between two people. The practice of arbitration was one of the better parts of the Wayfarer folkway, one that the Pilgrims had adopted as their own when they'd started coming back to Shadene to settle in this holy land and seek the blessing of the hills.

"Changes occur in people's lives, especially after traumatic events." Carib's voice was calm and dispassionate, neither attacking Salli nor defending her brother. "It can be hard sometimes to understand such changes. The first step is to talk about it."

"What's to talk?" She could be angry. It was all right.

She was aggrieved, not arbitrator. "Meeka is confused. He needs to come home."

She had a natural right to her emotions, and to express them strongly enough to make her point. Arbitration failed when the depth of a resentment was miscalculated. To participate fully was to take steps to ensure that they all understood how angry she was.

Or, how upset she was. Why should she be angry? If Meeka wanted to abandon his family's historical faith and turn his back on everything their parents had tried to build in Shadene, why should she be angry about it?

Centuries ago the Revelation had come to the Holy People, the hill people of Shadene. But humanity was weak and easily swayed by illusion, even in the time before the waking world was hidden from them by the veil of suffering that separated the truth from the land of dreams.

God had punished the heterodox by sending the Great Ice as a sign of danger. Then the Holy People had fled as Pilgrims from the mountains, fled to the west, where in the course of time the Pilgrims colonized the whole of the Great Prairie and crossed the Rift Desert to the other side of the world.

Pilgrims had grown rich and prosperous, and so fell into error once again: putting their trust in science and technology; traveling to other worlds and building great colonies there, till over time more Pilgrims had lived in the colonies than on Creation. God had rebuked their pride and their presumption yet again.

The colonists grew relaxed and lazy, and then the virus came that poisoned all air for Pilgrims save that of Creation's own atmosphere. The right mix of gases could be created in the colonies: but there was not enough to go around.

And the Pilgrim people fled home to Creation, leaving millions of dead and dying behind. Those who survived the trip took the discipline with humility and turned back to the roots of their faith, abandoning the illusions of science. To return to the holy mountains that had been set aside for them from the beginning of Time. To go back to Shadene.

There were people there, yes, but no Orthodox. There were only Wayfarers. The Wayfaring people had originally come to Shadene after the retreat of the Great Ice, from the islands far to the east over the Great Deep; they were not of the Holy People. Wayfarers were ethnically distinct, ignorant folk, whose understanding of the Revelation was imperfect. Heterodox.

It was another sign of the displeasure of God, Who alone could have allowed the holy land to fall into their hands; but the Pilgrims themselves had surrendered Shadene to the Wayfarers during the glory days of the colonies, and there was no going back on that.

Carib was waiting for her to say something. She hated the cold blue eyes of the Wayfarers—they were so heartless. Faithless. Soulless. They had made Shadene their country, but they had never truly belonged here. They were interlopers in the holy land. God had marked them as people of illusion by making them light: light eyes, light hair.

She spoke. "You must know that Meeka is to face the inquest hearing. There was an accident. A human soul was cut off from its body." Meeka had killed a man, but it wasn't Meeka's fault. The inquest hearing panel would see that clearly enough. Meeka would be exonerated. It was just a formality; the police investigation itself was already closed. Why wouldn't Meeka come back for the inquest?

Didn't he realize how bad it looked, that he had fled?

"Your brother has decided to go before the Jarrod court instead. This is an act of courage on his part. He rightly deserves praise and support from you, not hostility." Carib was calm, maddeningly so. "Are you afraid for him?"

She hadn't had time to become afraid for him. The idea was too new. Salli struggled with herself for long moments before she realized that it was best to be honest—howsoever offensive. This wasn't a civics lesson. This was about Meeka. Meeka was her brother, Pilgrim bred and born.

"The Jarrod court has no jurisdiction." Salli's voice failed; she had to force the words out, half-whispered. "No offense. But it was an enclave block. They had no business being there in the first place."

And Jarrod, the religious court of the Wayfarer heterodox, had no voice in the management of the Pilgrim enclaves. That had been arranged from the very start of the immigration period, more than two hundred years ago.

Pilgrims from west of the mountains were to be permitted to return to the land of their ancestors, the Revelation Mountains by the sea.

Pilgrims were to be permitted to bring their families and movable property and settle within the jealously guarded boundaries of Shadene, to develop pilgrimage sites and bring much-needed capital resources to maintain and repair old holy shrines. Some of the most holy places had been allowed to vanish into the forest for lack of money to keep them up; and those shrines and holy places Pilgrims were to be permitted to adopt.

But Pilgrims were not to be pressured to abjure their faith and confess the Wayfarer Dreaming. Nor were they to be subject to the religious law of the land, but were granted the right in perpetuity to cleave unto themselves in sovereign enclaves, to have their own church, to govern themselves by their own law.

"I think to be fair you'll admit that there's a question about that." Carib didn't sound angry; but his face suddenly looked twenty years older. "Wasn't that what started the incident in the first place?"

Yes, there was a controversy. True enough. It had been years. The secular state of Shadene had profited from the influx of Pilgrim money, Pilgrim labor. Now that the Shadene standard of living had been brought up to the standard of affluence enjoyed by Pilgrim nations, there were movements afoot to redefine the relationship between Pilgrim Orthodox and Wayfarer heterodox.

Now that the secular state of Shadene was rich, it had no further need of Pilgrim resources.

But Pilgrims had joined Wayfarers in the secular government, now, and knew how to protect their own interest. They had a right. The original enclaves were grossly underdrawn for a Pilgrim population the size of that in Shadene these days. Why should Pilgrims send their children to school with Wayfarers, to be tainted by the Wayfarer heterodoxy?

"Whether or not there was a controversy," Salli fell back on the letter of the law, feeling insecure in her position, "Meeka was just doing his job. And the Jarrod court has no jurisdiction. They could have claimed his body at the time, and they did not."

She had been afraid that the local authorities would lay claim to Meeka. One hundred years of coexistence had not changed the facts of life, and there was no question but that Wayfarer holding cells were particularly unpleasant places for Pilgrims.

A Wayfarer could slip a colored lens over blue eyes and dye his hair, but no amount of cosmetic could change a Pilgrim's dark eyes to light. They could not disguise themselves. It was mutually understood that Wayfarer and Pilgrim should not police each other; that was why there were police like Meeka in the first place.

And that was why there were avalanche soldiers, originally drawn exclusively from Pilgrim families to guard

Pilgrim investment in renovated shrines. Wayfarer heterodox believed that shrines should remain as they had weathered, all the holier as their dilapidation increased. There were elements amongst the Wayfarers that were not unwilling to resort to violence to protect heterodox sensibilities—or to jealously protect what were seen as Wayfarer shrines from Pilgrim attentions.

"Salli, it's good of your brother to make the gesture. The enclave's geographical boundaries were contested. He's doing an honorable thing by submitting himself to the Jarrod court. Why do you resist this?"

Carib was good at arbitration. His calm tone of voice, his reasonable argument made Salli question her own mind. It wasn't fair. She hadn't really had time to think about what Meeka had told her, or to decide how she really felt about it.

"Only Wayfarers come before the Jarrod court." In the uncomfortable position in which she felt placed, Salli could only resort to the most basic objection. "And Wayfarers are heterodox. My brother is Orthodox. He cannot go before the Jarrod court. The Jarrod court will not hear him—unless—"

Meeka had said that he'd met someone.

What if, this once, he hadn't meant a girlfriend?

And what if it went deeper than that?

The Wayfarer tradition was full of charismatic leaders. False prophets. Untrue Holy Ones. The Holy One had come down from the mountains to prepare the world for its waking, and had said that the Awakened One would come into the world to bring the new day. Wayfarers were heterodox, honoring many so-called Holy Ones for what piece of waking wisdom each might bring. True Dreamers, Orthodox Dreamers, knew that the Awakened One had yet to come into the world, and that the Wayfarers were a deluded and theologically promiscuous people.

Carib was watching. Salli took a deep breath. "If Meeka is not Orthodox, then he is not my brother." It hurt to say so terrible a thing. But it was true. She could not imagine tolerating a heterodox Dreamer in her family. Their parents were dead, true—their father just two years gone. Just as well. The shame alone would have killed them, to say nothing of the scorn and pity of the rest of the Pilgrim community.

"And yet you have liked the Wayfarer theology," Carib countered, mildly. "At least Meeka says so. He had a hard time accepting that, he says, but now he's willing to admit to you that he was wrong."

She could not answer. Had Meeka given himself over so to these Wayfarers, body and soul, so that the most intimate secrets a brother and sister might share became mere ammunition for the use of people Meeka had surely never even met more than six months ago?

"Wonderful poetry," she said offhandedly. But it was true. The Dream Lover theology was the finest of its kind anywhere in the world. It could not be matched for the intensity of the longing it expressed, or the richness of imagery it deployed to describe the union of the awakened heart with God. There was nothing like it anywhere in Pilgrim devotionals, not for centuries back.

The Pilgrim devotionals tended to be rather more literal and transaction-oriented than the pure, aching, god-intoxicated desire of the soul for knowledge of the awakened world that characterized the Wayfarer Dream Lover theology. And yet it was the Pilgrim devotionals that stemmed from the true Revelation, and the Wayfarer theology was just the primitive misunderstandings of an alien race come from the sea to the holy mountains well after the holiness had fled. "I like the poetry of the Dream Lover theology. Wonderful. It's of literary interest to me. Nothing more."

Nor would Meeka have been able to betray any information to the contrary to these people. Because Meeka didn't know. Salli believed the Dream Lover theology was consistent with Orthodoxy, resounding—even despite itself—with the clear bell-toned voice of the Holy One. But she had always found it expedient to keep that to herself.

"Will you entertain a proposal?"

She almost wished Carib would argue with her, instead of merely going to the next step of the arbitration. She knew she had nothing to be ashamed of. Her orthodoxy was unchallenged. But the Dream Lover theology had always been a jealously guarded secret in her heart; and she felt vulnerable and unhappy to have her fond interest exposed. "I'll listen, and you'll have my honest answer."

Formula. Still, arbitration was a useful tool only to the extent that people agreed to play fair and abide by the rules. Salli shook herself to settle her mind and folded her hands in front of her on the table.

"Your brother Meeka has been strictly tested, in these past few months. He believes his life has been irrevocably changed by a conversion experience."

As she had feared. Salli kept her face calm, listening as open-heartedly as she could.

"Come with us to Mount Corabey, where we are gathering for the Jarrod court. Meet with Meeka's teacher. Be there with him when he speaks about what happened. You will not be bound by the decision of the Jarrod court, of course. But it would mean a lot to your brother if you would at least meet the Holy One. He hopes that you will come to understand."

Salli thought fast.

She had not shot and killed a human soul, by accident or otherwise. She was not psychologically vulnerable, as Meeka was. If she met the Wayfarer Holy One who had caught Meeka in the snare of heterodoxy—and remained

Orthodox—maybe Meeka would recover his balance and wake to his duty.

Or maybe she would just get close to a Wayfarer Holy One, yet another in an endless stream of heterodox false prophets. She'd left her duty station without leave to find her brother, but she had not forgotten that she was an avalanche soldier. A new Wayfarer Holy One meant possible increase in terrorist activity at shrines and in recreational areas. The more she found out about this one the better she would be able to report to her superiors about it.

"Let's set a limit to this test." She wanted to be sure there was no ambiguity about when she would be free to go her way. "How long would you say makes a fair trial? One day? Two sermons?"

"We're eight days' walk from Corabey. The Jarrod court convenes when the Chalice cups the Star, that's nineteen or twenty days yet." Carib was prepared. "So we're talking twenty-five days at maximum, I think. If nothing we can do will change your mind, you could still be there for your brother. Come with us to the Jarrod court, Salli, and go whichever way you choose when the Jarrod court is over. In twenty-five days' time."

Fair enough.

She inclined her head slightly.

"Twenty-five days, then. All right, I agree." Salli stretched out her hand, half-expecting Carib to scorn to touch her flesh—a woman of different faith. He apparently had no objection to the contact, and clasped her hand in his with precisely as much force required to express relief and goodwill, without any extra edge of test of strength thrown in.

"I'll tell your brother. He'll be glad. Take yourself down to the hot springs, Salli Pilgrimsdaughter, just the thing for stiff muscles. It's a rest day, today."

Delicately put, that, acknowledging the effort it had

taken her to track these people this far in without being found out till the last—without reference to the awkward fact that she *had* been found out. Discovered. Discountenanced. Salli rose to her feet carefully, smiling even while every muscle she possessed protested at the movement.

"Thanks. It'll be welcome." She felt a little uncomfortable to be accepting a meal share from Wayfarer heterodox. The proper prey of the avalanche soldier was the Wayfarer terrorist; and though it went without saying that not all Wayfarers were terrorists, suspicion came as naturally as breathing. But she had agreed to arbitration. She was not here under false pretenses.

"I'll tell your brother to sling you a hammock, then." Carib nodded, and let himself out of the silent hall, leaving Salli behind to consider the morning's events.

She was stiff. She was sore. Her body craved the warmth of the hot springs, and since she could not comfort her soul, her body's comfort would have to do.

There would be time.

She would talk to Meeka.

And she would bide her time till she met Meeka's teacher, and see what kind of false Holy One these heterodox Wayfarers had turned up to create dissension.

Three

"Miss Salli."

Stepping carefully between berry-bush roots and fronds of fern and the long thin branches of ground-level shrubs, Salli smiled to herself. It was Fenka. She liked Fenka. She kept her mouth shut and walked on.

Meeka was ahead of her by three paces' distance; the path was old, very narrow, clearly almost never used. They could go faster if they went two by two rather than single file, true, but this was holy ground to Wayfarers and off-limits to anybody else. Salli was genuinely impressed by how much care these Wayfarers took to minimize the impact of their presence on the land.

After a moment Fenka spoke again, two people back in line, a touch of impatience in her clear girlish voice. "*Salli.*"

That was better. They'd had words about this, last night in camp. At first Salli had not minded formal address, wanting to keep her distance from these heteros in as many ways as possible. But it had been three days, and she'd started feeling silly. As well as unnecessarily unfriendly.

She was still angry at Meeka, and she was going to stay angry at Meeka, whether or not she hated to be out of eyeshot of her beloved brother. But there was no reason to be gratuitously rude to these heterodox Wayfarers, who had welcomed her into their camp without reservation—even after she had stalked them like prey of some sort in her late quest to find Meeka.

"Oh. Fenka. I'm sorry, hon, I didn't hear you."

Someone farther back in line snorted in suppressed laughter at the clear insincerity of Salli's tone of voice. There was no privacy in camps this small—and there were only forty of them. Twenty-seven men. Thirteen women. Fourteen, counting Salli.

"You should have your hearing checked. You won't be able to hear the demo team's clear-the-slopes."

Fenka's voice held only mock-resentment. Fenka was a nice person. All of these people were nice. Sympathetic. Supportive. Was it just because they were hoping to recruit her to their cause?

"Then they'd have to pull me out of six feet of snow half a mile downslope. And I'd be mosquito-free at last."

They flattered her with the respect they showed her technical skills as an avalanche soldier. Apart from that first meeting—clumsy as it had been, awkward, humiliating—no one had called her Pilgrim Police, or taunted her with any of the slanders Wayfarers pretended to believe about avalanche soldiers.

That they'd arrest a Wayfarer on sight at resorts on suspicion of terrorism because no Wayfarer could possibly have enough money to be at a ski resort for actual recreation.

That avalanche soldiers completing their training were forced to bleach their hair white and paint the skin around their eyes with blue vegetable dye and be "Wayfarer"—which was to say excrement—until the dye wore off and their hair grew out in a proper Pilgrim color.

None of that.

"Salli, why would a Pilgrim want to go into the mountains? It's cold up there."

Instead they asked apparently sincere questions about

training and motivation and experience. Salli welcomed the interchange. The more they knew about her the more comfortable they'd feel with her, and the easier it was for her to get them to open up to her in turn.

It was her duty to the Secular Authority to get all the information about these people that she could. They could turn out to be terrorists after all, and it was in the Secular Authority's best interest to know one way or the other.

The Orthodox nations of Creation were always on the watch for an excuse to intervene in Shadene, and Orthodox intervention would only mean the end of the secular state as they knew it. There was no shortage of radical Orthodox on Shadene's borders asking for nothing more than a good reason to invade, and help the government out . . . of power.

"I'm a little surprised you should ask. If you don't mind me saying so."

It was in the best interests of friendship and hospitality as well. If she knew enough about them to identify them and their creed when she got back, she'd be able to ensure that the Shadene secular authority knew enough to distinguish between these harmless heteros and any more dangerous radical groups.

"I may be Pilgrim people. No argument. But the mountains have never gone away, in our hearts. We pray the same, after all, 'I will look up to the hills for the truth.' "

" 'Because the Dreamer will come down from the mountains, and the world will awake.' "

The response was spoken in unison, and by everyone who'd heard. The effect was chilling. She hadn't gotten used to it. And she should have known, she reminded herself; because that had been her point exactly. They had scripture in common. It was the interpretation of the

scriptures that divided them into heterodox and Orthodox.

She shook herself to clear the eerie uneasiness of it and
continued. "Our family came back to Shadene generations ago. That's more than two hundred years of looking at the mountains close up, Fenka. I couldn't stand
the thought of not spending my life on the high slopes.
I knew from the moment I was old enough to remember
that I was going to be an avalanche soldier when I grew
up."

Carib's voice came from the rear, pitched to carry. He
was the party's guide and leader, so he always took the
drag slot to be sure that no one was missed or fell behind. "You should have been doing woman things instead. Baking. Sewing. Brewing. Learning the praise
songs. Not playing high-slopes ranger."

He was teasing her; she knew it, because the second
in command of their party was Pareek. Carib's aunt. She
led the walk-line, thirty people forward.

"You could always get Salli to bake." Meeka looked
back over his shoulder at her briefly, his tanned face full
of love. Just at this moment, Meeka seemed free from
concern and regret that she did not accept his choices in
life. "But brewing? She always had to experiment. Summer beer with garlic, because it's cooling, after all."

Salli sighed deeply, under cover of the laugh *that* always got. She still maintained that it had been a good
idea, in concept at least. And who knew why it hadn't
been tried before? Maybe it was too obviously a bad
idea. But maybe, just maybe, it was an "obviously" bad
idea that would turn out to be a wonderful idea once
someone made the creative leap of faith and actually
tried it.

Like bladderpipes.

What kind of a maniac did it take to shove a hollowed

shank bone into the slaughtered animal's own bladder, even dried and washed?

And whatever could have been going on in the mind of the first person that tried it?

Now the voice of Carib's aunt Pareek came floating back between the black-pine branches and the thin canes of the berry vines. " 'To the frivolity of the ignorant, there is no end.' " From the Admonitions; because in Praise songs the Scholar said quite plainly that the sound of merriment was grateful to the ear of God, and could lead to an Awakening in this world. Pareek took pilgrimage seriously.

Or maybe she was just sensitive to the embarrassment that any woman's brother could create for an unoffending little sister who was just doing the best she could to keep her brother an honest man.

" 'And the foolishness of the unlearned cannot be measured.' "

Salli rather liked the Holy Fool theology. Since everybody knew how illogical one's dreams could be on the surface, who better than a fool to penetrate the dream-illogic of the waking world and see through to the eternal Wakefulness that was the only true reality?

But even more than Holy Fool, Salli liked Dream Lover. The faith of her mother was the only true faith; Salli was as certain of that as she could be. That didn't change the fact that no scripture, Orthodox or heterodox, spoke to her heart of her soul's longing for the immediate presence of God as the Wayfarer Dream Lover theology.

None of the Orthodox mystics came close, but God spoke to the heart according to the needs of each child of the Dream. It was enough for devout children of the Word to raise their hands in praise, bearing witness to the marvelous means through which the voice of God spoke to the soul.

Salli turned her attention to setting her feet in the footprints that were already there before her, singing in her heart for the Awakening to come to all of these good people and cure them of their heterodoxy.

"Well, of course I'd never been to a Wayfarer funeral, Salli. You know how depressing it all seems. Heartless."

It was evening, and the supper dishes had been scoured and restacked on the shelves of the camp's kitchen. This camp was higher on the slopes of the Skirts of Holiness than the camp where Salli had been discovered; three days' walk, and the trees had all changed. No more giant palms. These were great evergreens and shrubby brewbushes, whose dead leaves littered the ground and cushioned every step of the old Wayfarer trail.

Meeka sat on the edge of the dumpslope with his knees drawn up to his chin, brooding over the ancient midden as he talked. Wayfarers had been using these trails for centuries. It had even been speculated that there might have been some contact, somewhere, somehow, between Wayfarer immigrants and the Holy People, before they all went west. That was as old as these trails were.

"They say it's the sign of a true believer not to mourn at a funeral, Meeka." She meant to draw him out, work her way into his soul, set him straight again. For that she needed his trust. She would show him that she could understand the alien creed and even respect it, so that he would not be able to reject her arguments out of hand. "Death is an occasion of rejoicing, because the soul is free to Wake. It isn't really any different from Orthodox, is it? We cry at funerals because we're bereft, not because anything awful's happened to the dead person."

Frowning, Meeka reached down to scratch the top of his foot. The dead fallen brewbush leaves that blanketed the camp rustled as he moved, and released their beautiful perfume of holiness. It was as fragrant as flowers, and yet it was merely deadfall; what more perfect sign of the compassion of the Holy One, that even dead leaves breathed blessings?

"Platitudes, Salli. All of my life, it's all been like a dream, and all this time I thought I was awake. When I was sleepwalking."

It hurt to hear him speak like that of their shared childhood faith. Rejection of the Orthodox felt a very great deal like he was rejecting her, specifically, individually, personally. Salli took a deep breath. She couldn't afford to let her hurt show.

"Well, go on with your story, then." Three days, waiting for Meeka to relax, waiting for Meeka to be ready to talk. Three days waiting for these Wayfarers to get comfortable enough around her to leave the two of them alone to talk. "You were telling me about the Holy One."

He slapped his shin decisively, as if to swat the distracting itch out of his mind; and folded his arms across his knees once more, hooking his chin over the long bone of his forearm. "Oh, right. So. I'd never been to one of their funerals. And I really didn't think anybody would want me at this one, but I wanted to pay my respects, say the Awakening for him. I was guilty, after all."

True, if in a more limited sense than Meeka seemed to feel it. He had fired the bouncer that had killed the man. It had been an accident. There was all the difference in Creation between being the unwitting, unoffending agent of someone else's mischance and being a murderer.

Salli kept her mouth shut. There would be time to challenge his misguided suppositions later.

"So I went to the liaison worker and asked if it would be permitted for me to just go to the riverside and be there when the fire was lit. Whether anybody would notice me. She thought that was a pretty offensive idea, really."

Meeka's residual discomfort was perfectly reasonable. The liaison worker—one of the Wayfarer religious leaders who mediated between Orthodox and heterodox in matters of ritual—had probably laughed at the very idea of a Pilgrim at a Wayfarer rite of passage, especially *that* rite and *that* Pilgrim. All the same Salli felt a deep pang of sympathy for Meeka, deluded though he was. It had to have taken all his courage even to approach a Wayfarer with a question like that.

"Then a few days later someone stopped me in the street on the way to the station. Carib. I was expecting him to spit in my face. Instead he invited me to the sin-eating."

So the liaison worker had at least passed on Meeka's obviously deeply felt need to make amends. Salli was impressed. The sin-eating was no longer a truly religious Wayfarer rite, if it ever had been; nor was it restricted to family. Still, it was a community gathering, and few Pilgrims had ever been included as a member of a Wayfarer community.

"Salli, I was scared witless. But I'd been invited. I couldn't not go. So I went."

Oh, he was a warrior, was Meeka. His heart was strong and true and his spirit was bright and clear. His thinking was a bit muddled just at present, but he was her brother, and Salli loved him right now—this instant—as much as she ever had, heterodox illusions or no.

"There I was, in the middle of the old city, after sundown. Half again as tall as anybody else there. The only 'black-eyed unbeliever' in the room, and it was a crowded room. Everybody doing his best not to stare, being polite. It was uncomfortable, I can tell you, but I was glad I'd come. And then—"

The light had fallen away, the sun gone down. Salli could not quite distinguish the exact expression on Meeka's face, but his voice was full of emotion, resonant with passion.

"And then Varrick came into the room, and everyone shut up. It was like a signal had been given, something secret, everyone quiet all of a sudden. Here comes this woman—she's not too tall, not too old, not too young, as Wayfarer as they come to look at her—walking through the crowd right to me. People backing up left and right."

Varrick. That would be the Wayfarer's Holy One. Salli had heard the name over the last few days, and wondered; but had restrained herself from prying until she was better trusted.

"Salli, she's got the most incredible eyes. They're like looking into the entire forest at once, and not even seeing the palms. She stopped in front of me, I couldn't stop staring at her, and she said—"

Meeka's voice faltered; he stopped, and Salli thought she heard him choke his emotion back down into his throat. She'd never heard Meeka so close to tears. It frightened her.

"She said, 'Courageous art thou among the ungodly, Pilgrim. The time may yet come for you to Wake to truth.' " Meeka's voice steadied and strengthened as he spoke on. There was no particular reason for Meeka to be feeling so emotional to begin with, though, surely. People quoted the Revelation teachings all the time. There had to be more to it than that.

"She had a piece of sin-cake in her hand. She put it in her mouth, put the edge in her mouth, and broke off a corner. She stuck the corner into my mouth, and I stood there like a doorpost. 'Wake up,' she said. 'Wake up and taste the truth, this *is* the Waking World.' "

Impressive. Salli felt an involuntary chill down her

spine. There was no questioning the effect the gesture
had had on Meeka.

"And it was like I suddenly tasted food for the first
time. Like I'd never had peppercake before in my life. I
could taste everything in it, flour and cream and spice.
I woke up, Salli. Just at that moment I realized I'd been
sleeping my whole life. My whole life."

Salli let the silence between them lengthen, listening
to the night. Meeka was dead certain. She knew that
now, as she had not before; it was discouraging information.

But.

As much as Salli empathized with the utter conviction
in Meeka's voice, as much as she wanted to respect her
brother's spiritual insight, still this was Meeka. And
Meeka had always been all-or-nothing.

Absolute conviction didn't mean the same thing in
Meeka that it meant in other people—all of Meeka's
convictions were absolute. And if she could only once
succeed in planting the whisper of a convincing coun-
terargument in his mind, Meeka could well be embracing the absolute truth of Orthodoxy again within a week.
That was just the way Meeka was, heart and mind and
soul.

Meeka was waiting for her response, and the silence
was becoming awkward. "So. After that."

She should endorse his feeling, praise the conversion
experience. She could not. It was heterodox and Wayfarer. She was Pilgrim and Orthodox. Meeka would
know.

Meeka let his breath out with a sound too fond—impatient—vindicated, to be called a sigh.

"After that I had to know, I had to learn all over again.
I was like a baby: I know I cried like one." The admission
was rueful in tone, not embarrassed in the least. If these
heterodox Wayfarers had separated Meeka from so

much of his self-pride, then Salli knew they deserved thanks for truly helping—if in unexpected ways.

"They took me in like an orphan of their own. At first I kept working, but the more I learned of the truth the harder it was to continue to support the inequities I could see all around me, every day. I knew there was no way to explain it to anybody, and I was hating going to work because it took me away from learning. The others in my unit were getting uncomfortable with me learning all about heterodoxy. Finally I just stopped reporting for duty."

Meeka made it sound as though the process had taken weeks or months, instead of days. But that was one of the things that happened to people under stress, wasn't it? Time stood still, or vanished like the mist on the hillside at sunrise in midsummer. Meeka had disappeared less than ten days after the riot, well before the hearing that was to examine the event and establish his guiltlessness.

"You could have let your squad know. You could have let me know." It was a logical objection, and Salli offered it calmly, without too much conviction. It wouldn't have been like Meeka to have let anyone know where he was going. Not once he had decided that no one from his former life could understand.

"Maybe I should have, Salli. I didn't see the point."

Behind them, in the encampment, Salli could hear the voices of the men raised in evensong. Meeka stood up. "I mean, here you've met these people, you've traveled with them, you must know they're godly folk. And still you refuse to so much as sit with us for prayer. So what would have been the use, Salli?"

She would not sit in a Wayfarer prayer circle. She could not. As much as she didn't want to give offense, as much as she had begun to believe that these people were harmless after all, still she could not shape her

mouth around the words of a Wayfarer prayer or psalm
without betraying her own soul's conviction.

They were just words, true enough.

But Meeka was not the only stubborn child that their
mother had borne or their father bred.

"Maybe once I can meet Varrick for myself. Maybe
then, Meeka."

Or maybe never.

Meeka left for prayer circle without another word, and
Salli sat by herself in the dark until service was over and
she could seek her sleepmat in the dormitory.

It had been seven days' walk at a pace that fully absorbed all of the energy that Salli could muster. Riding
backwoods bikes or the fat-wheeled three-legged bumblers might have been more efficient or quicker; but in
order to minimize the impact of their presence on land
that was holy, heterodox practice demanded that they
walk. As the days scrolled by her mind began to float
free of her body with increasing ease. Her body knew
what it was doing, it was walking, and no more than a
base level of awareness was required to accomplish that
successfully. Her mind ranged out to all sides as they
walked, her thoughts snagging from time to time on the
bejeweled branch of a berry tree or the splashing of water over pebbles in a stream.

It was both beautiful and holy in the woods, and Salli
was beguiled from the discomfort of her body by the
combination. Not everything that was beautiful was
holy. But was it not true that everything that was holy
was beautiful? What was sanctity, if not the unchallen-
geable experience of the reality of truth, in all its divine
glory?

Midmorning, and Aunt Pareek called a halt to their
progress. Lunch, Salli supposed, though it seemed a bit
early for that. First things first. One of the women in

their party was suffering from a painful bunion that had
half crippled her, and Salli had a numbing ointment in
her kit. Once she saw that the people ahead of her were
laying down their packs she turned back in the line to
find Hanjill.

One of the men had cut Hanjill a stick, a few days ago;
Salli to one side, Hanjill's daughter Roose to the other,
Hanjill limped forward into the campsite. It was a beautiful campsite, this, halfway up the slope to a saddle pass
that Salli could see ahead rising up through the gently
waving branches of the chucknut trees. The Linshaw
Pass, perhaps, she realized. Had they come so far so
soon?

Were these indeed the outermost slopes of the Arms
of Corabey?

Roose settled her mother on a mossy log bench, and
Salli shook herself out of reverie. Ointment. She had to
concentrate on unwrapping Hanjill's foot, the shoe cut
open and spliced to ease the pressure on the spur of
bone. Red and furious, the bunion looked painful indeed. Salli daubed around it carefully with the nerve-
numbing gel, holding Hanjill's foot, rubbing the heel
softly to distract poor Hanjill while the salve took effect.

After a few moments Hanjill sighed deeply and patted
her daughter's hand, which lay supportively on her
shoulder. "Oh, that's so much better. Fetch out my slippers, girl; I for one will not resent the waiting. Not too
much. So long as it is short."

What? Hanjill meant to trek on in her camp slippers?
Salli frowned, packing her kit. That wasn't a good idea.
The rough trail would destroy camp slippers. But maybe
Hanjill meant to wear them only for so long as it took
for the meal break?

No, Salli reminded herself.

It was too early for the meal break.

And nobody seemed to be working on a meal, no, it

almost looked like they were stopping here: but why?

Salli stood up and looked around.

The camp was a leveled yard shaded from direct sunlight by the interlacing boughs of the great chucknut trees, the ground a well-cushioned carpet of green moss. She could see Meeka with a team of three others raking up fallen chucknut leaves to use as tinder, heaping the deadfall into a pile at the back of the largest structure here. A communal hall, clearly. Very old-fashioned, perhaps very old; a beautiful campsite, yes, the crystal-cold water bubbling out of the breast of the earth across the smooth stone of an ancient basin—but why would they stop?

They were so close.

If what she thought she could see up ahead in the path they'd been traveling was the Linshaw Pass, then they were scarce two days from the lap of Mount Corabey herself. Their destination. They were going to Corabey for the Jarrod court, and to hear the wisdom of the Holy One.

Why would they stop?

Roose had brought her mother the desired camp slippers; Hanjill rose to her feet, tired and weary but no longer in pain, and took Salli's pack. "I'll go get you settled, Salli," Hanjill said; nodded once, and moved off briskly before Salli could ask why they were stopping. Hanjill could not quite express thanks to an avalanche soldier, no matter how welcome Salli knew the ointment to be.

Salli didn't mind.

To be cared for even as indirectly as in Hanjill's taking her pack into quarters was fully satisfactory as a measure of thanks, in Salli's opinion, all things being weighed and considered and balanced.

She wanted to know why they had stopped; she could ask someone, or she could go look for herself and see if she could discern the reason. Her training predisposed her to go and look and try to figure things out first, ask later.

She headed for the trail.

Since they were stopping, she was free until it was time to clean dishes. She had no other chores in the rotation until then.

Like much of the trail they'd been following, the way up to the pass was paved, after a manner of speaking, with a layer of pebbles; and had narrowed over the years to the width of a mere footspan. Salli trod carefully. The bracken-fern was nearly as tall as she was, and the cool gray gleaming of the boulders of ancient volcanic rock seemed to shine out behind the green-fringed veil and speak to her heart in a language long since dead to the dreaming world.

She climbed the steepening slope up toward the saddle pass, her eyes returning ever and again to the clear blue sky between the pass's grim black shoulders. She was eager for her first glimpse of Corabey. These mountains were still part of the Preserve, and no Pilgrim had set eyes on Corabey for decades.

The path grew more difficult; she had to concentrate more on the placement of her feet. But she was close. She was very close. Within a few meters she would be able to glimpse the uppermost rim of the Chalice of Heaven.

Salli looked up and saw Carib instead of Corabey, standing in the path in front of her. Blocking her path. Confused, she stopped, her frown meant for a question; Carib shook his head.

"No one may look on Corabey until the bell calls, Salli." A taboo, then. Meaningless. What was she to make of such nonsense? And still—a bell—"We'll wait. And then we will all go together. Don't worry, you can't be any more eager to cross into the Chalice than the rest of us are."

Nodding to signal her understanding, Salli closed the distance between them before turning off the track. He had a log seat there, did Carib; he'd pitched a lean-to, and his camp stove was carefully shielded in the brush. He was set up to keep a vigil, or to keep anyone from creeping ahead in the night. Or maybe both.

"Until the bell calls?" The bells, the holy bells, had an important place in Orthodox liturgy, calling the people to prayer, signaling the end of service. "When is that supposed to happen?"

The bells were like the morning call that woke one up, except that they were to represent the call that awakened the spirit from the earthbound Dream of suffering. Heterodox Wayfarers used no bells in liturgy. That was one of the signs that they were mere opportunistic invaders in Shadene.

Apparently content that Salli meant no violation of protocol, Carib stepped back down off the track to take his seat once more. Reaching around to the back of his stump he found his pipe, and tamped its bowl full of a shag-cut smokeweed.

"When it's time, Salli." He offered the no-answer with a smile that drained it of any possible intent to offend. "Soon, I hope. There's theories that it's something to do with the phase of the moon, but no agreement about which. All I know is that we may not, um, cross into the Chalice until we hear the—the voice of the prayer bell."

Something in the slow and halting way in which Carib spoke his last sentence gave Salli the distinct feeling that he was translating, in his mind, from Wayfarer into the standard Pilgrim tongue that had slowly become the common language of the four continents.

Well, the three continents. The Great Prairie, with Shadene stuck alongside its east coast. The Ice. The Long

Coast. The Islands weren't a continent per se; and Sanbrusca didn't really count.

Sanbrusca was nothing but mile upon mile of sterile salt-flat desert and alkali dust storms, and no one lived in Sanbrusca at all anymore. The scientific research stations had been abandoned after the Wrathful Warning had come upon them, three hundred years ago, and in the aftermath of that testing time the Orthodox had turned away from the delusions of science.

"Carib, you'd have to be talking about a really big bell." She was beginning to think she could grasp the secret here—

Nor did Carib disappoint, nodding in genial agreement. "As big as you are, Salli, or bigger. They're not all in museums, you know. In fact as soon as we realized that the government meant to sequester them people stopped remembering where they were in a hurry. Damnedest thing."

Prayer bell.

Prayer bell, he'd said.

There were only four or five of them left in all of Shadene—that she knew of. Genuine artifacts from the time of Holiness, the time before the Dispersion, the time when there were only Orthodox, and the hill people dwelt in Awakened knowledge of God. Prayer bells were great and ancient, yes, taller than she was, incised with figures in a lost language and each with its own tone; when the time of the Dispersion had come, when the Holy People had fled from the Revelation Mountains, they had left the great prayer bells behind—but never forgotten them.

And Carib said there was a prayer bell here, at Corabey?

She'd seen prayer bells, but only in museums.

How had they got a prayer bell—all thousands of pounds of one, tall as she was, and cast according to

some trick of primitive technology that had long been
forgotten—up the narrow footpaths of these slopes, and
to Mount Corabey?

Or—sweet Awakening—did he mean that there had
been a prayer bell at Mount Corabey all along?

Such an artifact would be priceless—

Wayfarers had come lately to Shadene. They were not
hill people, they were fishing folk from the islands far
to the west across the Great Deep, whose agriculture remained secondary to the harvest of fish and sea-
vegetables even after centuries as the only people in
Shadene. Maybe she should have realized that Wayfarers would have found bells, and made up reasons for
them to be there in the mountains.

Maybe some Wayfarer Holy One had integrated
prayer bells into some secret Wayfarer ritual in response.

It had often been said that had the Wayfarers been the
actual lineal descendants of the hill people—as they
were wont to claim—there would be more continuity in
rites and worship with Orthodoxy.

This was almost too much to think about, all at once;
so Salli said the very first thing that came into her head.

"I've never heard one rung." The only prayer bells
anyone knew about—any Orthodox knew about—were
secured as a public trust, sacred artifacts of the Holy
People. They could not be rung in museums. The Council for the Awakening, which governed the Orthodox
faithful, had given it as an article of faith that the pure
spiritual voice of the prayer bell was not to be invoked
in so dream-deluded and devolved a world as theirs had
become. Only when the Day of Awakening came could
the prayer bells be rung again by faithful, Orthodox
hands.

That was the ruling, at least.

She was to hear the voice of the prayer bell?

Could it be a true prayer bell, the work of the Holy People of old?

And if it was, would Meeka not wake from the dream of his delusions at its first peal?

Leaning back against the crossbranches of his log seat, Carib lit his pipe, drawing at it in careful draughts to assure a good fat ember-cluster. "You'll not be able to mistake it, Salli. Don't worry. You'll hear it loud and clear, when the time comes."

She had to be satisfied with that.

Her mind full of confusion and anticipation, Salli went back down into the camp, to wait with all the others till the bell rang.

In the night Salli dreamed a dream of Corabey, a Shadene maiden dancing barefoot in the tall grass of a subalpine prairie, dressed in green pine with snow-white clouds swirling rhythmically around her.

Prayer bells in her fingers like castanets, well, that made sense. Corabey was a mountain. Mountains were big. Salli could understand why—large as a prayer bell was—it would still seem a dainty bauble in the hands of divine Corabey. She was the harbinger of Awakening, the place where the sun first caught the peaks on the morning of the winter solstice, and in her hands prayer bells would chime like windcatchers.

They didn't sound like windcatchers.

Frowning in her sleep, Salli concentrated.

Pretty little bells like windcatchers should sing on a high clear note, and what she thought she heard was oceans deep rather than skylark-high. Huge and deep, heavy and ponderous, with a reverberation so strong and powerful that it muddied the tolling of the bell into one long drawn-out pulsation of continually reinforced sound. Mount Corabey herself seemed to dance more slowly, in Salli's dream, her playful pirouettes less light-footed moment by moment, as though the sound of her dancing bells created physical interference in the air against which her body struggled as she danced.

Slowly.

And ever yet more slowly, the clouds settling to the ground around her. Fog. The bells still chimed, though, they were not diminished, nor did the pulse slow as Corabey's body settled into rock.

Salli sat bolt upright on her palm-stuffed pallet.

The prayer bell.

She wasn't even sure she heard it, but the others in the long low-roofed sleeping hall had begun to stir; it wasn't just her dream. And if she stilled herself and thought about it, she heard it, yes, she heard the bell, a low rumbling reverberation without the obvious punctuation of a peal but no less powerful for that.

She'd better hurry.

All around her people were rising, dressing hastily, rolling kits into their travel bags. The bell was the signal. They could cross into the caldera, and behold Mount Corabey; and when they got to Corabey the Holy One would be there.

The breakfast meal was quick, and eaten standing. The Wayfarers broke camp in single file, passing the wellspring font one by one to rinse their mouths and wash their hands to greet the morning. But no one spoke, no one raised her voice; it was light enough to see the path, but not yet sunrise.

Salli took her place behind Meeka in the line, disappointed to see no apparent alteration in his bearing—no Awakening to the very sounding of the bell. The path broadened as it ascended to the saddle pass, a rocky wash scoured clear of vegetation in the spring floodmelt. The Wayfarers kept closely grouped as they climbed the long slow rise, Meeka keeping close beside her to help her if she stumbled.

That was a joke.

He was the one who had stumbled.

But he was still her brother, for all that.

Clambering over ever-larger boulders, scrambling in their eagerness, they hastened toward the Linshaw Pass. The voice of the bell had fallen silent, but their concentration did not flag; what was beyond, if not just Mount Corabey?

Then as they reached the pass and crossed the flattened saddle of it to where the path began to fall into the valley once again, the sun broke across the eastern peaks of the Lunedin; and the Wayfarers knelt down on the rocks one by one with their packs on, singing.

> Oh, like the sun that rises in the morning is the Awakening from this dream we live, and like a mother's voice to wake us is the voice of the Holy One. Saying, rise up out of your Dream of suffering.

Looking at what?

Salli hung back, not wishing to be obvious in her refusal to kneel and sing with heterodox.

She didn't see anything special.

The enchantment of the vista, yes, no question. The path fell away from the pass down into a gently rolling basin of alpine prairie grass, brilliant as a starry sky with the late-summer blooming and beautiful with gossamer wisps of early-autumn fog. There was a lake there in the middle of the caldera, a lake fed by streams from the flanks of the mountain opposite—too far away to see the streams themselves, but Salli knew they were there.

She could even guess where, because she could trace the wrinkles in the flanks of the mountain's garment by the trace of still-unmelted snow. It was spectacular, even breathtaking; but why should it evoke the grateful hymn the Wayfarers were singing?

*I have made smooth the pathway of the Awakened, come
to me now and sit in the divine bliss of the Waking
beyond words.*

Carib, the last of the party, came up beside her. He
had held back even while the line had broken and
breached and hurried forward, to make certain no one
went astray. Carib handed her the field glasses from his
pack as he went past, and pointed; then he knelt with
the rest and raised his voice—Salli was surprised to realize that Carib had a tenor voice—singing with the rest.

*Oh, Holy One, we have long dreamed and waited for
your coming. The imprint of your foot is beautiful to
me, how much more beautiful your blessed face, oh Holy
One.*

Salli thought that Carib might be weeping. His voice
shook. More puzzled now than ever she raised the field
glasses and focused on the place Carib had pointed to.
It was just rocks, bare rocks, black rocks, on the flank of
the mountain, a day's walk before them still it could be.
What?
Amongst the rocks—
There.
Amongst the rocks there was an open-sided shed
roofed with grass the same color as the grass that clothed
the slopes. That natural camouflage made it difficult to
pick the shed out by sight from where she stood, even
with Carib pointing it out to her. A shed, and in the
shadow of the roof a dim pregnant outline only imperfectly visible even with the field glasses—a bell.
The prayer bell.
Scanning to the left and right of the shed Salli picked
out the low walls of summer booths, nearly invisible
amongst the waving grass. Herding people would have

used those booths, driving the grazing animals to high pasture.

Once she found one wall it led her to another, and another, and yet a third again. This was too large to have been a herders' camp. There was a city down there in the caldera, a city at the foot of Mount Corabey, waiting for the pilgrims who would come.

We are coming, as you have summoned us. We are coming at your word to hear your will. We are coming in Faith to bring Awakening. We are coming, Holy One.

The final fierce chord of the praise song echoed back against the sides of the saddle pass.

Pareek rose to her feet before the echo had fallen to silence and started forward. Salli waited for her place in the line and moved out with dispatch.

She was within sight of her goal. She was anxious to arrive. Meeka would have to accept that he'd been mistaken. He would come back to the world with her, return to Orthodoxy, and stand before the Pilgrim Court to clear his name, and no Jarrod court about it.

It could not happen soon enough for Salli.

The moon rose before sunset, full and blue-white. The caldera they had to cross was filled with alpine prairie grass, rather than the old-growth forest through which they had come; the moonlight was bright enough to see the clearly long-trodden pathway, if only as a shadowy line through the tall grass.

The prayer bell was silent, but a sense of urgency drove them on regardless. No one spoke or slackened. Salli ate dried food from her snackpack and drove forward with the rest, eager for the confrontation that would come.

She lost track of the time.

It was easy trekking; the farther they went, the better
the pathway, and Salli could see the long lines of summer booths stretching away across the broad caldera to
either side. A summer city of this extent would have
been visible from the air, and still it had gone unknown
all this time—because flight had been abandoned with
the colonies, three hundred years ago.

So important a place, and to be lost to history ... even
if it was a Wayfarer camp, and not of the Holy People,
it belonged to the ages.

Suddenly it seemed a high price to pay to Salli, the
space program for sanctity.

If the colonies had failed, did it have to mean divine
displeasure? Was it the will of God that the history of
the holy land be half-abandoned for lack of rediscovery?
Had her mother truly been a Promise-Keeper, or rather
a martyr to a tragic historical misunderstanding?

The path grew wider, easier to discern, but they
slowed down regardless because the slope had started
to climb. The moon lowered full in the western sky, blue
and luminous as the dream of hope. The eastern sky was
lightening, and it became hard to tell just where the light
was coming from.

The grassy fields, the rocky slope took on a flattened
one-dimensional sort of unreality, and the sound of
dawnbirds stirring began to break through the steady
susurration of their breathing and the walk itself. Rock
shifted underfoot with a faint crunching sound, and the
path grew steeper as the landscape grew shadowed.
They had passed the lake, now, crossing the alpine prairie in the old caldera to climb into the hem of the skirts
of holy Corabey.

Gradually it became possible to make out where the
flat rocks had been set into a footpath among the jumble
of gravel and pebbles; but the climb still slowed as the
slope of the ground increased. In the one corner of her

mind that was not completely obsessed by the trek itself
and the physical demands of walking all day and then
all night, Salli wondered at the stamina of the others in
her group. Carib's aunt Pareek was an older woman. Yet
she was at the front of the line; no one had fallen back.

She could see the outline of the hills through which
they'd come, to the south. Salli could make out the color
and texture of Meeka's shirt, dampened with sweat and
sprinkled with dew and with pollen from the flowering
of the grasses through which they'd passed. The sun was
rising.

Then the pathway widened, leveled, flattened out into
a shallow waterfall of black-slate steps that terminated
in a broad flat apron of black rock—and before them was
the bell, standing in its shrine shed on a pedestal of
smooth-grained rose-toned granite.

Standing before the bell, a figure in white, a strong
square-shouldered person with long dark hair. In skirts.
It was too dim to see her face. The Wayfarers with whom
Salli had come so far all lined up at the forward edge of
the apron and knelt; and Meeka knelt down, too.

Salli stood and stared in dumbstruck wonder, punch-
drunk and half-stupefied with fatigue.

This was the Wayfarer's Holy One, then, this the person who had changed Meeka's life, this the false prophet
who had made heterodox pariahs out of men who had
been stout pure Orthodox for seven generations?

There seemed to be people all around, filling up the
apron behind her; maybe others had followed them,
through the night. Maybe the other people had been here
already, assembling now for morning prayers?

Salli looked back over her shoulder. Yes, unfamiliar
people on the apron, lining the path up which they'd
come. Silent and waiting and kneeling in reverence, and
only Salli herself still on her feet before the Wayfarer's
Holy One.

She would not kneel to a false prophet.

She was not in the presence of the Holy One.

The woman who stood before the bell raised her hands, bending her arms at the elbows, with her palms facing out.

Salli was not twenty paces from where she stood, not thirty paces from the great bell.

"Behold," the woman said; and it was as still as the moment of Creation, as silent as the single breathless instant before the dream became matter to mold into Creation. "Behold. She rises."

The sun cleared the saddle pass east of the mountain, flooding the slope with light.

"Behold, she rises, like the Awakening."

It seemed to Salli that the sun rose within the body of the woman, so brightly was the sun reflected in the white garment that she wore. Her palms seemed to pulsate with brilliant white-gold light, and Salli didn't understand how that could be. Was she holding mirrors?

The crowd of kneeling people spoke the response with a fervor that shook Salli to her core. "Let us also wake, oh, Holy One."

The sun grew brighter moment by moment, its reflection in the woman's face and hands and clothing more brilliant breath by breath. Salli couldn't understand it. Salli had her back to the sun, and the reflected light from the figure of the woman was almost blinding. And the woman who stood there smiling at her was not even squinting. How could she face the sun and not be blinded?

"Awake, my children. Awake, my sons, shake free the delusions of this dreamworld, and know yourself for what you are."

Salli frowned and took a tentative step forward, trying to make sense of what she was seeing. The white light on the hillside was more overwhelming than that of any sunrise Salli had ever seen. She could hardly face the woman in white without having to turn away, even if she shaded her eyes with her hands.

But the rest of them weren't shading their eyes.

Meeka was on his knees right there beside her, and Meeka looked right at the woman without flinching or faltering even as the brilliance of the reflection grew and grew. With an expression of profound transcendent joy on his face—and recognition.

Salli could no longer see anything except the face of the woman enveloped in light, calm and serene. The woman nodded as Salli stared, as if in agreement with a statement that Salli had yet to make.

"Awake, my daughters," the woman said. "Rise up from your Dream of suffering. And see the light of truth."

Trembling, terrified, confused—but impelled by an urgent need within her—Salli stumbled forward, to touch the outstretched hands of the Holy One.

Salli touched her hand.

The fabric of time and space fell away from before Salli's eyes like a paper-thin gauze frayed to the vanishing point, like a film of algae swept from the surface of a pond, like threads of spider's glidesilk in the wind.

She became Creation.

The boundaries of her sense perceptions exploded into limitless Space, and she saw and heard and smelled and knew forever.

The ground beneath her feet dissolved away into the stuff of illusion. Her body ceased to exist. Pure spirit, pure energy, without form, Salli was everywhere in Creation all at once, seeing everything, knowing everything, understanding everything. In that instant Salli looked into the core reality of the created Universe and saw her own face mirrored back from every single tiny speck of matter that was or had been or was yet to be.

She was as one with the fabric of the Universe.

And because she was as one with created Space she existed within the mind of the Creator, and stood in the Creator's living presence.

She was too afraid to move.

And yet she could not but reach out to touch the consciousness of the Creator.

It was more huge and vast and infinite than the known universe, but that was not what really surprised Salli; what surprised Salli was a twofold recognition.

The Creator held her in conscious mind, and knew her for who she was; and the substance of the mind of the Creator was transcendent love.

What am I that you should take thought for me?

Staggered by the blessing, Salli fell down to her knees, clutching at the woman's sleeve with both of her hands. Shuddering.

She heard the voice of the Creator speaking wisdom and uttermost love. Salli could not speak, mute in the grip of an experience too overwhelming to fit into the narrow confines of mere language.

"Holy One," Salli cried out, finally, after what seemed a thousand years. She could say nothing else, but she knew, she knew the Holy One would understand all that she could not say. "Oh. Holy One. As it was promised. You have come to us."

The pilgrims behind Salli began to sing, chanting with a faith as deep as the roots of the mountains.

The Holy One smiled, her face full of love. Leaning down, she pressed her lips to Salli's forehead, and sealed the promise between them forever.

It was too much for the imperfection of the physical mind.

The light brightened beyond all understanding, and Salli went forward into the light, and left her body lying abandoned on the ground.

Four

The little breeze was warm, and carried with it the sweet perfume of fresh-mown grass mingled with the fragrance of the tiny snowsflower. Salli felt as though she lay afloat in a warm ocean, rocked gently beneath an awning and as safe as a babe in her great-uncle's arms. Stretching, she opened her mouth to drink the warm scented air; it was delicious, but it made her thirsty. Her mouth was dry.

Salli opened her eyes.

The sun shone at an angle across the dappled-print fabric that stretched over her to form the roof of the enclosure. She lay in shaded luxury on a pallet built of prairie grass with her back to the mossy wall of an ancient summer booth; there beside her head, a covered dish and an unglazed ceramic jug with an old-fashioned straw stopper.

Slowly she sat up.

She felt as weak as a blanched spring onion, her arms and legs as limp as steamed lettuce. The stone wall of the summer booth was cool against her back, and the warm breeze was as soothing as milktea in midwinter. If she reached forward, just a bit, she could grasp the basket handle of the jug, and drag it slowly up across her lap to slip the straw plug off on its chain of braided grass to take a drink.

Water.

Cool water, sweet water, pure water chilled in the jug by evaporation, and Salli drank and drank and drank—mouthful by mouthful—until she was full.

When the breeze shifted she could hear a sound, as though from one particular direction; and all seemed silent else. Where was everyone? Had they abandoned her? No, that couldn't be, no one would have so carefully disposed and provided for her if they meant to run away.

The sound seemed to be that of a voice.

Her hat lay at the foot of the grass pallet, together with her gear. Someone had changed her hiking boots for camp slippers: that had been kindly done, but now as she woke up moment by moment she grew impatient to understand where she was and what was going on.

Something had happened to her. She knew that.

She could not quite remember what it was, but she knew that it had been overpowering, and the most important thing that had ever happened in her life.

The world had changed. Her life had changed. There was something huge and wonderful outside this summer booth, and though she wasn't afraid that she might lose it, she was nevertheless anxious to remember what it was.

The wind breathed, and paused, and sighed once more, and Salli knew what direction she wanted to go in. She rose to her feet, only a little unsteady; took a final drink—deep and greedy, sweet and satisfying—then ducked her head out from under the fabric tenting that roofed the summer booth, and headed toward the voice. The autumnal slopes of Corabey rose close behind her; Salli could see the rising rock, black and russet and tan with the late-summer foliage. The voice came from the opposite direction.

"And I ask you to ... your heart ... could win your love?"

She was getting closer. Salli could begin to make out words, phrases. The summer city had bloomed while she had slept; each booth marked off as occupied by the ceiling cloth of one group or another. But nobody stirred. There was only the wind: and the voice.

". . . only one word. Nonsense. Complete and arrant nonsense. Do these take me for an idiot? Do they take you for children?"

A woman's voice, clear and strong, carrying on the breeze. The scent of water: the lake in the caldera, then. Salli remembered having gone around the lake. It had been at night. She had smelled it, green and wet and holy in its purity.

"And yet I know of no other explanation. Well. I have this to say to you, and if you will be guided by me you will hear these words and consider them most carefully."

One last long avenue of summer booths and tall grass, and Salli stepped into the clearing at the lake.

There were dozens, hundreds of people there, sitting on the ground, and on a platform at the water's edge—

Salli remembered.

The Holy One.

Not just another Wayfarer false prophet, not any mere religious teacher with too enthusiastic a following or delusions of godhood.

The Holy One.

And Meeka had been right all along.

"The teaching of the Return is that the world had fallen into delusion, and that the desolation of the colonies was a sign. This I say to you, now. The teaching itself is a delusion. The desolation of the colonies was a sign of nothing but a failure to account for the effects of habituation. And in turning our backs on learning and the search for knowledge and understanding, we show unspeakable ingratitude toward God."

Salli didn't want to interrupt anyone's concentration. She didn't want to draw attention to herself. But she had to hear what the Holy One was saying. She had to get closer. Finding a narrow, winding path between the seated congregants, Salli worked her way down toward the lakeshore, moving as meekly as she could manage.

"The world is the real world, it is only you who are dreaming. The reality is here, for you to touch and taste and smell. It was not created thus for you to piously ignore the wonders that await your every step into discovery."

She found her place ten meters from the pond and sank down onto the ground.

She could not take her eyes off the Holy One.

Plainly dressed in loose-cuffed shorts, her hiker's socks the same taupe color of hikers' socks from one end of Shadene to the next, her loose hair lying in flat relaxed waves across her shoulders—this ordinary-looking person, this simple Shadene Wayfarer, this unremarkable woman was the Promised One.

"It is a sin to scorn the riches of the world, it is a sin to have no use for science. I am come to put this right before too much time is lost and harm is done. Children. How could the wonders of this world exist merely to draw you into error? Such teaching is false teaching, and no true orthodoxy."

Salli had never heard such radical suggestions in her life.

And she knew without question that they were true.

"We must have science. We must have medicine. It is a sin to have the means to reach the stars, and not aspire to them."

This was the Holy One.

And nothing Salli had meant or intended to do in her whole life mattered now.

The day's teaching had ended, the congregation had dispersed. Salli sat alone in the grass at the side of the lake with her knees drawn up and her head buried in her folded arms. The breeze stilled, and reversed itself; the light changed as the sun tracked across the Circuit of Heaven.

The sun went down.

Still Salli sat, her mind so full of the great echoing reverberation of her experience that there was no room for hunger, thirst, or even an awareness of the passage of time.

The Holy One.

All of her life she had spoken prayers and said the litanies, her faith more the cherished habit of a well-socialized young adult than that passionate—wild and ecstatic—union described by the Dream Lover theology. Now that she knew what it was like to join her waking mind to the consciousness of the Creator, how could she doubt that Varrick was the Holy One?

How was she to understand that after all the centuries of waiting the Holy One had come at last to be here and to be now?

Overwhelmed by remorse at having doubted Meeka's conversion, swamped by chagrin at having breathed the same air as the Holy One for these months gone past in ignorance of Varrick's existence, but most of all still shaken body and soul by what she had experienced, Salli lay down on the grass and wept.

The cool dirt smelled comforting and reassuring. She dug her fingers through the root mat of the tall grass to work them deep into that black earth, wishing above all else to take root and find transformation. She could be a tree, a reed, a grass, and glorify the Creator with every breeze that passed.

She no longer wanted to be Salli Rangarold. Salli Rangarold had doubted the Holy One, and had approached her with selfish motives in her heart, intending to learn about Varrick in order to woo her brother back and have good information to provide her chain of command. This was a sin, and Salli wept in shame, the hot salt tears soaking into the cool fertile soil.

She cried herself out in shame and sharp regret; and then she lay there, without the strength or energy to rouse herself and go back to the camp. She was thirsty now, again.

How was she going to find her way back to the booth where her gear was?

Drifting in and out, on the border of consciousness, Salli awoke with a sudden start.

People.

Coming toward her.

"I'm so sorry." Young female voice, familiar. One of the people Salli had been traveling with, Carib's daughter Enis. "I promised to stay with her while she slept. But she slept so soundly, and so long, and I wanted to hear the teaching. It was so selfish of me, and look at what has happened."

People coming toward her through the grass, with bright glowing night torches whose soft white light identified them as being solar-powered. Salli was suddenly painfully aware of the fact that her clothing was rumpled, her face at least blotched—and quite possibly dust-streaked as well.

Then she heard Meeka. "It's all right, Enis, there's no harm done. My sister can outsleep Return Day fireworks when she makes up her mind to it. You couldn't have known that she was going to wander off, and she was seen listening to Teaching herself, so you've got that in common, don't you?"

This was unhappy confirmation of Salli's suspicion—they were looking for her. And she in her condition. She was going to have to reveal herself; she could tell from the tone of Meeka's affectionate cajolery that Enis was very much upset.

As reluctant as Salli was to sit up, she was more reluctant still to be stumbled across while lying on her belly in the grass. Well. It was one thing or the other. She would feel better if she made the move.

Slowly, stiffly, Salli rolled over onto her back and sat up in the summer grass.

There were three people looking for her. Enis and Meeka: and even in the uncertain light from the torches Salli recognized the woman called Varrick. There might have been some other people there as well, but Salli had eyes only for Varrick.

"Salli, is that you?"

The Holy One.

Enis rushed forward to help Salli stand up, her shadowed face difficult to read in the light cast by the night torches. Anxiety. Relief. Guilt. A little resentment. Maybe—Salli told herself—she was imagining the resentment, projecting what her own feelings might have been. It didn't matter. She owed Enis an apology, whether or not Enis was angry at her.

"I was having a dream." It was one of those things that sounded perfectly reasonable in a person's own mind, and perfectly idiotic when spoken aloud. "Mount Corabey. Dancing."

She thought that had been it, anyway. "When I woke up I heard the Teaching, and I had to get nearer. I'm sorry, Enis. I shouldn't have wandered off like that, but I heard the Holy One—and I—"

And she couldn't keep her voice steady. The Holy One

was there, not two steps from her. Enis was holding her, stroking her back soothingly, but suddenly Salli was overwhelmed all over again with the memory of what she'd felt when Varrick had touched her.

Her knees gave way, she knelt down in the grass and buried her face in her hands. "Oh, Holy One. I have sinned against you, I have been dreaming, don't let the woman I was keep me from your teaching—"

There might have been a signal; Meeka and Enis were there together, raising her up.

"Nonsense," said Varrick.

It was not the voice of transcendent reality, the voice that could wake up the world.

It was the voice of a teacher, a little hoarse, tired, resonant with love and forbearance.

That was all.

There were no showers of starfall in Varrick's voice, no movement of mountains, no dissolution of desert into ocean.

Salli relaxed, and listened to Varrick's scolding gratefully.

"Nonsense, young woman. You're not expected to be psychic, only to know the truth when you hear it. And for that you have to hear it. That's why your brother wanted you to come here with him. Yes?"

"And you should listen to me," Meeka added, ever one to take advantage. "Because I was right. Wasn't I, Salli? Come on, you know it's true."

An old joke, it grounded Salli at last. She could be comfortable. She could. Well, maybe she could not be comfortable in the presence of the Holy One, but Meeka's joke had connected the here and now after the shock of her experience with her family history, her previous life, and given her back her framework for reality. She knew who she was. She knew where she was.

She knew that she was hungry.

"Go on with you," the teacher admonished Meeka. "You're going to meeting, I think? Now that your sister is found."

"Batchelder drums," Meeka agreed, grinning, and stepped away from Salli with a final hug of reassurance. "I'm learning the lore. It's great."

"We'll let him go, and then we'll go get something to eat." Varrick said it to Salli with as easy a confidence as if she had known Salli forever. She was the Holy One. She *had* known Salli forever. "Just wait a minute, though, Meeka. Batchelder. Is that men who aren't married? Or who won't marry? Or is it men that no one will agree to marry?"

The old argument, the old joke. The Hilde Batchelders had been a fraternal service order at some point in the fairly distant past. The word itself, *batchelder*, had never been translated to everyone's satisfaction, and academic controversy still raged over the issues of whether the Hilde Batchelders had been artisans, freemen, or mercenaries of some sort.

If Varrick knew, she was not letting on.

Meeka just smiled—smiled, and at the Holy One—and went trotting off into the night, in the direction of the summer booths. Now that Salli had stood up she could see lights, there, through the tall grass, lights muted behind fabric roofs in booth after booth after booth.

Hundreds.

How many people had come to Corabey?

Had they been here just one day, or longer?

"They're a wild bunch, the batchelders," Varrick said to Salli, shaking her head. It might have been ruefully, but it was hard to tell for sure. "We'll get someone to keep an eye on them. Salli. Come and eat. Then you can tell me how you tracked Carib as far as you did, avalanche soldier."

It seemed a reasonable request.

Salli was happy.

"As you say, Teacher," she agreed, meekly.

To be in the presence of the Holy One was to be in the abode of sanctity, in the mansion of bliss.

Further than that plain fact Salli had neither desire nor energy to wonder.

Since the day that the bottom had dropped out of her world Salli had worked with the camp's security. It was what she was best at, as an avalanche soldier; and it was something she could do without too much mental effort, which left her mind free to think deeply on the event that had recentered her worldview and anchored it so unexpectedly in so unconventional a religious teaching. Most of all it was a task which brought Salli to Varrick on a regular basis, as she participated in the Wayfarer's system of negotiated conflict resolution.

And she got all over the camp, seeing as much of it as she wanted. Security work gave Salli access to features of intense interest that she would not have enjoyed as a mere pilgrim. The knowledge she gained would have been useful, perhaps, to the Shadene secular authority in establishing a profile for this new cult. But it wasn't a cult. And Salli only cared about the Shadene secular authority to the extent that she wanted to protect Varrick's people against any intrusions for as long as possible.

Negotiated conflict resolution bid her today to the shrine shed, and from there through to the cave and Varrick's presence. The shrine shed was set against the slope of the mountain, the bell suspended from a huge crossbeam that looked as though it had aged iron-hard. The foundation posts of the shrine shed were massive and close-grained—a good thing, too, Salli had decided.

There was no telling whether avalanches were frequent at Mount Corabey, but the signs were all there.

And the shrine shed looked to be able to weather the worst of them.

At the back of the shrine shed, where it abutted against the living rock of Mount Corabey, instead of a blank wall or an open wall there was a passageway through the rock. A short corridor led to a shallow flight of stairs that bridged a black chasm of unknown depth; then the passageway opened up into a high-vaulted cave, dimly lit by sunlight that found its way through open places high up on the south wall.

It was very pleasant in the cave, if cool; the chasm that underlay the shrine shed was apparently deep enough to function as a well for cold air, and the air currents in the cave teased that pleasant chill into the cave for everyone's enjoyment.

Varrick lived in this cave.

Varrick lived here and took council here; there was room for fifty to seventy people in the cave at once. There was a raised place at the back that was level with Salli's shoulders. A ladder leaned against one side, and its flat surface—twice as long on a side as Meeka was tall, and him Pilgrim—was covered with rugs and wooleries for comfort.

It could get chilly in the cavern at night, and when it did they built the fire up in the base of the platform and vented the smoke out behind it. There was a natural chimney of some sort there, clearly enough, because although Salli had helped build the fire more than once over the course of the past week she had yet to see the woodsmoke draw within the cave itself.

On this raised platform Varrick ate and slept, consulted her theology students, presided over conflict-resolution meetings. On this raised platform Varrick sat now, facing a caveful of angry elders on one side and her batchelders on the other.

"Holy One, your wisdom surpasses that of common man, and I your student do not mean to challenge it."

The elders were all ages, actually. People of responsibility and authority, or rather influence, within the camp. In this case it was a woman not much older than Salli who spoke—Jeluga Regh, standing before the elders with her hands clasped in front of her and stating her case firmly.

"I am concerned about the attitude of the batchelders. We are your children, Holy One. But we are also good law-abiding citizens of the state of Shadene."

And Salli was glad to hear it. Being at Mount Corabey was slightly against the law, but that was a relatively minor thing compared to the real issues that faced the state of Shadene from within and without and threatened the public order . . . not to speak of the survival of the state.

During such hearings the security post was at the foot of the ladder up onto the teacher's platform. Salli edged forward to have a better view of Jeluga, who was wrapping up.

"I see no need to tolerate this reactionary, absolutist rhetoric on the part of your batchelders. We are not at war with church, state, or Pilgrim. To the contrary, we mean to coexist peacefully. The ranting of these batchelders is a bad influence on young and impressionable people. I speak for all of those here assembled with me when I seek your teaching on what is best done."

Varrick was sitting cross-legged at the foot of the platform, a narrow strip of untanned flesh shining pallid and incongruous where the pose tugged Varrick's socks down her shins a bit. Now she shifted her weight—her foot had apparently gone to sleep—and drained her glass of water, setting it down beside her near-empty pitcher before giving Jeluga the nod.

"Thank you, Jeluga, Elders. Let us now hear the batchelder representative's argument."

The details of the problem had been worked over in advance. Varrick had already been briefed on the specific incidents that formed the basis for the elders' complaints. She'd met with elders and batchelders separately before this, passing arguments back and forth until both sides declared themselves content that Varrick knew the complaint and the defense.

All that was left was to complete the formalities, and for Varrick to announce the compromise solution that had been developed over these three days past.

"We appreciate Elder Jeluga's concern, Holy One. But we have done nothing wrong."

The batchelder spokesman was a Wayfarer named Muirje, short, powerfully built, with black eyes that goggled a bit in his face—an enduring legacy from the last days of Shadene's poverty, just a generation gone. He was a very personable sort. He treated her with patronizing amusement, but Salli liked him immensely.

"Although we are united by your Teaching, Holy One, we are all still our own people. Elder Jeluga is charitable, and finds it easier to live if she ignores the signs of conflict that lie plainly before us all. There are powerful forces in the world that are inimical to our autonomy. We speak of that conflict, Holy One. We seek to find others who see the world as we do."

Meeka stood with the batchelders, looking calm and relaxed and at peace with himself. Salli was glad that he'd found a place to belong: Meeka needed to belong. It was fundamental to his character. And typical that, once having embraced this new Teaching, he would go overboard and take things to extremes. Yes, the Orthodox nations of Creation would take advantage of instability in Shadene to push conversion to theocracy—an Orthodox theocracy, needless to say. That didn't mean there were plots to destabilize the government and make that happen.

Now Varrick spoke. "If we cannot deal peaceably amongst ourselves, there is no reason for anybody to believe we can deal peaceably with other Teachings. Muirje, people generally interpret accusations of conspiracy as expressing hostility on the accuser's part. How can I permit you to walk through my camp and talk about Pilgrim persecution, and about Shadene secular authority collusion with the Pilgrim Police to the great despite of poor innocent Wayfarers? I have no room in my Teaching for victim theology, Muirje."

It was the batchelders amongst Varrick's people who resented the Pilgrims most, the batchelders who felt that they were discriminated against, the batchelders who claimed to believe that Creation was plotting against them. And Meeka had embraced their thought; or at least they had embraced Meeka, and he seemed to feel that their view of the world and his accorded miraculously well with one another.

For herself she found the batchelder rhetoric tiresome, as did Elder Jeluga and the others. To be scrupulously fair, Salli had to admit that she had enjoyed privileges not extended to Wayfarers, and just by virtue of her status as a Pilgrim.

But she didn't think there was a gigantic conspiracy of any sort to keep Wayfarers down and disenfranchise them of their own land.

Muirje bowed his head, accepting rebuke on behalf of all the batchelders. It had all been worked out beforehand. So Salli knew what came next.

"Is there a venue for us to speak, Holy One, so that we may find like-minded thinkers who have come to your Teaching?"

Oh, all right. We'll shut up in public. We can say anything we want in private, after all. So how do we go about finding like-minded souls? Because we think there's a problem, Holy One, and we intend to be ready to protect ourselves.

"You shall have platform time twice a week, when we do community announcements. You will review your remarks with Elder Jeluga or her representative before you speak. She has no authority to censor, change, or cancel, but if there is an objection, we will be forced to reconsider."

Make sure your speech is innocuous enough and you're home free. The people you need will find you. It is just those people who read three pages into each paragraph who would be likely candidates for the batchelders, after all.

Now Muirje and Jeluga bowed their heads in unison. "Thank you, Teacher. It shall be done so."

Varrick sighed, puffing the air into her cheeks until she looked like some deformed aquarium fish.

"Salli. Let's go fill water jugs before noon meeting."

The batchelders and the elders alike were filing out; there was no more business that morning, but it would soon be time for Varrick to speak to the congregation. Meeka winked at Salli on his way past; Salli acknowledged his greeting with a nod, but she couldn't muster a smile.

Varrick noticed, of course.

But Varrick merely shook her near-empty jug of water and suggested, "Walk with me, Salli, I need to go out to the springs." And held her peace thereafter, until she and Salli had left the residence cave and started upslope and east for the cave that sheltered the wellhead from which Varrick drew her water.

"Problem, Pilgrimsdaughter?"

Varrick's question was half-teasing, but affectionate. For whatever reason Varrick always made Salli blush when Varrick called her that. And sure enough, Salli flushed, and grinned at the teasing, and frowned once more—almost simultaneously.

"The batchelders, Holy One." She'd paid attention in her avalanche soldier training classes. She could remember the lectures on the formation of terrorist groups—Bern Travers's lectures. Partly because Travers was an interesting lecturer. Partly because he could be considered to be an attractive person, in a mongrel sort of way—and a curiosity, Shadene father, Wayfarer mother. But mostly because his backwoods skills and his psychological acumen alike were unquestionably top of the line.

"Meeka seems to become more and more single-minded the more time he spends with them. I can't credit all those absurd conspiracy theories. I have a hard time believing that my brother actually seems to have accepted them."

Varrick placed her feet carefully on the slope; it wasn't steep—less than thirty degrees—but the surface was irregular enough with rocks and clumps of autumn vegetation.

"There's nothing to be done about that all-or-nothing mentality, Salli, it's the curse of the male animal. On or off. Up or down. Yes or no, wet or dry, black or white."

All right. Salli got the idea. Varrick was being a little extravagant, a little unfair, but she'd made her point.

"Meeka's a policeman, Holy One. Absolutists aren't welcome on security forces. Anybody's security forces." *And shouldn't you be concerned that these batchelders, who look to nominate themselves as your security force, seem to be comprised of absolutists?* she wondered, silently.

They'd reached the cave mouth; Varrick stood aside to let Salli go in first. It was a narrow cave mouth, but there was plenty of room inside; and the water was indescribably delicious—

"Jarrod's coming," Varrick said, joining Salli in the cave. It was cool, and the water welled up fast and full enough to fill the little hollows all around the brim of the basin in the floor. People had been coming here for the sweet water for a very long time; the cave's floor was hollowed by the knees of countless water-bearers before them.

"I think your brother is going a little overboard because he's very uncertain right now about what will happen. Wait for Jarrod, Salli. Once that's over with, he may recover his sense of balance, don't you think?"

It sounded very reasonable, and Salli welcomed the suggestion with an eager heart. But it didn't really provide an answer to the problem. Meeka's stronger fanaticism was only part of the issue. Once Jarrod court was over, Meeka might relax; but what about the rest of the batchelders?

Kneeling down at the edge of the well basin, Varrick drank the icy water from cupped hands before filling her pitcher.

Varrick was Holy and Awakened, Salli reminded herself.

And she could revisit the issue once again, after Jarrod.

Finally it came, the day of the Jarrod court, the day that would free Meeka of his burden of guilt and anguish and hurt.

The sun was brilliant in the cool blue sky, as far north as it would ever be; for it was equinox, halfway to midwinter, and already the sun had started to track back south above Mount Corabey. Varrick's people had assembled around the lake; Varrick stood on the platform at the water's edge from which she spoke her Teaching, while Meeka with his Advocate waited on the shore facing the crowd.

Meeka was pale, and Salli's heart ached for him. *It will be over soon*, she promised him, willing her thought to reach him through telepathy. *Life will begin again. Soon. It will be soon.*

"Children," Varrick called; and the crowd responded as if with one voice.

Teacher.

"Children, we have come today to hear the serious matter of the burdens on the soul of a man from amongst our congregation. You know this man, he is your brother Meeka, but you may not know the grief from which he suffers."

Actually Salli felt that more people knew what the trouble was than didn't. Meeka stood out amongst Varrick's congregation in a variety of ways, and he had not been shy about confessing himself to anyone who expressed any curiosity as to what he was doing there. Varrick's speaking followed the formulae, more or less.

"Oh my beloved, children in faith. While we live in illusion we must have law. Hear now the law of the Jarrod court as we proclaim its jurisdiction."

There was a group of elders standing at the foot of the crowd, at Varrick's right. One of them—Carib's aunt Pareek—stepped down to the lakeshore and spoke, turning to face the crowd, raising her voice.

"The law says that the faithful shall be judged by the faithful, and the law of the heretic or unbeliever shall have no force among the godly. We are all faithful here, and will hear the plaints of faithful in this Jarrod. If any shall object, let them speak and be heard as guests beneath these skies and this sun. Meeka Pilgrimson, come forward."

One step forward was about all Meeka could manage, with the crowd as thick as it was. Meeka lowered his head, as if in submissive resignation; but his expression seemed tense, to Salli. Beside him, Muirje—the batchelder who was to speak as Advocate—responded in due form.

"This man is Meeka Pilgrimson, who comes before you to answer for the death of the body that housed a human soul. And if no one feels he has more right than I to speak for Meeka, I will be his advocate."

Salli's attention had been focused on Varrick and the elders. Now she realized that there was a commotion of some sort at the back of the crowd. People were still arriving, it seemed. And at least one of them was still pushing his way resolutely forward—a short man, wearing a climbing hat that concealed his features, his personal kit dusty and stained and showing evidence of a long trek through the woods.

When he was within three ranks of the front row the man spoke.

"I contest the jurisdiction of the Jarrod court over this matter."

The people who stood in front of him moved to allow him access to the lakeshore. Something about his voice suddenly bothered Salli, and when the man came through the ranks to stand at the water's edge at last she realized what it was.

She knew him.

Not intimately well, perhaps, but well enough to know who he was—and to be able to guess immediately why he was here.

"Who are you, and why do you rebuke the Jarrod court?" Varrick asked. There was no hostility in her voice; Salli guessed it was just formula. At the same time Varrick did seem genuinely surprised. Had she not then foreseen this development?

She was the Holy One; how could she not have foreseen it?

"My name is Bern Travers, Teacher. I come to speak on behalf of the Shadene Secular Authority."

Bern.

She'd attended his training classes; he gave seminars

on crowd management, sensitivity training. Marksmanship. There was a joke in Bern Travers being a sensitivity training instructor: Bern was a half-breed. His father had been Orthodox, but his mother was Wayfarer, and Bern took after his mother in matters of faith. He managed to look Pilgrim enough to get Pilgrim students to listen to him, though.

"The Shadene Secular Authority yields to the Jarrod," Muirje said, and there was an edge of angry aggression in his voice. "You have no cause to challenge these proceedings."

Bern nodded, reaching up for his broad-brimmed climbing hat to take it off. There was no telling whether he was agreeing or merely uncovering his head in respect for the Jarrod court, the gesture was that smooth and that methodical. "The secular authority yields to the Jarrod court. That's true."

Bern's voice was mild and reasonable, and he had the teachers' trick of speaking softly enough that people quieted themselves to hear. Some of Salli's troop made fun of that in Bern: typical, they said, of the underhanded and manipulative Wayfarer in his blood. Salli hadn't ever thought that was a fair criticism.

And Bern was still talking. "Still. I don't mean to offer any offense. But this is not a true Jarrod for secular authority purposes. And I would like to argue against hearing this case anywhere outside Hilbrane."

Hilbrane, the ocean-fronted capital, the oldest city in Shadene. Where the secular authority had its headquarters, and its high court. There were murmurs in the crowd, for all Bern's experience in mob management; Varrick raised her arms, her palms turned outward to quiet the assembly.

"No offense is taken," Varrick said firmly. "Speak upon your argument, Bern Travers, and the Jarrod court will hear and deliberate."

Meeka looked confused, standing with his Advocate in the middle of the witness space of the lakeshore and yet all but ignored and invisible. Salli's heart went out to her brother; she resented Bern for interfering. Meeka couldn't know. Meeka hadn't done sensitivity training with Bern, not ever.

Bern walked past Meeka toward Varrick's platform as though Meeka wasn't even there. "Teacher, and children of the Wayfarer teaching. Salli."

Surprised to be noticed, Salli blushed at the note of mild superior surprise in Bern's voice. Then blushed more deeply, angry at herself for coloring in the first place.

"Teacher, the killing was done on disputed ground, and by the Pilgrim Police. We all know what these two things mean. It is already an unsettled year, Teacher. And it is vital that we show the world no weakness, because there are Orthodox in Creation all too willing to solve our internal conflicts for us."

Because the riot in which Meeka's unfortunate victim had met his accidental death was one of the smaller of this year's crop, and each year the Orthodox states questioned the long-term stability of the state of Shadene. The riots grew worse in the summertime. By and large Wayfarers could not afford to go to the mountains to escape the heat.

"Now to try this man before this court, which does not have the authority of the Wayfarer churches behind it, creates an incendiary situation. It sets church against church, Teacher, because the Varrick Teaching has never been examined and declared sound doctrine. Best to manage the problem as a civil one, Teacher."

Surrender Meeka to the secular authority to avoid sectarian passion, in other words, and to validate the Shadene secular authority's judicial practice. Let Meeka be judged as a citizen, so that the issue of the land in dispute could be quietly turned aside, and Shadene show itself on the world stage of Creation as a state in control of its population.

Varrick struck her palms together sharply; the crack of the sound was startling. "You approach me as the servant of the degraded Word."

She had their attention, right enough. Salli grinned to herself: *Take that, Bern, here's more than one Wayfarer can work a crowd.*

But she wondered at herself for the thought.

Varrick sounded angry. "And now you insult me. Now you give offense, because you ask me to stand down from my teaching and defer to a civil court. I am angry, Bern Travers. I will hear no more of this."

Angry, because Bern had asked the Holy One to do a politic thing rather than simply stand on her rights. Of course for Bern the politic thing was the right thing. It was his job to be politic.

Or was something else going on?

"Teacher, I ask to be forgiven." Still calm, still quiet; Bern apologized for the fact that she had taken offense, not for having given offense. He was insufferable. *I'm sorry you feel that way about what I said*, not *I'm sorry I said something that made you feel that way.* "I didn't come to insult anybody. But Meeka Rangarold Pilgrimson should stand trial at Hilbrane, and at no other place. It's the only solution to an already difficult situation, one he didn't make any better by—"

By running away. By failing to report and fleeing, as though he had done something wrong. Had he done anything wrong? Salli wondered, suddenly.

She could remember being angry at him for his inexplicable behavior, for his apostasy.

Now she was apostate as well, with less excuse; she had not fled blood-guilt. Should she wonder at herself?

Every time she reached back to Salli-before from Salli-now her memory of her experience of Creation stepped before her, and reminded her that her whole universe had shifted in a very real sense when Varrick had touched her hand.

This was not apostasy.

There was no right or wrong.

There was only the Holy One, and the Holy One's mere presence transcended all.

"No more," Varrick repeated, and the crowd closed in on Bern where he stood. "Put this mocker of the Word away, I do not wish to see him. Jarrod will have to wait. We cannot rule with anger in our hearts."

No.

Poor Meeka—

And yet Varrick was right. The mood of the crowd was irritable; violence seemed to lie close beneath the surface, held in check by respect for the Holy One. Salli couldn't see Bern, he was surrounded. She hoped he wouldn't provoke a fight.

"Meeka Pilgrimson," Varrick called. The crowd fell back to clear the witness space. Bern was no longer there. "Meeka, I'm sorry to make you wait. Let no one chide the Pilgrimson for that he did not speak at Jarrod. There will be another time."

Meeka was pale and looked mulish. Angry, yes. What right had Bern to come and intrude on this matter? What did Bern care?

Now Meeka would wait to be relieved of guilt, Meeka would have to hold his grief within until he could speak a public confession, make his plea aloud. The guilt of it had been eating on him like poison in his belly for months.

"We hear your word, Holy One," Muirje said. "Let Meeka Pilgrimson be accepted among us until then, and no blame put on him."

More batchelders came up out of the crowd to put

sympathetic hands to Meeka's shoulders as he turned to go.

"Salli." Pareek—starting toward the swelling flank of Mount Corabey, starting for the shrine shed, and the other elders with her—beckoned for Salli where she stood watching Meeka go. "Come to council, Salli. Varrick has asked for you."

So black and bitter was Meeka's scowl that Salli—all coward for that moment, her heart quailing before the savagery of her brother's evident rage—welcomed the call to go with Varrick, and keep apart from him.

Because it meant that she'd have a good excuse for keeping away from Meeka, equally as much as she would sit with the Holy One.

Five

Entering the shrine shed and going left-wise around the great prayer bell respectfully, Salli stepped down into the council chamber to find her place on the lowest hewn-stone bench.

Varrick was already sitting on her raised platform at the far end of her residence cave, cross-legged, hands folded, staring at the floor. She looked like a saint in meditation; except that the saints in meditation were usually shown wearing gowns of some sort, and Varrick almost always wore trousers—more practical for hill-climbing.

The room filled quickly.

Varrick didn't speak.

Somebody slipped through the seated audience, crossing the open space in the middle of the room to lean forearms and elbows on the speaker's platform and whisper up at Varrick. Was it Muirje? Salli frowned, but couldn't decide for sure; it was dim in the council chamber, though it was bright morning outside.

There was a little breeze that blew from deep within the mountain, stirring the air in the cave; Salli concentrated on the simple pleasure of it, cool air, like the refreshment of the spirit in the presence of the Awakened.

Whoever it was who had come to speak to Varrick, Varrick nodded, and he went away—but deeper into the cave, not outside into the sun. Salli hadn't seen anyone go deeper into council than this room, before, but why should it surprise her that there were passageways beyond—especially given the evidence of the breeze?

Varrick raised her head and looked across the room at Salli.

"You know this man, daughter of Pilgrims?"

Varrick sounded dubious, even worried. Salli shifted where she sat, uncomfortable, but unable to discover why she should be. Bern was nothing to her, or she to Bern. He had been surprised to see her, maybe.

"Bern Travers is also a teacher, Holy One. I met him in the Academy." The Sillume Academy, that was to say, a school for avalanche soldiers. "A troubleshooter for the Shadene secular authority." She wanted to say something more about him, something that would explain to these people about Bern. He was one of the people who always seemed very sure of himself. But he had the credentials to back him up. "He's very well respected."

As if that meant anything. What a stupid thing to say. Varrick frowned, and Salli felt miserably certain that it was at her gaucherie. "He seems to remember you particularly, Salli. It isn't fair to ask you, but I wonder if you'd mind. What do you think of his being here?"

Well . . . Salli started to open her mouth but shut it again, thinking fast. Bern. Had come to take Meeka to Hilbrane, to the secular court there; had come alone, but . . .

"He would believe it best for the civil order that Meeka not be judged by any Jarrod court." Well, Bern had only said as much, hadn't he? "But if he couldn't win Meeka to come back, he wouldn't want an incident. I doubt there are troops."

Of course that didn't begin to answer the questions that were raised by Bern's appearance. Bern might have come alone, as she had, to try to win the point by an

appeal to reason. That didn't mean others weren't waiting to see if Bern was successful or not. Nor did it answer how Bern had found them.

"We will shift our teaching." Varrick raised her head,
raised her voice, so that the entire chamber reverberated
at the sound.

Salli could believe she heard the bell, outside, behind
them, answer in like wise; but it had to be her imagination. Such limited energy as any given voice would
carry surely could not stir so massy a thing as the great
prayer bell to respond to the vibration.

"It has been coming time to speak out to Creation, and
this man's arrival shall be taken as evidence that the
outer world will hear us. Because they know we're here.
Perhaps we will all go to Jarrod at Pellassa, and see
whether any secular authority tries to take Meeka Pilgrimson away from his true Dreaming there."

Salli listened in misery. Varrick's voice was clear and
full of challenge, and that could only mean trouble. And
yet this was the Holy One. Who else should challenge
the complacency of the imperfect truce that governed
Shadene?

Why would Varrick permit conflict, unless it served
the end of a true Awakening?

Bern's unexpected appearance had unnerved Salli, set
her off-balance. It was all too easy even for an Awakened
soul to doubt the wisdom of the Teacher; first the batchelders, now this. Salli shut her eyes to say a small prayer,
humbled in her heart at the realization of how easily the
soul could fall into delusion yet again in the very presence of the Holy One.

Then Varrick spoke her name.

"Salli. I want you to stay behind with this Bern Trav-
ers. I dare not leave him imprisoned here alone, nor do
I think it prudent to leave any of these people with him.
There is no way to tell. Something might happen."

What?

The Holy One was leaving her here?

She could not break into tears of anguished protest and throw herself at Varrick's feet. Not here. Not now. Varrick would know how Salli felt, already. All she could do was swallow and submit.

"I am true to your teaching, Holy One." It was as strong a protest as she could make; and it was only the formula for acquiescence. To hear was to obey. "I will stay with Bern, as you instruct me."

She had not stopped to think, in all these days, that she might not be near to Varrick forever. Until Bern said something, it hadn't occurred to Salli that Wayfarer Holy Ones without benefit of church certification led furtive, carefully concealed lives of preaching to small groups in private homes, unpublicized, ignored by the authorities.

That was the root and cause for the glad passion that had driven Carib's party to kneel in tearful prayer on the stony surface of the saddle pass, that had driven them to walk all night after having walked all day to come into the presence of the true Holy One. Varrick was their Holy One. And to imagine being parted from her was maddeningly, piercingly painful for Salli.

Varrick rose to her feet, turning to climb down off her platform. "Elders, break camp and clear the area. Go out as quietly as you came in, we invite no trouble. Once the faithful are safely removed from Corabey it will not matter if the soldiers come. Salli, come with me. I will talk to your Bern Travers."

This was just a sop to Salli's feelings, in light of the unkindness Varrick showed in making her stay behind. Salli followed Varrick out of the council chamber, mute with misery. She was not to be allowed to go with Varrick. She had to stay behind.

And yet of all these people, all of these surely hundreds of people who had arrived at Corabey over these past few days, of all of these people only a few could reasonably go out with Varrick if they meant to pass without creating problems. Any entourage would mark Varrick as the ringleader, the figurehead, identify her as the Wayfarer's Holy One and make her vulnerable to be apprehended and sequestered by Synod—the Wayfarer church authorities—or the Shadene secular authority.

It was part of the bargain that the Shadene government had made with the Wayfarer religious establishment when Pilgrims had first started to return to Shadene. Both Wayfarer heterodox and Pilgrim Orthodox in Shadene agreed to checks and balances to keep the uneasy peace between them.

Only after examination and licensure were heterodox teachers to be allowed to speak in public of the great Awakening. Teachers who sought to speak their piece without official sanction were to be treated as mere demagogues, and silenced accordingly.

Varrick walked quickly from the shrine shed up the hillside, and people made way for her until she had climbed past the outskirts of the temporary settlement with Salli in figurative tow behind her. Salli had not climbed so far up the slope before, and weighed it as she went with a half-unconscious attention born of her five years as an avalanche soldier.

Bare slope.

Low vegetation; some brush, no trees—the ancient religious sites of the hill people were almost always characterized by the absence of old growth.

There were people waiting at a rock that sheltered a cave mouth, but Varrick didn't pause to speak to them. She went straight in, and Salli after her had to stop abruptly to avoid running into Varrick where she stood.

It was dark.

Varrick stood silent for a moment, and Salli's eyes adjusted to the dim light in the cave.

This was a small cave, made peculiar by the heavy wooden grate that divided it in two—back from front. There was a ledge to sleep on behind the grate, and Salli thought she might smell running water; not a bad cell, for a cave, but a cell nonetheless, and within the prison— Bern.

He'd stood up as Varrick had come in, or at least he was standing now with his hands wrapped around the old worn slats of the wooden grate. They would be as dense as iron with age, Salli guessed, blackened as they were by time—and how many other such clutching grips? For his own part Bern looked a little more dusty than he had earlier, but Salli could see no sign of any injury.

Nor did Bern sound hurt.

"Eldest. You honor me." In fact what Bern sounded was hungry, in some way. The hunger of the soul, in the presence of the Holy One. "I hope you won't deny me your sweet teaching. I've been hearing about your word for more than a year, and couldn't get to see you until now."

Varrick folded her arms over her brown mock-tunic, apparently amused and irritated at once. "Some nerve, Bern Travers. You show up uninvited at Jarrod, and thanks to you these people all go home without it. You challenge my authority lay and religious, and who knows how many troops of Pilgrim police are lurking out there in the woods? And still on top of it all you want to hear wisdom."

It was too dim to see if Bern blushed. Salli stared, fascinated. Was it just a shadow, over his cheek? Bern wore a beard, there was that. So it was all that much more difficult to tell.

"My oath is to the Shadene Secular Authority. But my mother raised me up godly, poor woman. I've got to do what I hope is best for us all. And still I can't help but hope to hear the prophet speak, will you shut the dream-gate against me?"

Strange. Bern sounded sincere. Salli had almost never heard Bern Travers sound quite serious, let alone sincere. It was hard to reconcile with her memories of him in class. His dedication was all in what he did, not in how he did it.

"Bern Travers." Varrick sounded as though she was still deciding what to make of him. "It's an odd name for a Wayfarer. It's an odd name for a Shadene."

The Holy One challenged reality. It was her way, and part of her Awakening. Salli hoped Bern could accept the questioning in that light; because otherwise he might mistake Varrick for prejudiced.

"We all walk between worlds, Holy One." Bern sounded almost disappointed, if as calm and reasonable as ever. Salli wondered if she was imagining it. "Some of us more obviously than others."

Varrick blew the breath out of her lungs, puffing up her cheeks. Deciding. "You shall hear teaching, like an honest man. Will you answer some questions before I leave?"

Now Bern stepped back and sat down on a rock. There was nothing in the cell with him, but Salli saw what she presumed to be his pack near the outer wall of the cave. She was glad to see they'd brought him his things, and glad to see that they hadn't put the pack in the cell with him.

The cell would not have held Bern long if he had had his pack—he probably carried his kindle-saw, and that would make short work of even old dense wood. There was a question in Salli's mind how long the cell could hold him even without it.

"Of course, Teacher. And no, I don't have any Pilgrim police waiting for you in the woods. If there are any, they didn't get here following me."

That begged the question. "How *did* you get here?" Salli demanded. It had taken her weeks to focus in on the Shadene party with whom Meeka had been traveling. How had Bern found Meeka?

Of course, if Bern had been hearing about Varrick ...

"I've heard rumors about the teacher, and the bell. It seemed a safe assumption, and if Meeka wasn't here, I would still get to hear the teacher. I asked after you, Salli. It all added up."

Typical. She had spent the time and effort to find Meeka, sacrificing her job—her oath of service—everything to find her brother. And Bern had just looked for her. Conservation of energy.

Varrick shook her head, as if in amusement. "If you tell me as an honest man that you haven't been followed, I'll be satisfied. We're still leaving. You may come and sit with me in Pellassa when I preach, if you would like."

Bern rubbed a thumb over the beard at his chin in a way that indicated he was about to make some particularly careful distinction. Salli had learned that in class.

"There could be troops, as I said. I haven't seen any. And I did my best to make sure I wasn't followed. I took the long way in."

Memory of countless arguments in class gave Salli the key to what was on Bern's mind. "But you have trackers on you. Hand them over, Bern, all of them, and no signaling as you do."

Varrick was staring at Salli, now, with amused astonishment. Bern frowned: but reached into his shirtfront, pulling the flat orange palm-sized tracking transmits out of some inner pocket. Passing them through the ancient grate to Salli, Bern met her eyes with something like a petitioning expression on his face. Salli didn't understand; but she was distracted by something important, and put the moment's heart-contact to the back of her mind for later.

"Unactivated," she told Varrick, somehow proud. "None of the seals are broken. There is no danger here, Holy One."

Varrick stepped up to the grate, quite close. Salli wanted her to keep her distance; Bern could easily seize Varrick by the throat to force them to release him. She corrected herself as soon as she realized what the thought in her mind was. This was the Holy One. Bern would not dare lay hands on a teacher.

"Come to me here," Varrick demanded. "And receive blessing." Bern knelt at the grate, his forehead pressed to the old wood. Varrick stood silent for a moment, meditating.

"Child of Shadene. Child of the alien." Her voice was full of the peculiar power that Salli heard every time that Varrick preached. "You have more difficult a path than many, Bern, and yet you forget the strength of your birthright. Now I advise you to keep to your chosen way. Wake up, Bern Travers. You will see the sunrise, in your lifetime."

The sun's transit across the sky had carried it far up into the sky, and for an instant the sun's light shone full into the cave, to reflect back from Varrick's shoulders with blinding brilliance.

Salli put her hand up to her eyes and turned her face away. It was only the sun. It could only be the sun. A woman could not burn blue-white like a torch. No human could carry such a light within her: but it was the Holy One, and Varrick was not human, not in the normally understood sense of the word.

Flesh and blood, yes, demonstrably, and Salli knew that Varrick was flesh and blood from watching her for these days past. But the power of the Awakened One shone from beneath the dream-illusion of flesh and blood, to be a sign and a portent.

Except that Varrick did not believe in signs, and rejected portents. . . .

The moment passed. Bern knelt still with his head bowed and his forehead pressed to the bars, as if to be as close to Varrick as possible. Varrick turned around.

"Keep him here for me until we're clear of camp, Salli." Varrick's voice was full of tenderness and regret. She knew what she was asking, but she asked for it regardless. "Give us a day's start, and then walk out. That will be enough time for everyone to get clear. Come to me in Pellassa; I will look for you there."

There was no answer and no arguing. Salli nodded, because she did not trust herself to speak.

Varrick left the cave.

Bern stood up, slowly, some minutes after Varrick went away. Turning without comment Bern sat down on the ground at the back of the cave, facing the wall.

There wasn't much to do in a cave when all the entertainment to be had was watching Bern. Bern was going nowhere. The vent chimney in the ceiling was far beyond reach, and surely too narrow for Bern to get up through even with his generally slim frame. No shoulders. Well, he had shoulders, but they fell away from his neck at such an abrupt slope that they almost might as well not have been there at all.

Bored and depressed, Salli was sensitive to sounds on the slope outside. She heard Meeka coming; she thought she recognized his footsteps in the gravel, even climbing. She didn't have long to guess if she was right, though, because Meeka called out for her.

"Salli, are you there? Teacher said I could find you."

A joke, from their childhood. As though the Holy One was a classroom teacher. Salli stood up to go to the cave mouth; Bern surprised her by speaking, for the first time since Varrick had left.

"It's your brother, Salli."

No, it was her brother Meeka. But that would have been a joke, evidence of bonding or companionship. She felt neither bonded nor companionable where Bern was concerned.

He didn't seem to have noticed. "I'd like to speak to Meeka if I could. Would you ask him for me?"

She'd just bet Bern would like to speak to Meeka. Part of Salli was quite willing to let him; he could see how well he did, where she had failed. But Meeka would just be provoked. There was no point to it.

"I'll let him know." That much Salli could promise honestly. Ducking her head beneath the heavy stone lintel of the cave, Salli went out into the early-afternoon glare; it was Meeka, yes, of course, coming up the slope, and with his pack on.

His pack reminded her, and she put her arms around him and hugged him fiercely. Poor Meeka. He had been waiting all this time to make public confession at Jarrod. And just as he had thought that the burden of guilt that he had been carrying was coming off at last, some special agent from the Shadene Secular Authority had come to ruin it all for him.

Meeka clung to her as she to him for long moments. But finally he put her from him, very resolute, and set his pack down on the ground between them.

"I'm going, Salli." And had come to say good-bye. "We'll travel to Pellassa, to appeal to Synod. I should have known they wouldn't let me speak. I should have expected this."

Sallie still could not believe that Meeka's bitter resentment was to be validated, particularly when it shaded over into paranoia. "Which 'they'?" she asked; not pretending that she didn't know, but not willing to let his claim pass unchallenged. "You think there's a conspiracy here after all? I think Bern's on the level. This is just like him."

Meeka scowled. "You and your friends at the avalanche headquarters. It's only a matter of time before you realize it for yourself, Salli. The Secular Authority is not at all what it would like you to believe it is."

Conspiracy theories abounded. One of them was that the Shadene secular authority was a cover for Pilgrims trying to take over Shadene, to the ultimate disenfranchisement of all heterodox. Another theory held just the opposite, with the secular authority a subtle ruse to conceal the covert actions of Wayfarers as they schemed to deprive all Orthodox of liberty, if not their lives.

"Wants a word with you, Meeka." It seemed to Salli that this was a wonderful opportunity to bring that up. "Bern Travers. You could just go and ask him what his intentions are, why not?"

Snorting in derisive disgust, Meeka stooped to lift his pack to his shoulders. "As if there'd be any trusting anything he said. No, thank you, Salli. But Salli—if I don't make it till the next time I see you—"

Then he wouldn't see her, of course. The phrase was nonsense. Its implications were irrationally terrifying.

"Meeka!"

"If I don't see you again. If they get me. You carry on, Salli, you fight them. Avenge me if they cause my death, little sister, promise me this much."

This was ridiculous. Meeka was off center, unbalanced, too easily moved to extremes—the burden that he carried made him stagger beneath the mildest of breezes. It was crazy even to suggest that he would be killed rather than be allowed to testify that the land was truly Wayfarer land, and the murder under jurisdiction of the Jarrod court. Madness.

But Meeka was her brother. It was madness, but it frightened Salli, and she cast about her for something to say that would reassure them both before Meeka went away.

"Don't be so melodramatic. The worst that's going to happen to you will be having to sit through the opening remarks before Jarrod is in session."

Meeka didn't smile at her joke.

"You'll find out soon enough, Salli." He was well wrapped up in his dignity, settling his pack across his shoulders. "I won't say I told you so. I just hope I'll be there to see you when it happens. Regrets to your friend Travers, Salli, and I'll see you in Pellassa. Unless."

Unless someone assassinated Meeka first.

Salli could not credit the very idea. But she didn't want to argue with Meeka just as he was going away.

Another hug and a quick kiss, and Meeka was down the slope and gone, and nothing left for Salli to do but go back into the cave and keep Bern company.

Soon someone came into the cave carrying Salli's pack and two rolls of bedding, one of which Salli threaded through the bars to fall on the floor within the cell for Bern. She had to unroll the bedding to make it work; the grid was too close to admit the bedroll all intact. Bern turned his head at the sound, and condescended so far as to stir himself and come help make the transfer; but he didn't say anything. He wrapped himself in the blanket and sat back down on the floor, leaning against the sidewall this time. He looked worried, Salli thought. Could he be depressed at the failure of his mission?

Later still someone brought supper, and a cold packed meal for later on. It was awkward trying to get food through the grid to Bern, who didn't seem much interested anyway; so Salli quit worrying about it. She wasn't particularly hungry herself either.

Things got quiet, outside.

Salli knew when the sun went down; the air smelled different—there was a draft of air circulating through the cave from some vent somewhere above. It would get cool. They were in the mountains, after all.

Wrapping herself up in her own blanket Salli laid her head down on her pack and went to sleep.

There was a rodent in the cave. Salli heard it scratching stealthily, working away at some piece of grain or hard-shelled seed. Scraping. Rodents didn't bother her, rodents had a right. She rolled over on the cold hard floor of the cave to go back to sleep, and the rodent-scratching stopped—as she'd expected. Maybe she'd scared the night chewer off. Maybe she'd just scared it into silence for long enough for her to fall back . . .

Scratching.

Salli opened her eyes wide in the dim light. There was only a little moon, outside the cave, and still less of its light made its way through the narrow cave mouth. She could see the cave mouth and the relatively lesser darkness beyond, but that was as far as the light went.

So she'd have to find the rodent by listening.

A few moments' pause, and as Salli evened out her breathing—to reassure the rodent—it started eating at whatever it was again. Behind her. Between her and Bern. If she thought about it, she could hear Bern's breathing as well.

Odd.

Bern's breathing was on top of the rodent's attempts to eat its supper.

Or else—

The rodent moved.

Salli caught her breath, to concentrate.

Bern was still asleep, to judge from the sound of his breathing; but—the sound of his breathing had moved, as well.

Everything came together in a flash. It wasn't a rodent. Bern was working his way out. He knew she was awake;

he would know that she knew he was working on the four latches that secured the doorport grid to his prison. She had the dart gun in her pack, she could hit him with a dose suitable for any midsized predator, and that would keep him down—

There was a sharp click, echoing in the still silence of the cave.

The latch.

If she could get to her pack, she could get her darts. The nightbeacon could blind him, temporarily. It would blind her, too, but she would be expecting it and could shield her eyes.

Deciding, Salli unwrapped herself from her blanket on the floor and rolled over to her pack on the other side of the cave.

She only made it halfway.

Halfway across the floor a tremendous crash startled her into temporary immobility, and immediately following the crash a large heavy object landed square on top of her. Pinning her down. A heavy object, and a body— Bern Travers's body, scrambling out of the cage to snatch up his pack and flee.

Bern had stalked the Holy One to Mount Corabey.

She hadn't been supposed to let him out until such time as all of Varrick's encampment had been gone long enough to infiltrate back into the cities, before Bern could call the pilgrim police—or, more realistically, the Shadene Secular Authority—down upon their heads.

And now this.

She'd been asleep, not paying attention, not alert enough. If she'd been thinking . . .

Now she had betrayed the Holy One, if only by omission.

And how would it look, that Bern had escaped her custody? Wouldn't it seem obvious collusion? A day's lead, Varrick had said, and then walk out. It hadn't been half a day, since the camp had fallen silent. Bern would call in the secular authority. It would seem to everyone that Salli had conspired with Bern and the secular authority to draw Varrick into a trap.

Salli lay on the ground with the gridded doorport on top of her, stupefied by the immensity of the mistake she'd made, unmindful of how ridiculous it would look to anyone to see her in so undignified a position.

How could she have slept through the jailbreak?

Why hadn't her brain woken up when her body had?

She could hear the night outside the cave, but only very indistinctly, the sound muffled by distance and muted in the still, dead air. There was no breeze, not anymore. Once the sun had gone down and the temperature had equalized between the cave's interior and the slope of the mountain outside, the breeze had stilled. It was a shallow cave, or else it would be different.

Footsteps.

Lying on her back, staring into blackness, Salli thought that she heard footsteps outside the cave mouth. Her imagination, surely. Bern had run out of there with such haste and determination that he could well be halfway down the mountain by now. She couldn't be hearing footsteps.

But she was.

If it wasn't Bern, since it couldn't possibly be Bern, then who was it?

Had Varrick left someone to keep an eye on her? Had this been a test of loyalty, one that Salli had failed? No. That would have been unworthy of the Holy One. Varrick knew that Salli was her true student, or Varrick knew nothing, and Varrick knew all things—or she was not the Holy One.

Or Varrick, who was the Holy One, who knew all things, had known Salli would fail her; and that had been why she had left someone?

Because there *were* footsteps, and coming into the cave. Moving slowly and deliberately. Not trying to cover or conceal their presence. Someone coming into the cave, someone crouching down beside her head, someone reaching out to lift the grid out of Salli's stubborn grasp.

Bern?

Someone who cast the grid aside and set the night torch down close beside her, checking the pulse at her throat.

"Salli. Are you all right?"

It *was* Bern.

This made no sense.

"Come on, Salli, say something. Speak to me. Raise your left hand, anything."

No. She didn't think so. Instead she thought she'd lie here and stare at the rough rock ceiling. It would serve him right if he took a scare, for having run over her the way he had. And the unreason of him coming back after having been in such a hurry to get away was more than Salli's rattled brain could grasp.

Bern swore to himself, some Wayfarer phrase for "outlander." She'd heard him swear before, though not as grimly as this. His face was strange in the low light, the shadows cast by his cheekbones shading his eyes, his whole face muddied by reflection from the neat little beard and moustache that he wore. Salli raised her head to look at him, intrigued; the movement gave her away.

"Oh. Salli." Rocking back on his heels, Bern watched her for a long moment—as if trying to decide if she were still dazed. "Can I help you? I want to get out of here, let's go."

She didn't want his help. She rolled onto her side and rose to her feet under her own power. If they traveled together she could slow him down, and maybe it would be all right. What was she thinking? He had probably already called for Secular Authority security forces.

She took her blanket up from the cave floor and stumbled out into the night, with Bern following.

Early yet, yes, as nights went; the moon just rising. Bern had dropped his pack near the cave mouth, but Salli couldn't see his comm gear. She hadn't heard him call, now that she thought of it; and wouldn't she have done? Maybe it had been a pulse signal. Or maybe she hadn't heard because she'd been unconscious for a moment.

"It'll be warmer downslope, Salli." Bern had his blanket and her pack in hand, and held the pack out for her. "Let's set up camp down by the prayer bell. We can still get some sleep before morning."

Before the security forces arrived. She followed without comment, wrapping herself in her blanket and her misery alike while Bern built up a fire. He was in a good mood, now, rubbing his hands together briskly as he sat down facing her. Salli could only stare.

"Better?" he asked, as if angling for forgiveness. She had betrayed the Holy One, and Bern was the proximate cause of that betrayal. There could be no forgiveness.

"You must know what this means." She did not have to let him sit and bask in the warm glow of his cleverness. He had bested her. She didn't have to pretend it was all right. "There will be more riots."

Bern shook his head. "No. No, there don't have to be more riots. She said she'd take your brother to Pellassa. I believe she'll do just that. It could still be all right."

He was being obtuse, and that irritated her. "Don't play games with me, Bern, I know how you teach already. You've called the secular authority. You have no intention of waiting for Varrick to follow through."

Her bitterness at herself for failing made her words even sharper than she had meant them to be. Bern sobered.

"I haven't called the secular authority, Salli. I haven't called anybody. She said to give her a day's grace to clear the camp. We can hike out in the morning, but I want a good look at that bell, first."

If he had no intention of leaving before morning, why had he awoken her so early in the night?

"I don't understand." And that was putting it mildly. "You were in an awful hurry to do something."

Bern took a moment before answering, shaking the blanket out around his shoulders. Once he was settled to his satisfaction he met her eyes, across the warmth of the campfire, and folded his hands over his crossed legs thumb tip to thumb tip like a monk. Bern had little hands. He had little ears, too, and they were flatter against his head than the ears of anyone else Salli had ever met.

"I had to get out of the cave, Salli. I thought I was going to be all right, and I was doing okay until the air stopped moving. If I hadn't gotten out when I did, I would have started screaming. I'm afraid of dark places, Salli. Claustrophobia. So now you know."

What are you going to do about it?

She didn't know what to say. She was too grateful to him for honoring the task that Varrick had laid on her to consider using the information to tease him, though, at least just then. Uncertain as to how best to respond, Salli yawned, making a great show of being ready to go back to sleep.

Afraid of dark places. Bern Travers, who walked between Pilgrim and Wayfarer afraid of neither, who managed mobs with one quiet word and who handled avalanche-detonation charges as though they were paper lanterns. Bern Travers, afraid of the dark.

"So wake me up when breakfast is ready."

Where was Meeka now? What was he feeling, having come so far to face the Jarrod court, denied the catharsis of public confession and the formal acknowledgment of error and forgiveness that he needed to get on with his life?

Where was the Holy One, and what priceless teaching was never to be Salli's because she had been made to stay behind?

Pellassa.

She would go to Varrick in Pellassa.

Salli yawned again and fell asleep.

Six

Salli awoke to the homely fragrance of paperbread baked on a flat rock, hissing slightly as it blistered in the moist morning air. She was stiff from sleeping on a thin pad on the hillside; she did not feel the least bit interested in having any discussions of whatever sort with Bern.

Nor would Bern expect her to engage in any before she had rinsed her mouth. Climbing up to the cave that housed the wellhead Varrick most favored, Salli washed her face and cleaned her teeth so that she could speak the Word with respect and reverence.

It was strange to be in this place with Varrick gone. Standing to rinse her hands, Salli felt a keen appreciation of the age of the place as a weight upon her shoulders; how many others before her had stood here, in this exact place, to speak Awakening?

"Behold, she rises, like the Sun. Like the sun across the dark land is the word of the Holy One that wakes Creation from its Dream of sin and suffering. Oh, Holy One. May we also rise, and wake to the new beginning."

All the days she had been there, Salli realized, she had not said her morning-prayer prayer even once. She had said a Wayfarer prayer with Wayfarers. She had not spoken Orthodox in all this time, and yet she stood in the place where the Orthodox had first written the prayers

113

and devotionals of the Pilgrim people. She hadn't thought about it while Varrick had been there, not more than superficially. How did the cave walls of this ancient city feel, to be used by Wayfarer heteros?

"Salli!"

Bern's voice called for her across the slope, and shook her out of her musing. "Salli, you'll miss breakfast. Hurry it up."

She was hungry.

She'd been too heartsick at being left behind to eat last night.

Bern had paperbread and sweet-seakelp chutney, packed in as a fruit leather and reconstituted in a tin of hot water. It was good. Salli seated herself and wolfed down her breakfast. Despite Bern's implicit threat to close the meal line, he showed no signs of wearying of his chore; but sat and mixed paperbread batter and spread fruit chutney on hot crisp curls of chewy bread until Salli had stuffed herself well and truly.

"Good appetite," he noted, neutrally, putting the cooking things away as Salli lay half-stupefied with satiation, her feet pointing uphill on the slope to aid digestion. Salli ignored him. Bern had been raised by a Wayfarer mother. Wayfarer women were supposed to eat voraciously.

"There's half a packet of good strong tea left in my mealsack," she suggested, rather than dignify his comment with a response. "Good for the metabolism."

For a moment she thought she might have pushed too far, because there was a sudden silence from the Bern side of the breakfast fire. It didn't last long.

"Don't mind if I do. But you should be more careful, Salli, or have you forgotten?"

Forgotten what? Salli didn't answer. She was too full to think. After a few minutes Bern crossed over to the Salli side of the slope and passed her a mug, sitting down beside her, facing downslope while she faced up-slope. She had to sit up to drink. The tea was hot and sweet and strong, near-scalding—perfect. Salli sipped three times, and Bern spoke.

"Now you have to marry me, Salli. After all. I've made you tea and you've drunk it, bread and you've eaten it, in all the old stories you'd be pregnant already."

Oh.

Remember *that*.

Well, it was perfectly true that ethnic Shadene married by feeding the women of their choice. But there was more to it.

"Where's the roof over my head and the cover to my bed? The fire on the hearth, well, I'll grant you that one, on a stretch." It was a good breakfast fire, in fact. Very tidy. Very compact. Efficient. "You'll have to do better than that, Bern. As if. And I don't care what the old stories say, there is more to getting pregnant than eating a man's paperbread in the morning."

Bern grinned at his feet, squinting a little at the sun that shone against the side of his face. "Oh, well. It was worth a try. Let's get out of here, Salli, but let's go visit the bell, first."

He had said he wanted a closer look at it. It didn't take long to clear up their small camp; and once Bern had covered the drowned fire with the rocks he'd moved to build the fire pit there was little left to show that they'd been there, even to the critical eye of an avalanche soldier. People had been using the site for centuries. But it was no less a holy place for that, a place in which it was not respectful to leave evidence of their sojourn.

Packed and ready, Salli followed Bern down to the shrine shed, setting her gear down on the black-slate-flagged apron downslope. She'd had all the time in the world to study the bell herself; it was interesting to

watch Bern, seeing it through his eyes all over again as
if it was for the first time.

It was big.

It was taller than she was, and so big around that
Salli's reach encompassed less than half of its diameter.
Weathered with age to a dull bronze-colored patina, yet
the relief images with which it was decorated could still
be made out. The mountain. The bell. The shining glory,
come spilling down the mountain like an avalanche. The
faithful, gathered to witness, their hands held out palms
forward in religious awe.

> *The voice of the bell is the voice of the Holy One, calling
> to us to rise and come forward. Children of the moun-
> tains, bear witness and wake.*

It was one of the oldest surviving scriptural fragments
in the entire world, the explanation and the exaltation of
the place of the prayer bell in orthodox theology.

Salli's morning thoughts were still with her as she
studied the bell, wanting to fix every image on its surface
clearly in her mind now that she had to leave. The surviving bells that were known to the world were all the
same size, more or less. But none rang the same note. It
was part of the mystery, and that simple fact had been
used in recent decades to encourage tolerance amongst
the Wayfarer people of Shadene and the Pilgrims. None
of the bells rang with the same note; was this not a sign
from the ancients that not all the people must be Orthodox?

"Where do you think the hill people went, Bern?" Salli
asked almost timidly, not wanting to insult him. It was
an old controversy. "Do you think they're still with us?"

Centuries ago the Pilgrims had fled from the mountains, and found themselves masters by default of the
great prairie that was central to the greatest continent on

all of Creation. Centuries ago these mountain camps had been abandoned, had fallen to ruin, and their technology with them; and when after centuries Pilgrims had come back to the Revelation Mountains there had been nobody there.

Nobody, that is, but Wayfarers, aliens from the islands on the other side of the world, new come to Shadene and just beginning to explore the mountains. Completely ignorant of what historical treasures were contained in, represented by, camps such as this at the foot of Mount Corabey. Ignorant, or uncaring, and how could they not have cared unless they'd been ignorant?

"You mean the whole sea-exodus joke." Bern's response left no doubt as to what his feelings were. There were problems with the hypothesis that the Wayfarers had sailed here, true enough. There were no island people quite like Wayfarers.

Nor did Wayfarers seem to have any sailing technology beyond that required to harvest the rich coastal waters for fish and seaweed; and that was a mere matter of sculling and shallow hulls. If the Wayfarers were island people, they'd forgotten all about it since their arrival.

Well, why not?

The Pilgrim governments west of the Revelation Mountains had resolutely turned their backs on air traffic of any sort after the Prodigals had returned to Creation; so who was to say that a technology could not be abandoned—and then forgotten—and all in the space of a few short generations?

Salli didn't answer. She didn't see any need to. But after a moment Bern lowered his head around the side of the bell to look her in the eye, very fixedly. Pale watery eyes, like his Wayfarer mother. Red-rimmed just at present, because of the fire no doubt. Somewhat baggy as well; hadn't he slept?

"I don't think they went anywhere, Salli. I think we're

still here. It's the simplest solution. Just not political."

One of the theories was that the hill people had simply moved down to the coast during the time of the Great Ice. And it had cooled, dramatically, at about the time that the hill-camps had been abandoned. But if the hill people, the Holy People who had sent the Pilgrims west of the mountains so many centuries past, if they were the same as Wayfarers—well—

Well, one simply didn't know what to think, except that it meant that Wayfarer heteros were closer to the true Dream of the Revelation itself than Orthodox Pilgrims. That had whole cartloads of repercussions, none of them politically acceptable—to Pilgrims, at least.

No, it was impossible.

Sooner or later they'd find an Orthodox hill-burial that was unequivocally from the time of Revelations, rather than yet another ethnic Shadene, Wayfarer burial from a much later date that just happened to be sited on or near some evidence of the true Holy People.

Sooner or later the archaeological evidence would come to light that would tie the Wayfarers once and for all to the island raiders from the other side of the world.

Till that time . . .

"Step back, Salli, cover your ears."

Salli took cover behind one of the great pillars that supported the roof of the shrine shed and covered her ears, horrified.

Bern struck the bell halfway up its height with the great wooden mallet-beam that hung suspended in its cradle of rope to one side of the bell. From where she stood Salli could see from the violence with which the mallet rocked in its cradle that Bern had struck it with considerable force. She feared a bell tone with the force of earthquake; and the tone was intense and powerful, but sweet and light for all that—it didn't deafen her.

The vibration rattled Salli's bones regardless.

The prayer bell echoed and reechoed again, and slowly—slowly—slowly the echo began to die away. She could hear the falling of pebbles and small stones, shaken from their resting places by the reverberation of the bell and cascading in tiny rockslides down the slope.

Finally, Salli ventured to cant her head around from behind the stout wooden post that had intercepted the worst of the shock wave and split it, passing her safely on either side. She wanted to know where Bern was, right now. She needed to be sure that he had no clever ideas about doing that again.

"Always wanted to do that." His cheerful, if somewhat shaky, admission was all the proof Salli felt she needed that the theory that the hill people were Wayfarers was ridiculous. "Every time I've seen one in the museum. Want to have a go?"

No one whose blood and bone was the same bone and blood as that of the holy hill people, the people of Revelation, could ever strike a prayer bell with such perfect insouciance. Just to see what it sounded like.

Prayer bells had been holy to the hill people, and were holy to Pilgrims yet, and that Wayfarer heteros disregarded so vital an element in the ritual was all the more proof that the Wayfarers were ignorant of true Revelation.

What would Varrick's teaching be, about the bell?

Surely when it had rung, the night before they had crossed into the Chalice of Heaven, surely it had not been rung just to see what it sounded like?

Carib would have known.

Carib would have told her.

"No thanks, Bern, one go's quite enough." And her ears were still ringing, even protected as they had been. "Come on. We can be to the far side of the lake by evening, but we'd better get started."

Salli shouldered her pack and set off down the slope.

No, the hill people were gone. One way or the other. The last remaining inheritance of the hill people lay in the veins of the Pilgrims, to whom the Revelation rightly belonged. They had to tolerate Wayfarers, in the interests of peace. But the Wayfarers had no rights.

And now that the Holy One had come, it would all be sorted out, and no further claim from any Wayfarer to any site in the Revelation Mountains need be entertained again.

Never again.

Walking away from Corabey with Bern would have been a vacation, had Salli's mind not been so full of conflict: concern over her brother, longing for the presence of the Holy One.

They climbed out of the caldera going north and west, shunning the low and easy southern Linshaw Pass for a narrower and steeper egress which cut the avalanche soldiers' defense grid inside of two days. Bern knew where he was going: and once Salli saw the avalanche soldiers' marker posted at a stream crossing, so did she.

This was easy trekking, in a sense. The paths were narrow but fairly well maintained, and there were rangers' huts to be found for people who knew where to look for them. Carefully camouflaged, out of respect for Wayfarer sensibilities—and to cut down on incidents of vandalism.

By evening of the third day since they'd left Corabey, Salli and Bern came up on Allin Springs and the old baths there. It hadn't been Allin Springs forever, no, but one of the first Pilgrims to find the place during the past century had left a note tucked into the moss to the effect that he was all in, and the name had stuck.

Allin was a hot springs, as old as the mountains themselves, and had been in use for as long as there had been people in Shadene. The oldest construction was hill-people work, and no Wayfarer immigrant since had improved on it. Reaching Allin Springs in the late afternoon, Salli and Bern both dropped their packs—as if by mutual consent—and stripped to get into the water.

It was wonderful.

Salli wanted never to get out. The hot alkaline water seemed to dissolve all of the glue that held her bones together at her joints, and with it all of the tension in her back and arms and legs and shoulders that had built up over days of hiking and camping on hard ground.

Gradually it dawned on Salli that she was alone with Bern beneath the great bell of Heaven, with nothing between her skin and his but hot water. Hot sulfurated water, yes, perhaps, but still—

It wasn't the least bit improper to share a hot springs with a person of the opposite sex, she reminded herself sternly. Not the least bit. Of course one usually went on hot-springs hikes with four or more people, and a certain degree of respectability lay in numbers; still. She and Bern had been hiking for days. They were tired.

That was all.

Few people could be considered physically appetizing after so many days in the woods, without a single chance to get in a really good wash. Yes. That was right.

She'd been watching Bern idly, not paying attention to herself watching him. Nothing personal. He had an interesting body, well, interesting in the abstract way that any unclothed male body was interesting, of course, and no more than that.

It occurred to Salli that she was perhaps spending rather too much time studying how the round curve of muscle shaped the upper portion of Bern's pale naked chest. She blushed, and raised her eyes to find some safer sight anchor well past the far edge of the soaking pool.

Bern spoke, and Salli met his eyes by instinct, powerless to prevent the color from blooming even more deeply in her cheeks.

"Say, Salli."

She had already begun to blush, and now she felt that her skin was so red as to provide light in the long dim shadows of the twilight woods. Her imagination of what Bern might think she was blushing about only made it worse.

Still, Bern spoke slowly and contemplatively, without any hidden amusement she could hear. Maybe he couldn't see her blushing. It was getting darker, after all.

"About your unit. Let's talk. I did a little flower arranging, sort of behind the backdrop. I hope you don't mind."

On the other hand Bern wasn't making any sense. Had the heat addled his brain? "Tell me what you're up to, Bern, and then I'll tell you if I mind."

He stretched himself in the water, his arms a straight line wrist to shoulder. It was a very natural gesture, a very Bern-like gesture, but it looked quite different when it was unclothed.

"Wee-ee-ll. It's like this. You're away without leave, we know that."

She was more than merely away from her unit without leave. She had left her unit of assignment and her area of responsibility as well, to go find Meeka. The avalanche soldiers could dismiss her from service for being away without leave, and she would lose her pension. That was not so much an issue, young as she was. Though it was a good pension.

What was more to the point was that the Shadene Secular Authority could conceivably imprison her for the crime of having abandoned her area of responsibility. Fellertown Lifts was not heavily patronized during this time of year, so no actual lives would be endangered by

Salli's absence—she had been confident of that. But there were matters of principle at stake.

"Go on."

There was more to this than the obvious, Salli was sure of it. Bern was devious and underhanded. There was always more to Bern's musings than their surface meaning.

"But you're away without leave to find your brother, and I wanted to find him, too. I think we both wanted to find him for the same reasons, at least to start out with. So it didn't work out that way. So what?"

Neither she nor Bern had talked Meeka into returning to give witness at a hearing or stand before the court of the Shadene Secular Authority, he meant. She thought.

"But that was why you left. So I told them that we were working on the problem together. Because we were, really. In a sense, at least."

Salli felt an initial rush of gratitude toward Bern for covering for her. She squelched it as firmly as she could. For one, she had already noted that Bern had brazenly taken advantage of her anguished search for Meeka to accomplish his own ends. For another, this was Bern; so there was more.

"And."

"Yes, well, and. Of course, they had to carry you as away without leave, or blow the mission. And they'll expect you back, Salli, for debriefing, prior to return to duty."

Salli turned this concept over in her mind, examining it from several angles as she drew circles in the water with the fingertips of her left hand.

"So come back to the avalanche soldiers with you for debrief, Bern, and pretend it was all a secret mission all along. Saving my job, my pension, maybe my freedom. Or go straight to Pellassa, where the Holy One will be waiting to see me."

"There, you see, I knew—I knew you would say something like that." Bern's emphatic gesture, his slapping of the table's surface with the flat of his hand, was spoiled completely by the fact that the table's surface was the surface of the soaking pool. All he got was splashing. "But Salli. Think. It's more than just your job, your pension, your freedom. This is a Holy One, a new Wayfarer Teaching. You know what kinds of trouble that means."

Of course she did. That was what avalanche soldiers were all about, at least in one sense. Bern wasn't suggesting anything new. She'd promised herself when she'd agreed to go to Corabey with Meeka that at least she'd gather evidence for official use, to help the secular authority decide whether Varrick was dangerous or not.

It was just that all of those careful rational thoughts belonged to the reality that had defined Salli's life before she'd met the Holy One.

"Bern." She could hear her voice tremble. She didn't like it, but there seemed to be little point to standing on her dignity when she was naked in a pool of water with this man. "You've met the Holy One. You've spoken with her. How can you suggest I shun Varrick?"

What was a job, a pension, freedom, set against the once-in-a-millennium chance to hear wisdom and Awakening from the mouth of the Holy One? The true Awakened One, the one and only, the true orthodox Awakened One, and no Wayfarer promiscuity of Holy Ones about it . . .

Bern was nodding. Maybe a touch too vigorously. Maybe a touch. "Yes, but Salli. Think what it could mean, not to you, but to Varrick. You owe it to the Holy One to debrief. Render unto the secular authority that which rightfully concerns the secular authority. Be fair, tell me you can see it that way."

It was in her power to smooth the path of the Holy One in Shadene, by providing what information she had to the authorities. Varrick had never preached violent overthrow, or exclusion of heterodoxies, or chosen people, or any of the theologies that had caused trouble for them in the past. Varrick's Teaching was much more radical and sensible than any of that. *Trust your own heart. There are no signs, nor any portents. Open your eyes and you will see. Only sleepwalkers need clutch at guideposts to tell them where they are.*

Of course, if Varrick was right, the entire teaching of the Orthodox Church was a mistake, and the plague that had destroyed the colonies three hundred years ago had not been sent by God to focus people's attention on religion. It had just been a plague.

"Bern, it isn't that I'm not grateful for the out." He needn't have done that. He could just as easily have left her out on the wrong side of a killer overhang with no bolts set and no reasonable attach in sight. "How long would I have to spend, though? Because it hurts. Being away from Varrick. Hurts."

Odd, but she had no hesitation in saying such things to Bern. Could she have said them to anyone else, anyone else at all?

"Nine days to debrief, Salli, and I come for you on day ten whether they're done or not. I'll arrange your transport to Pellassa myself, on the Authority's books. Please."

Nine days.

On top of these days spent traveling, and days yet to come in travel, how many days before she could sit once again in the presence of the Holy One?

But Bern's request was more than reasonable, under the circumstances. Really. Salli could find no fault with the idea that she had not already brought out for discussion. She was trapped.

"All right. Nine days in debrief. And you come for me on day ten, without fail, Bern, you promise."

Pushing herself out of the pool, Salli pressed for re-assurance, unsure of how serious she was. Bern answered her seriously, so she didn't have to decide whether to push it or not.

"Done deal. Last one into the cabin gets to wash the dishes."

All right, she'd give the Shadene Secular Authority nine days.

But she'd be longing for the Holy One every minute.

Debrief quarters were comfortable but spare, well insulated from any outside distractions. There was a time sheet on the wall so that Salli could track the hours and the minutes and the days, but no newsfeed, no print stock, no on-screen presence to bring her word of what was happening outside. Sallie grew to wait for the debrief team, itchy and bored, but they weren't much good. They just went over the same material. Over and over and over again.

There were three people on debrief, and they were never the same three people, in order to avoid any loss of detail information as a result of an unconscious supposition on Salli's part that she'd already mentioned an incident that she had in fact only just then remembered. Three people, one who talked, one who watched, and one who watched the one who talked and the one who watched and Salli. Three people, always different, but the same thing over and over and over again.

What do you know about Meeka's contacts with the heteros? When is the first time you noticed something odd? What did you do when he was reported missing from his assigned duty? Why did you do that? Whom did you seek out for information?

Tell us how you located your brother. Describe the people in the Wayfarer party. What do you remember of

*conversation en route? How do you see their motiva-
tion? Can you recall the first time you saw Varrick?
How many people were at Corabey when Bern Travers
stopped the so-called Jarrod court?*

*What was your reaction to your first meeting with
Varrick? Is there something you can describe about her
that explains your conviction that she is the Wayfarer's
Holy One? What is the substance of Varrick's Teaching?
What did people talk about in between times?*

*How was your camp supplied? What did you eat?
Where were the toilets? Where did the toilets drain?
How large was the bell? When was it rung? Tell us
about the inscriptions on the bell. Were there other artifacts? Did anyone remove anything? Did anyone con-
sume anything? Did anyone spoil or destroy anything?*

There were breaks at regular intervals, and Salli would
take a jog around the running track that connected to
the debrief suite through an airlock. There was never
anybody there. The running track itself was completely
enclosed by walls of wobbleglass, and the light outside
the wobbleglass never varied.

*What was the organizational structure of the camp? Tell
us about the people who you noticed as wielding influence or authority. What remarks were exchanged con-
cerning the Shadene Secular Authority? Did you at any
time see, hear of, or suspect the presence of offensive
assault weapons? Were there any maps? Did people
watch the night skies for surveillance kites?*

Every so often Salli slept, and every so often Salli ate,
and though there was a time sheet on the wall and a
ticker on the table where she sat to be debriefed Salli
forgot whether she had turned the time sheet, and
whether she needed to reset the ticker. It didn't matter.
She didn't care.

In a very real sense Salli welcomed the absence of cues to the passing of time. It was only nine days, she knew that, because that had been her agreement with Bern—and she couldn't imagine that she could possibly have any more than nine days of debriefing in her. Not for this. Yes, it was important, but all the same it was hardly as though they'd been terrorists.

Her job was to make sure that the debrief team understood that fact so clearly that there would be no possible room for misapprehension, even though they mistrusted her judgment. She knew they did. There were no overt signs, no, none whatever, but it was their job to question—not her motives—but the validity of her perceptions.

> *What do you remember of your first meeting? Tell us about Varrick. Did she seek you out? What did she say to you? Were the others friendly? Was there any change in their behavior toward you? Did you see any change in your brother's behavior?*
>
> *What was it that convinced you that she was the Holy One?*

Slowly, without Salli much noticing, the focus of the debriefing started to shift.

> *What was your physical state that first morning? When you met Varrick for the first time. How long had it been since you had slept last? How long had it been since you'd eaten or rested? How much fluid did you get to drink while you were crossing the caldera?*

Salli's brain was becoming numbed and confused after day after day of intensive debriefing. She didn't know why they were asking the questions. She just did her best to answer them. But since this was debriefing, it didn't matter that she answered the questions; the next team would just come in and ask the same questions all over again.

Are you familiar with the effect of fatigue on the conscious mind? Do you remember your psychology classes in school? What is the effect of prolonged sleep deprivation on the sentient brain? How long does it take for exhaustion to create a species of walking psychosis?

Struggling to remember, struggling to respond, Salli fought her own confusion and the inertia of the debrief itself, focusing always on giving a fresh answer. Always the same answer, but carefully considered and newly validated each time.

That isn't what you said before, Salli. You said two days just now, whereas you said three days before. Try to remember, Salli, which was it?

The debrief teams were supportive, careful, sympathetic. They stopped asking questions when Salli got confused, when she got irritated, when she was tired. The debrief teams had a job to do, that was all.

Salli had lost track of what that job was, because the questions did not seem to make sense.

Let's talk about your relationship with Varrick. How did she treat you? Differently than the others? Were privileges extended to you alone? What was your feeling about that at the time? How did you explain that to yourself? Did any others say anything to you? Why do you think that nothing was said?

She was sitting at the table, playing with a broken piece of sweetwafer. Her cup was to one side, only halfway on its coaster, its contents stone-cold after hours of neglect and muddied at the bottom with the crumbs of dipped wafers gone by. The person who asked the questions was an ethnic Shadene, to look at her—blond hair, blue eyes, pale skin. She put her questions earnestly, but without any cues of urgency or anxiety in her voice.

"When you first met Varrick, after your journey across the caldera . . . There was a light, you said. What was it about the light that seemed supernatural to you? Could it have been a reflection?"

Salli woke up.

She could see that light, that brilliant white burning light; it was in her field of vision now, and at the center of it was truth.

Which the Wayfarer debriefer did not believe to be true.

They thought she was deluded in her conviction that Varrick was the Holy One. Deluded or worse, brainwashed, accidentally or deliberately manipulated into mistaking Varrick for an Awakened One—when the truth of the matter was that Varrick was not *an* Awakened One, Varrick was *the* Awakened One, the true Orthodox Awakened One come at long last.

The shock left Salli breathless. She could only stare.

"Salli, do you hear me? Is something wrong?"

Numbly Salli raised the fragment of sweetwafer to her lips. It was sweet, and crumbly. She tasted it as if it was for the first time ever.

How long had she been asleep?

How long had she been here?

"What day is it?" she asked. They would tell her, if she asked. "Aren't we about done with this? I can't think there could be anything left that I haven't told you. Three times. At least."

"I'm sorry if I've said something that offended you." The debriefer's voice was as calm and smooth as ever;

but the words were there. They knew what they had
been trying to do. They probably thought it was in Salli's
best interest to persuade her to rethink what had happened to her. A temporary walking hallucination, created by fatigue and physical deterioration—hunger and
thirst.

Much more easily explained away than an Awakening.

Pilgrim stock were not expected to Awaken to any sort
of heterodox reality, let alone an unsanctioned one, but
Salli knew something that they didn't know. Yet. Salli
knew that Varrick was the Awakened One.

"I'm not offended." She could be as patient and calm
as anybody. "I just want to know what day it is because
it seems to me we should be about done."

Her interviewer pushed herself away from the table
and stood up.

"We're done if you say so, Salli. This is your tenth day
of debriefing, and your brother's asking to see you. Outside. If you want to go."

Her brother?

Meeka?

Why not Bern?

And how could her brother come here, and not be
forcibly detained for debriefing himself?

She'd told Bern nine days, she'd agreed. Nine days.
Whether or not Bern had kept his part of the bargain,
nine days were up. This was day ten.

"In that case I want to leave, now. I'm expected in
Pellassa."

The interviewer nodded, stepping away from the table. "We'll send an escort, then. Half an hour to pack?
Do you want more time than that?"

The recorder and the monitor were already at the
door, waiting. Salli shook her head, a little confused at
the lack of any resistance. She had almost expected them

to pressure her to stay and be debriefed until she could no longer hear the voice of the Holy One in memory in her mind.

"No, thank you. Half an hour will be fine." She had only the gear she'd walked in with, after all. And she was an avalanche soldier, or at least she had once been an avalanche soldier. She knew how to pack quickly and well.

The debrief team left the room without another word spoken, no nod of acknowledgment, no thanks for her time, no well-wishing.

The heartless coldness of it all made Salli want to run after them, call them back, change her mind, just to gain some signal that they recognized her feelings and valued her cooperation; but that was all just a debriefing trick.

She didn't have to fall for it.

They could hurt her feelings, but they could not change her mind; and with the small comfort of that knowledge Salli went to pack.

An escort came just as Salli was lacing up the last panel of her rucksack. It was lighter now than it had been before; she had carried gear into the mountains that was no longer hers to carry—things that avalanche soldiers were issued for their use, but that remained the property of their units.

There was the signal at the door; Salli lifted her rucksack to her shoulder and keyed the admit.

Her unit.

Morrissey, and the rest of her own team—Carpi, Solt, Techam, and Ware.

They had sent her own team to escort her off premises, the bastards; and Salli felt a surge of fierce resentment. She had deserted, yes. But she had done her best to make up for it in debrief, to the extent that it could be done without revealing information that the Shadene Secular

Authority might be able to use to compromise Varrick or her Teaching.

She deserved better than to leave debriefing this way; and fixed Morrissey with a hostile glare across the threshold, past the opened door.

Her team stood impassive and stone-faced. Morrissey himself seemed to search her face for clues as to how he could make sense of all that had happened, his expression a mixture of confusion and hostility on his own part.

Angry and frustrated, Salli attacked. "I was told my brother was here, Squad Leader." "Team Leader" she could have said, since that was the capacity in which Morrissey appeared. But that would have been more confrontational than Salli truly felt. It wasn't as if she was blameless. She had deserted. She had not explained.

"Outside, Sal—Miss Rangarold. With a crowd of well-wishers."

Morrissey's tone of voice was cool and unemotional, but not condemnatory. Reserving judgment. Suddenly Salli wished that there was time to stop, time to explain. She owed her team better than this. Couldn't she at least have written a note? And she hadn't.

"Let's get going, then."

There was no time, at least not now. If Meeka was here he was here at risk, because he was a deserter in his own way; and failing to appear for his hearing made him a fugitive in the eyes of the Shadene Secular Authority. With a crowd, Morrissey said. A riot about to happen.

The best thing she could do for all concerned was to get out quickly. Resettling her pack on her back Salli started forward, and her escort led on down the featureless hallways.

It was quite a hike, as it turned out, through blind corridors each as sterile as the last until they came to the apron of a loading dock whose pulldoor was closed. Not a very large loading dock. Salli cued the climber, and the pulldoor began to track across the loading dock.

Cool air flooded in; cool air, and bright sunlight. There was a wind up, outside. Salli could hear its rustling through the boughs of the trees that were obviously to either side of the loading dock.

The pulldoor tracked all the way to the back end of its pocket and stopped.

It wasn't wind.

It was a riot.

Out beyond the loading dock there was a motor yard, and a chain fence at the other side of the motor yard securing the outer-compound perimeter. In the motor yard, between Salli and the fence, there stood a company of avalanche soldiers in riot gear, silent and self-disciplined and formed up at right angles to the loading bay and the fence beyond. And just to the other side of the perimeter fence, a crowd of people, chanting the angry cry of an enraged mob, brandishing the basic weapons of an inner-city riot.

Planks.

Staves.

Rocks wrapped up in thin cotton fabric, swung around in a cloth sling to be flung at the heads of the pilgrim police.

Puzzled, Salli stepped forward across the pulldoor's track, into the light. Midafternoon, she guessed, one corner of her mind assessing the light and the angle and the pale color of it.

What were all these people doing here?

And how was she to find Meeka, in that crowd?

Had the debrief team conspired to let her die a casualty of a street fight, if they could not shake her new-found faith in any other way?

Lessons from mob-management classes sped through her mind, slowly enough that she remembered she had taken them, too quickly for her to grab any one idea and make it hold still for long enough to do her any good.

Ground and cover? No. That was shock wave. Low crawl and side breathe? No, something else. Mark and move was a warning order, lock and load was a grenade, dress and cover were marching orders. What was she supposed to do?

Nothing.

She was supposed to do nothing.

The mob was on the other side of the fence. She was inside the building. It was bright outside. They could probably not even see her. There were more traps between her and them, though; now that Salli could see them better she recognized with horror that the avalanche soldiers were the rest of her unit. Her own former unit. Now she could be sure that there had been an element of spite to this.

Now that Salli's eyes could focus better—having adjusted to the light—she could see that there were people other than the avalanche soldiers just inside the fence. As Salli watched and stared one of the people by the fence started running, and Salli was quite sure that that was a mistake.

Never run from a mob.

A mob will follow.

A mob was a wild animal, composed of people who as long as they were part of the mob weren't people. That was important. Decent people could do things that would shame them forever, when they found themselves melding into a mob's being.

Bern's lessons, but it was Meeka coming for her, Meeka running across the motor yard calling her name. "Salli! Salli! Salli, are you there?"

Salli knew what to do now, she had to get to her brother. Scarce noticing the supportive hands of Carpi and Solt letting her down to the yard, Salli turned to face the scene, finding her balance just as Meeka reached her.

"Salli." He embraced her, folded her into a hug so fiercely fraternal that she could have wept. His clothing was dirty, she smelled oil and grime on his jacket, and also smelled the sharp onion bite of dried sweat gone sour for lack of airing. It was not a smell she knew as her brother's, but she could abide it because it came with him.

"Meeka. They said you were waiting." And this crowd with him, protection against an arrest attempt. "What's going on?"

He put her apart from him at an arm's length, then hugged her once more. As if he had thought that he might never be able to hug her again ever. But as soon as he did he turned her, and started to jog toward the fence with an arm around her shoulder.

"No time to explain right now, Salli. We've got to get you well clear of this place. We've both got to get out; we've become dangerous, imagine that."

It made no sense.

They had to pass in front of the long line of avalanche soldiers to get back to the gate. Captain Jule Clemens, her commander. Colonel Janelric. Morrissey and her team joined the platoon in line as she passed, grim-faced and resolute, not forgetting to leave a gap in the line where she should have been standing—it was brutal.

It was hard for Salli to discipline herself, but she was an avalanche soldier by training if no longer in fact; she could show steel as well as any of them. She hurried with Meeka, and kept her gaze fixed resolutely forward.

The crowd at the fence started cheering as they neared. The guards at the gate opened the small pedestrian gate just in time for Meeka to push Salli through ahead of him, closing it just as soon as Meeka had cleared the threshold.

This mob had something to do with her? And with Meeka?

Things had been quiet, utterly quiet, intensely one-on-one for the past ten days. Salli's head was reeling from the sudden onslaught of chants and yells, a mob, all of these people. Numbly she let herself be bundled into the back seat of a surface car, grateful for windows that were blacked opaque and for sound dampers that shut the wild yells out.

The surface car began to move, and Salli put her head back against the seat brace. Meeka had not come in. Meeka was in the front of the car, maybe. Meeka was in another car, maybe. If Meeka was hunted it was prudent practice to separate, true enough.

What had happened?

What could be happening?

And how long would it be before she could sit once again in the presence of the Holy One?

Seven

The surface car didn't move quickly, but it kept moving for hours. It was a high-security surface car, which meant that Salli could not see much through blackened windows; the barrier between the passenger compartment and the front of the vehicle was locked in place. She didn't know where she was going, or who was taking her there.

Could this all be some obscure kind of insanely convoluted plot?

No, Meeka had come for her, and Meeka knew as well as she did where she had to go and why. But where was Meeka now? she wondered. She'd make sense out of the riot at the debriefing center, the stone-cold row of avalanche soldiers, sooner or later.

Her days and nights had gotten a bit displaced, after ten days of intense debriefing under artificial light.

Salli lay down on the back seat of the passenger compartment and went to sleep.

After a while she woke, alerted by a change in atmosphere of some sort. How long she'd been asleep she did not know. The surface car had stopped moving. It was quiet. The recycled air in the surface car's secured passenger compartment had gotten stale; she had a headache.

Pushing herself stiffly up into a seated position, Salli

ran sleep-clumsy fingers through her uncombed brown hair and thought about what she was going to do next.

She wasn't going to learn anything new by sitting in a surface car that could well be abandoned, for all she knew.

Wearily, warily, sleep still heavy on her, Salli slipped the privacy-secures and opened the surface car's passenger door.

Cool air; but very welcome that way, and fresh as well.

No light except for those within the passenger car: then those went off, so suddenly that it seemed clear to Salli that someone had turned them off.

"Don't be alarmed, Miss Salli."

Well intentioned as the reassurance doubtless was, the shock of hearing the voice so close, so unexpectedly, made it hard for Salli to suppress a gasp. A gulp, at the very least. An unfamiliar voice, heavily accented, pitched high as a woman's but with a man's characteristically rough timbre—and coming out of black space right next to her head, just outside the car—if that was not an alarming experience, what was?

Salli didn't trust herself to answer. The voice apparently believed this meant that Salli was listening, paying attention.

"We've got to be very careful. Your brother is hunted, especially after yesterday morning. If they know where you are, they will seek him through you, and therefore you need to be also hidden away. My name is Geril. We were together at Mount Corabey."

Salli tried to take it all in and make sense of it. Waking moment by moment, she found her sense of self-sufficiency woke even as she did; and for now she did not feel endangered.

"What has been happening since we left Corabey, Geril?"

Now the subtle glow of a low-observable lantern came into view, handed through the door into the passenger compartment. There were conclusions to be drawn from all this play of lights and darkness; they were in a covered structure, from the sound of voices and the relative stillness of the air, but the people she was with still wanted to avoid the lights in the passenger compartment. So it was night, when a stray beam might escape an unsuspected chink or crack and betray their presence. Night of what day?

"Here, you should change, Miss Salli. The car will be here in two hours."

Now a stack of clothing, passed in to her from the greater gloom outside the car. Her eyes were adjusting to the low-observable light. She still couldn't see much of anything. That didn't mean that others near her couldn't see better; so Salli hooded the light and began to change in the dark, feeling her way through the stack of clothing.

From the sound of the voice outside the still-open door, whoever it was had put his back to the car out of modesty. Respect for her modesty. She should have known better than to have imagined that a Wayfarer would take advantage.

"The Holy One gave the signal to vacate, and we packed out. There were patrols in the woods, but our party wasn't molested. They were looking for your brother, to bring him to court."

And they hadn't found him. Obviously. Or he couldn't have mustered a mob for protection and come for her. Once out of her clothing and into fresh underwear, Salli considered, then chinked the light open just a bit. They wanted her to change to help escape identification. She didn't need to draw attention to herself by wearing her split skirt backwards.

"Then the announcement was made that your brother

had confessed the Varrick Teaching and desired to stand before the Jarrod court. The Secular Authority censors caught up with the news releases before too long, but it got out all the same."

Split skirt, work shirt, heavy socks, boots. A hood. They had her tricked out as a lay sister—well, that made sense. Anyone could see she was not a Wayfarer by looking at her. She had the black eyes of the Holy People, the hill people, eyes that were the color of earth and rock and certitude. Not like the eyes of these Wayfarers. Lay sisters wore hoods to filter out the distractions of the world's illusions, and one would do to hide her Pilgrim eyes very well.

"Once it was out there was no calling it back. It's been a contentious year already. You could say your brother has polarized public opinion, Miss Salli. And there's a lot of curiosity about the Varrick Teaching."

There was clear contempt in that word, *curiosity*. Salli could understand completely. Curiosity was a poor motivation to seek truth, as likely to impel one to seek mere diversion as the soul's true learning—and people who took a new Teacher for diversion were beneath notice. Even by Wayfarers who could not know the whole truth of it, that Varrick was not *an* Awakened One but *the* Awakened One.

"You'd not been heard from, but that secular authority man Travers had been spotted. So you had probably gotten back. The Holy One was expecting you in Pellassa. We began to agitate to find out where you were and why you hadn't been allowed to follow your conscience."

Salli stopped with the hood only half-pulled-down over her face. It hadn't been like that. She'd gone to debrief of her own free will; or had she?

She'd made a deal with Bern.

And Bern had failed to follow through and keep up his end of the deal.

"I thought it best for the Teacher to do what I could to allay the secular authority's concerns." That much Salli could be sure of. "I've heard her teaching. And I'm an avalanche soldier. I figured I could tell them that she wasn't a disturbing influence."

If people had been rioting, what credibility could such a claim have had?

Geril the Unseen laughed softly, bitterly. "And the faithful know, Miss Salli, but ignorance in the heart of the untutored is fear. Teacher's given them all more than one chance, and they've chosen dream over reality every time."

The secular authority and the heterodox Wayfarer church were not inclined to accept Varrick at face value, then. So the days Salli had spent in debriefing had been of no use to the Holy One and had kept Salli from her for all of that time. Discouraging seemed too mild a word for it.

"I'm done." She'd finished changing, and folded her old clothing into a neat stack beside her on the bench seat of the surface car. "Now what?"

Geril reached his hand into the passenger compartment, and Salli passed the bundle of discarded clothing to him. Her personal identification papers were in her blouse; she thought of it only as Geril took the discards away. It didn't matter. Salli Rangarold was nobody to her anymore. Salli Rangarold had been an avalanche soldier, but even that had proved to be of no use to the Holy One, from Geril's information. Now Salli was going to have to learn a new identity, one that she could devote entirely to the Holy One's teaching.

"We've got a transfer car due soon, Miss Salli. You'll be traveling as a student of the Holy Fool, going to Pellassa to hear the Index Teacher. This is the first time in twenty years that Saurdish has spoken to the faithful in assembly, and the crowd will give us all plenty of room in which to hide."

This was a surprise of sorts. Salli sat in the back of the surface car, thinking about what this all meant to her. Saurdish was the Index Teacher of the Holy Fool, the acknowledged master of the creed during his lifetime.

If this had been last year, at this same time, Salli knew that she would have thought seriously about coming to Pellassa—on whatever pretext she could devise to spare embarrassment—to hear Saurdish speak. And now?

Was Varrick's teaching compatible with the Holy Fool theology?

Varrick said that there were no signs, there were no portents, there were no warnings from on high of a punishment from God. Specifically, that the plague that had devastated the colonies more than three hundred years ago had been a natural disaster, with no more meaning in and of itself than that the wonders of the world were not all to the benefit of mankind.

The Holy Fool theology answered such questions with the formula that defined the teaching, "How should I know the workings of the mind of God? I am a fool. I only stand and marvel. How wonderful are thy works, oh Lord, and beyond the understanding of your fool." It was appealing.

Nothing could shake Salli's absolute conviction: Varrick was the Holy One, and she thirsted like a pilgrim in a salt desert for the sweet refreshing sustenance of Varrick's teaching.

And yet she felt an uncomfortable, regretful fear on behalf of Index Teacher Saurdish, and hoped against hope that there would be a reconciliation between the Holy One and her devoted Fool.

The arena was the largest in Pellassa, the Synod House where the Wayfarer heterodox held their annual doctrinal examination exercises. That had never made sense to Salli; of what use to anybody was a doctrine that was being tested, refined, reaffirmed year after year? Wayfarer heterodox did not believe in the infallibility of revelation. That was only part of the problem.

She had more immediate problems to contend with, however.

The place was immense.

There were easily thousands of people there.

How was she to find Varrick?

It had taken her six days to cover the few miles between the debrief facility—which turned out to have been at Sigat, at the foot of the mountains. Six days traveling as the guest of Wayfarer heterodox, people who took her to their bosoms without question; people whose hospitality she accepted with a twinge of discomfort, knowing there was no other way for her to get through to her brother and to Varrick.

She was not part of the Wayfarer heterodox community. She was the Orthodox daughter of Orthodox parents; it was only for a lesson against prideful assumption that the Holy One had chosen to return as a Wayfarer.

Six days of traveling under protection, carefully hidden in plain sight as a pilgrim traveling to hear the Index Teacher. Six days of realizing, slowly, but with increasing concern, that the Secular Authority had lost control of the situation.

Meeka's case—the question of how to characterize the death of the Wayfarer street fighter in the first place, of how to interpret Meeka's conversion experience, of whether Varrick was a genuine teacher or an opportunist allowing herself to be used by a man just trying to dodge responsibility in return for the publicity she got—had become far more than what it seemed on the surface, complicated though that was.

Meeka's case should have been a simple one of making a decision on how to characterize the precise block of residential housing in which the killing had taken place and how to characterize that killing itself accordingly, with a simple and straightforward conversion to penalty for Meeka's actions that would fall reasonably and rationally out of the process itself.

What had become of Meeka's case was no less than an index teaching of its own, in a sense, a touchstone that combined and set into opposition the whole of the secular authority in a traditionally religious state, the whole of the Outer Cloud, the existence and status of Pilgrims and the autonomy and influence of the Wayfarer heterodox.

It all came at a bad time.

The rhetoric had been heating up for some time, and the societal pressures within Shadene were only exacerbated by the high profile of Meeka's case.

Reported incidents of vandalism and violent confrontation were already on the rise; the Orthodox states of Creation renewed their offers to assist Shadene in transition from a representative elected government to a religious government almost daily.

Here and now, however, here in the huge arena of the Synod House, there were no apparent tensions—except for eagerness and anticipation. These were all Wayfarer heterodox by definition, an audience self-selected for homogeneity—followers of the Holy Fool theology.

Salli had walked past the Security check and into the arena without being noticed as anyone out of the ordinary by the Security who manned the traffic-control points. Just another body to count, so that the arena could be closed if it reached maximum safe capacity.

Once inside the huge roofed amphitheater—three-quarters buried, below street level, and still towering over its ancillary outbuildings—Salli broke from the people she'd come in with, and made her way slowly down onto the arena floor. She didn't want to endanger anybody by staying with them. She was better off in the company of people who had no idea who she was, whose denial of involvement could be honest, genuine, and sincere.

Much better.

She was in a certain amount of personal danger, being there; though not sought by the Shadene secular authority as a fugitive, still the secular authority could reasonably be expected to track her to get to Meeka—which Salli could no more afford to let happen than Varrick's party could. Varrick's party itself had hived into cells for similar reasons, with an added mission to protect Varrick herself.

There was no assurance that Salli would find who she needed to find here, that she would be able to make contact without showing her hand to secular authority observers.

Still she was more excited than anything else.

The arena filled, and Salli found a place down on the floor with a mixed crowd of people packed so tightly that no place went unclaimed for long. There was the sharp keen smell in the air of too many people keyed up to fever pitch; for a moment Salli thought she sensed or smelled something anomalous, something out of place, and turning quickly to locate the source saw a man in a forester's hood who might have been Bern Travers.

But he was looking away from her, and Salli sank down in her place a bit to hide her height more effectively. Who cared if it was Bern? She had lost faith in him. He had promised to come to take her away from debriefing, and he had not. Bern was no longer someone she could trust, and after all there was no reason for it to be Bern at all just because his shoulders and the angle of that round narrow head looked familiar.

When she checked behind her surreptitiously with the

reflection in the small hand mirror that all Holy Fool theology affirmers carried with them, there was no sign of the man.

Time wore on. Salli grew restless, along with the rest of the people in the great hall. The arena was filled top to bottom, and crowds of people yet eager to get in from what Salli could glimpse of one entrance. The crowds were still pressing into the arena when the fire marshal finally closed the doors. Then the lights were lowered, and the entire room fell silent.

Even the shuffling sounds of people settling, the nervous coughs and throat-clearings that ebbed and flowed again like the sound of surf on shore—even that died out.

Into the waiting silence came the Teacher, Saurdish, the heterodox Index Teacher of the Holy Fool theology, climbing up a flight of stairs below the raised platform of the central stage to seat himself on the rug-draped chair that stood alone with a low table center stage, waiting for him.

Salli felt her heart swell with emotion and with love. The Holy Fool threatened no one, judged no one, found fault with no one. The Holy Fool was God's own idiot child, and Saurdish was his Teacher.

Saurdish was old and moved slowly, with great deliberation but without hesitation. Settling himself in his chair, Saurdish leaned forward, the proximity cameras focused on his pale blue eyes and his snowy white moustache, the furrowed forehead and the glossy shiny expanse of his nearly bald head.

"Good day to you, children," Saurdish said; and like the voice of the ocean, like the voice of the wind, like the powerful rumble of thunder each voice under the arena roof responded as if with a single voice.

God has blessed the day that brings you to us, Teacher.

Saurdish smiled broadly, and launched into the cate-

chism of the Holy Fool. "Who then comes as a seeker
after knowledge of God, in this world of illusion?"

And Salli, who knew the answer, lifted her voice together with the others in joyful response.

*Only an idiot would seek certainty in the world of dreams.
Let me be your idiot, oh Lord.* She gave all of her cares over
into the Holy Fool's keeping, and sat happily in the moment for as long as Saurdish spoke.

The local authorities did not seem to have quite managed to close the arena doors after all. People continued
to press forward past the rows of seated listeners, kneeling on the uncarpeted poured-floor wherever there was
space. In a small quiet corner of Salli's mind that worried
her. There would be problems if the building had to be
evacuated. There were more people inside now than
could be adequately cleared through the existing exits in
an emergency.

But that was only a small corner of Salli's mind.

The greater part of her attention remained firmly concentrated on Saurdish himself, and she spared the cautious worldly voice with her as few scornful thoughts as
would suffice to quiet it. These were all faithful. What
problem could arise? Nobody here was thinking of anything except receiving teaching from the Holy Fool's
preacher. Secular concerns were for the Secular Authority.

There wouldn't be time for any problems to develop;
the Teaching was drawing to a close anyway. "So much
for the teachings of an old fool," the Teacher concluded.
All too soon. Saurdish would have been well within his
rights to speak his set piece and leave; everybody respected his age and infirmity. That he did not do so—
that he called for the queries of the faithful, having said
what he meant to say—was bittersweet; sweet, because
he would stay and speak to them; bitter, because al-

though delayed now by an hour or so for questions and elucidations, the only eventual outcome was the end of the teaching.

"Talk to me now, my children; how am I to make sense of the world?"

It was the call for challenges, for points of theology. Demands for solutions to the problem of pain, for instance. Other heterodox Teachings addressed the problem of the existence of pain in different ways. Orthodox held pain to be an illusion, part of the confusion created by the failure to realize that the world was an artificial and imperfect state; the Holy Fool just shrugged, and said that the problem of pain was that it hurt.

"Teacher, I crave wisdom. How are we to understand the Pilgrim's place in our lives?"

Stations with open transmit lines had been preset all over the arena, and lines formed at each for people who wanted to seek an answer to a specific question. This question was so generic as to almost be part of the Teaching itself, even as the question-and-answer format was part of teaching both heterodox and Orthodox.

The Index Teacher smiled benevolently, warmth and love beaming from his multiply magnified countenance on twenty or thirty screens throughout the arena. "Oh, children. It's not for a fool to understand. Are they here? Very well. Are they gone? Even better."

This old saw was worth a laugh, howsoever dutiful. Salli could not quite join in. She was a Pilgrim. Meeka's conversion experience aside, nothing that had happened to her had challenged or changed her allegiance to the faith of her forebears. If anything, Salli's own conversion emphasized, rather than minimized, the delusions of the heterodox; Varrick was *the* Holy One. The one and only.

Once the laughter had died down a question came from far at the back of the arena, a woman's voice, calm and considering.

"Why should the Holy Fool scorn the Pilgrim, Teacher?"

The arena quieted, the background noise hushed. This was not part of the standard catechism. Salli composed herself for the reply, stifling a pang in her heart; the voice had reminded her of Varrick.

"The Pilgrims' proudly proclaimed Orthodoxy is a flawed teaching." The Holy Fool did not have a foolish answer for this, it seemed—perhaps the issue was so delicate that all Wayfarer Teachings had to conform to a single central point of view, in order to be registered and acknowledged. "It is a perfectly good teaching, but it is wrong. The destruction of the colonies for the impiety of pride is proof."

And the horror stories told by refugees fleeing from the grotesque suffering of the colonies had given birth to the Sacred Promise, and terminated both space- and air-transport programs forever.

More than three hundred years ago.

The staging satellites that had been positioned between Creation and Doctrine—the nearest planet, the first colony established in this system—were still there, still linked in perfectly synchronous orbit, still shining faithfully in the night sky. Waiting for Pilgrims from Creation who would never return to build a base on the broad and potentially fertile plains of Doctrine.

"And yet a fool can never tell."

The voice was the same. There was a small surge in the murmurous sound of the crowd, reacting in mild wonder to the fact that the speaker had not yielded the floor to another question but was arguing instead.

"In fact the Holy Fool has said that the sunrise means only that the sun has risen, and no other meaning is necessarily communicated by the Creator than that. Would not the Holy Fool also say that the plague that struck the colonies may have been nothing more than a plague that struck the colonies, and not a sign from God?"

Salli felt the small hairs at the back of her neck begin to prickle, rise. She was beginning to suspect that she knew where this argument was going.

"And if it is so, then the historical occurrence of the plague that struck the colonies would have no bearing on the spiritual value of Pilgrim Orthodoxy. Why then should the Holy Fool not embrace the Orthodox, Teacher?"

The broadcast screens were unforgiving, focused on the face of the Index Teacher. Some of the transmit cameras were scanning the arena, looking for the woman who spoke; they hadn't been able to find her, at least not yet. That was odd. There were only a limited number of open transmits for people to use in the arena.

Saurdish was frowning: but—whether because he was aware of how closely everybody in this arena would scrutinize his countenance, or because he was so truly one with the Holy Fool that he felt no personal resentment—his frown looked benevolent, concerned, caring. "You have asked and I have answered, daughter. This poor fool does not understand your question. Can it be that you have another purpose in mind, than the receipt of teaching?"

One of the single most inflammatory statements Saurdish could have made, and yet he made it sound so calm and reasonable that his questioner was able to respond and make her voice heard even as the crowd woke slowly to a realization of what was happening.

"In all Teachings there is no single truth, Teacher. I have come to speak the Varrick Teaching, if the Holy Fool has no better reason for refusing to call Pilgrim Orthodox as good as Wayfarers in the sight of God. If the Holy Fool cannot answer let the Holy Fool seek the convocation of the Synod to hear the question."

All of the cameras that Salli could glimpse were scanning the crowd now, looking for the speaker. And now a chanting had begun on the floor, so low at first as to scarce make itself heard over the increased level of background noise that accompanied the speaker's challenging words. The chant itself was a challenge: *Convoke. Convoke. Convoke.*

This was a blatantly political, carefully staged effort on somebody's part to force the Holy Fool to call for convocation of Synod to evaluate the Varrick Teaching. Salli recognized what was going on with dread and discomfort; surely there were less brutal tactics than these available?

But others in the arena, well-meaning Wayfarers who had come only to hear the Index Teacher Saurdish speak, reacted as strongly, but with fewer reservations.

Convoke. Convoke. Convoke.

People around the chanting section were rising to their feet, raising their voices, shouting the chanters down. The chanters would not be shouted down. One of them raised a voicehorn to his lips, and how he had smuggled that past Security was a puzzle to Salli.

Convoke. Convoke. Convoke.

The crowd was getting angry, and rightfully so—it was obvious that there were people trying to disrupt this event, subvert it to serve their own purpose. Nobody liked feeling used. More than voices were being raised now; on a monitor Salli could see people starting to shove each other. The Index Teacher had left the center stage, but the crowd was not quieting.

Convoke. Convoke. Convoke.

A second and a third bloc had picked up the chant, making it more obvious than ever that this was a planned disruption that had been carefully thought out in advance. Arena security was refocusing the monitors on the chanters, taping for future use in legal proceedings no doubt. The noise in the arena was deafening, and above all Salli could hear the artificially amplified chant singing defiance and mockery in the ears of the Wayfarers who had just come to hear Saurdish speak.

Convoke. Convoke. Convoke.

Salli could hardly hear herself think. The noise had risen to maddening levels. She had to get out. Where was the nearest clear exit? All around her people were on their feet, turning to see, trying—she supposed—to understand.

Maybe if she stood up on her chair seat.

Not as if she was the first to have had that idea—still, Wayfarers in general not being so tall as Pilgrims, Salli had an advantage of height as she climbed onto the thin seat of her assembly chair. She had the farfocus glasses that people brought to such events in order to see the stage more clearly; she put them on to check on the exits, and saw with a sickening feeling that the exits were jammed. The doors were open, but nobody was moving. People outside were pushing to get in as strenuously as people inside were pushing to get out.

People were going to be trampled upon, injured.

People were going to be killed.

This could not have been what Varrick had intended—and yet—what other outcome could she have expected, she, the Holy One, who knew the past and the future?

Had this been Varrick's doing?

Steadying herself where she stood with a hand to her neighbor's tolerant shoulder, Salli swept the arena with her farfocus glasses as she had been taught to visually search an avalanche runout zone for clues to where the bodies might have come to rest.

Five separate groups cried out for convocation now, and each of them surrounded by a crowd of agitated and hostile heterodox Holy Fool devotees. Salli wondered about that, but put the question into the back of her

mind. Abstractly speaking such mundane and purely
political stunts should pass over a Holy Fool and leave
no trace of having ever existed: an intriguing topic for
meditation later, once this rapidly-developing riot had
run its course.

Convoke. Convoke. Convoke.

The pushing and shoving that preceded an actual me-
lee had developed to the extent that people were excited
and angry, faces flushed, clothing disarranged. Being
pushed made people hostile and prone to react on instinct, without thinking. Being pushed back somehow
always affected people as though they had just been
pushed without provocation. The avalanche, as it were,
was primed and set to go.

Salli scanned the uppermost tier of the arena, hoping
against hope to find an exit that was not blocked, some
means of letting the pressure out of this explosive situation before it was too late to stop a catastrophe.

No luck.

But as she worked her visual sweep of the third field
from her left something that she saw stopped her cold
where she stood, an icy sweat of dread chilling her from
head to foot.

Meeka.

Her brother, with a voicehorn, the headscarf that had
shadowed his Pilgrim features pulled down around his
neck like a bandanna. Meeka, flushed and white in the
face at the same time, shouting through the voicehorn
into the very faces of the angry Wayfarers who confronted him.

Convoke. Convoke. Convoke.

Salli could not take her eyes off of her brother's face,
transfixed with horror.

It had come to blows, now, as people tore the chair-
backs from the arena seats and used the cross-braces as

clubs. The bloc of chanting dissidents was losing coherence, as it was attacked; Meeka staggered once, twice, three times under the angry ferocity of a Wayfarer's blow, but yielded neither his balance nor the voicehorn.

Convoke. Convoke. Convoke.

What Meeka could not see—what Salli could not take her eyes from—was that the people at his back were falling, one by one, as Wayfarer heterodox attacked those who had disrupted their special event and insulted their Teacher. This was territory, faith, tradition, and the righteous anger of people who felt themselves unjustly attacked; this was war—and Meeka was not ethnic Shadene, Meeka was Pilgrim, Meeka was more hated for his face and frame than even his companions in disruption—

She saw the raised crossbar behind Meeka's back, and screamed his name.

There was no hope that he might hear her.

She saw the crossbar fall, she saw it driven down across Meeka's head with as much power as fury could muster in his assailant. She saw the blood come to Meeka's mouth, she saw him topple, and the staves and beams and crossbars that she saw being raised and brought down again and again over the place where Meeka had fallen were bright with blood.

She could no longer see Meeka.

She knew that they were murdering him.

The surface beneath her feet gave way and Salli fell, cushioned against some nearby body and too heartsick to think twice about it.

Screaming could do no good. There was nothing she could do to stop or stay Meeka's murder at the hands of these Wayfarers.

She no longer heard anything, saw anything, felt anything.

Adrift in a shocked space of helpless horror Salli screamed: and let herself be borne along the human tide that carried her, no longer caring where she would end up.

Eight

Salli awoke with a strangled start, choking on a mouthful of warm fluid. Even as she woke someone raised her up into a seated position and thumped her between the shoulder blades with more concern than care—

"A *little* spoonful!"

It was a woman's voice, fierce and admonitory. An older woman, and with an accent that Salli had grown familiar with over the past few days. Wayfarer. Ethnic Shadene.

For whatever reason it could be, she found the sound of the woman's voice comforting.

"Yes, Mama, you're right, and I'm wrong. Again. Now help me with this, you don't want the mother of your grandchildren choking to death before I can so much as marry her."

The words ran over the scorched streambed of Salli's mind, and vanished into mist without a trace of residue to mark their passing. Meeka. Meeka, and the bloodied clubs. The riot. Her brother. Dead. She choked again, but on her own cries this time, swallowing the screams that she still felt swollen in her belly before she embarrassed herself in front of people that she did not know.

"Where am I?"

She croaked her question, her throat raw with grief and choking. Somebody was holding her up, someone who kissed her forehead so quickly that she almost thought she had imagined it.

"Sh, sh, there, now. Better. Yes. See, Mama, she's not going to die, here. Can you swallow this, Salli? Careful, my mother's already completely disgusted with my nursing skills."

She must have imagined the kiss. Yes. And the little scratch of a moustache, and a fragrance of body heat that seemed familiar if innocuously so. No Wayfarer had offered her such intrusive intimacies. Swallowing a spoonful of hot broth carefully, Salli made up her mind to open her eyes.

The soup was soothing, whatever it was. Salli blinked her eyes open with an effort made easier by her desire for more of the elixir. "What is that stuff? Let me have some more, please."

Right now.

The room was dim and the ceiling low, in the fashion of Wayfarer winter quarters. Close and cramped. Easy to heat, and lined with braided mats of sea grass for insulation, hanging on the walls, layered on the floor, tacked to the ceiling.

Very traditional.

The older woman who stood in the narrow doorway frowning in concern before withdrawing, ethnic Shadene, also very traditional.

But none of the rest of the situation made any sense, for in the midst of all of this old-city Wayfarer dream she lay in the arms of Bern Travers. Who was not old-city Wayfarer, and where had he come from, and what was he doing here?

"Take the whole mug, Salli, there. Can you hold it all right? Here, let me help you."

Her hands were shaking. Bern steadied her grip with his hands over hers, as tender as a nursemaid. It was a laugh; this was Bern Travers, here.

But Bern was talking. "It's my mother's, one of her specialties. Good for shock. Or a sore throat, or a bruise. Someday I'm going to get her to admit that it's all just the same broth of swamp-apple and sweetreed. She just changes the seasonings to make you think it's different."

Talking, almost babbling, and he had not let go of her; he still sat at her side with his arms around her. She couldn't remember having asked him. She couldn't remember how she'd got here, for that.

"Bern. What's happened?"

"Nothing we can do anything about for a little while yet. The city's locked down, Salli, there's been an awful riot. It only started at the Synod House. There's been a lot of tension, and things got out of control in a hurry."

He wasn't moving; no, he seemed perfectly comfortable with her leaning into him. It was just her sitting weight, there was that. But still it was odd, or at least there was something odd going on, even if she hadn't yet quite put her finger on it.

"Meeka was there." In the Synod House; she'd been there, too. How had she gotten out? The exits had been jammed. "I saw him go down, Bern. One of those idiots yelling 'Convoke, convoke.' Is there any record—"

But she'd seen Meeka go down, and he wasn't going to be getting up again. Bern's regretful shake of the head only confirmed what Salli already knew, even if his actual response was neutral.

"It'll take weeks to straighten out, Salli, people were there under assumed names. I was there. But your brother wasn't. You weren't. Those tickets were issued by name, in advance. It was quite a shock to see you there, I'm just glad I did see you in time."

Wait a minute.

She was angry at Bern.

Salli handed the half-emptied mug of broth over to

Bern and settled back more deeply against his shoulder, scowling.

"Start at the beginning, let's just. You were going to come and fetch me from debriefing. Nine days, you said, and you'd come for me yourself, and instead what? I had to wait for Meeka to come. And then to walk out past my own teammates, Bern, it was ugly. I want to think better of you."

Surprised as she was to hear the sincerity in her own voice, Salli realized that she meant it. She wanted to think well of Bern. He'd promised. She'd believed him. She hadn't realized until now how bitter a blow her disappointment had actually been.

Bern turned away to set the mug down to one side, but did not shift his embrace. "And I want you to think well of me. But I was detained. By the time I broke out of the hospital you were gone, and I really had no charter to find out where you'd gone to. I called on Varrick, and believe it or not she received me. Promised to give you my message when she saw you. I've been waiting ever since, and then this Holy Fool thing came up."

And she hadn't gotten back to Varrick yet. She didn't owe Bern any explanations; but it would only be common courtesy to fill him in. "The people Meeka was with felt that I had to hide to help him hide. It made sense. You're saying they were paranoid?"

What was she doing in bed in this dim room, this quiet room in what seemed to be someone's home?

What was she doing resting in Bern's arms, as if she had a reason or a wish to be there?

"Not paranoid, Salli, not a bit. But it wasn't my charter to find your brother. I gave my report. Varrick meant to bring Meeka before the Jarrod court. For that the Jarrod court had to give her credence, though, and there's a problem with that."

And now there would be no Jarrod court for Meeka.

No reconciliation with the community, ever. Meeka was dead. Bern might have more to say, but Salli did not want to hear it.

"The issue's academic." She swallowed the salt tears down with an effort. "You'd better leave, Bern, I'm going to cry. Oh. A lot. You don't want to be here."

Bern rose to his feet, as if to go; but no, it was only to reorient himself. To take her into his arms face-to-face rather than serving as her backrest. "You're mistaken," Bern said, with absolute conviction. Absolute firmness; utter tenderness. "There is nowhere else in Creation that I'd rather be right now. Cry all you like, Salli. Just don't shut me out. Let me share your grief."

Making no sense.

Again.

Salli didn't care.

She buried her face against Bern's shirtfront and cried as she hadn't cried ever in her life. Meeka was dead. She was alone.

There were not enough tears in the world to express the desolation of her sense of loss.

When Salli woke up she was by herself in the room, the door left open, the small sounds of human occupation comfortingly familiar in the background. She remembered where she was and how she'd come here well enough; but it was too bizarre to be credited.

Bern Travers?

Talking to his "mama"?

And where then was she, if she was in the house of Bern's mother, in a small closet of a room smelling faintly of leather-dressing and the musky underfunk of the male animal?

Taking up a fistful of bedclothes, Salli breathed in deeply, suspicious.

Bern.

If he wasn't actually living at home, he had clearly stayed over sufficient nights recently to communicate his smell to the bedclothes. They weren't soiled by any stretch of the imagination, except where she herself had bled on them from one of the multiple scrapes that made her sore from head to foot. She didn't remember any of those. She only remembered confusion and struggle, accidental blows, inadvertent injury, all only dimly sensed around the edges of the huge and horrible fact of Meeka's violent death.

She hurt, she ached, she was stiff, she was sore, but she was thirsty, and the water jug that had been left for her on the side table was empty. She was going to have to get up, and that was going to be awkward because she wasn't dressed. Well, not in any clothes that she could recognize as hers; whoever had put her to bed had stripped her down and washed her feet, and Salli could only hope that it had been Bern's mother. And not Bern.

She sat up slowly, taking her time and fixing her attention on the nightstand as she waited for the room to come back into focus. A low glow-lamp, one of the old-fashioned Wayfarer kind with a globe made out of the dead shell of a roundsnail. An old glass valet dish with a wrist-chron and a Pilgrim's ring, also old, so old that the engraving on the ring had rubbed smooth and there was no telling what shrine it had originally come from. A partially disassembled firing mechanism from a crowd-control grenade, carefully wiped clean of its residue of irritant powder . . .

The bed was low to the ground, and it was easier to slide down off it to her knees and rise to her feet from a seated position on the reedmat rug than to try forcing the badly leveraged stand from the edge of the bed. She was wearing someone else's good thickweave smock, the kind with the long tails and no collar—as dressed as she needed to be, really, all things considered.

Someone's rather dilapidated reed slippers were half-hidden beside the bed, and Salli slipped her feet into them. Bern had small feet. But he was a man, and what was small feet on a Wayfarer male made reasonably sized feet on a Pilgrim woman. Her feet were on the narrow side, which helped.

Salli padded over to the door—the reed slippers creaking at every step—and pushed it open cautiously, determined to find Bern and confront him. She wasn't quite sure what she meant to confront him about, but there was so much to choose from that it was an uncertainty of abundance rather than a loss for suitable issues. The hall was narrow, but long; she could hear voices at the end of it.

"No, Mama, you owe twenty-eight for greens this month. The bill's correct. You're transposing again."

Bern's voice, and as Salli crept up on the kitchen at the end of the hall she could see him sitting at a table with his mother and a stack of account books. And a bead-counter. The bead-counters that were sacred to Pilgrims and used to devote repetitions of prayers were used by heterodox Wayfarers to do their accounts.

It was just another instance of proof that Wayfarers were alien to the holy land. Exposed to religious artifacts in the absence of cultural understanding of their meaning, Wayfarers had assumed the sacred furniture was no more than a handy tool for calculating who owed whom how many fish at the end of the season.

Salli knocked on the doorjamb and went in.

"Now sign the last one like a good mama, and we're done with accounts for this month," Bern was saying. "Then I'd better be checking on—Salli!"

The cool measuring eye Bern's mother focused on her made Salli blush. But it wasn't her fault. This was all Bern's fault. "Hello, Bern. Mam Travers, excuse me, I don't believe we've met."

An idiotic thing to say if there ever was one. She was sleeping in Mam Travers's son's bed. The roof constituted an introduction, surely.

Mam Travers took it all in stride. Was Bern in the habit of bringing strange women home to his mother? Salli wondered.

Mam Travers simply stood up without the slightest hint of discomfort. "But my son has told me all about you, Salli. I'm very sorry about your brother. Bern, you be sure she doesn't go hungry from under my roof."

Bern had risen in turn by this time, bundling the account books into a carry-sack with a bemused expression on his face. "Yes, Mama.—Don't fight with the plaits shop this time, please."

Mam Travers took her account books and left.

Bern gestured toward the place his mother had vacated; Salli sat down.

"Your mother said to—"

"We need to talk before—"

They were both trying to talk at once, shutting up as abruptly as soon as they realized the other was speaking.

Silence.

"Yes, as a matter of fact, I—"

"You must be starving, let me—"

And again.

Salli eyed Bern warily, wondering how to break out of this. Bern raised his hand, almost shyly. Salli nodded. "The chair recognizes Bern Travers."

Bern's eyes disappeared when he smiled, and his grin split his face. It had always struck Salli as a little alarming. It looked painful. It was unnatural for a man to show so much tooth when he smiled. "Thank you, Teacher. You must be hungry, let me get you something to eat. And we need to talk. Why didn't you wait for me, at the debriefing center?"

This wouldn't do. She was angry at him for not having

made good on his promise to come and fetch her. For all Bern had done she might as well have still been there—had she not realized independently, on her own, quite by herself that the time was gone.

She wasn't about to let Bern turn the issue into blame on her side. "You said something about the hospital, Bern."

Bern turned from the table and stood up. "Small explosion. Nothing more than inconvenient, but they insisted on keeping me on ward. I was worried when I found out that you'd gone with your brother and the rest of those batchelders. There's been ugliness, Salli. I suppose a riot was inevitable."

A riot was never inevitable. Bern would never have accepted so fatalistic a pronouncement in class. That would be the tenth part of one's grade right there. Right off the top.

"I'm thirsty, too." She wouldn't go so far as to accept what might have been meant as an apology, in a backhanded Bern sort of way. *Small explosion* sounded a little worrisome, but with Bern himself minimizing every step of the way she wasn't going to push it. He looked as though he was still in one piece, and she would probably just have to wait for the rest of it. "I'm hungry, yes, but I'm thirstier than hungry. If that makes sense. Can I have about a gallon of water, please?"

Bern was busy amongst the dinnerware. Glasses. Meatsticks. Napkins, mugs for hot kelp tea. "Worked out for the best, maybe, strengthens your position. Rescued by the batchelders, I mean, Salli. Listen. We could really use you. All of Shadene could really use your help."

He set a glass of water in front of her, and a pitcher of water was filling in the sink under the hand pump. Cracking a bladder of juice he poured another glass full of bride's-blood, sweet and thick and grainy; opened a cupboard and took out a miracle melon, slicing as he talked.

"I'm not going to pretend that I have your best interest at heart, Salli, not after what you saw happen to your brother. I'm only just thinking of the state of Shadene. I don't want you to have any illusions about that."

Miracle melon grew on the salt flats, but the sweet pulpy flesh inside was as fragrant as flowers and utterly pure of any taint of salt or bitterness. Sweet as the sunrise on midsummer morning. Miracle melon was the best thirst-quencher in all of Shadene, with the single exception of water. Salli accepted a dish of melon chunks and devoured the dripping cubes greedily, juice running down her arm to her elbow and soaking into the sleeve of the smock she wore.

"So what do you mean, Bern?" Meeka was on his mind? Was he afraid that she might take his behavior as indicative of something more personal? Oh, surely not. Not Bern Travers. Just because he'd sought her out, and saved her from a riot, put her to bed in his bed, dressed her in one of his old smocks—there was no reason to suspect that anything might be going on in the dim recesses of his murky brain.

What had he said to his mother?

Not just now, but earlier, and about grandchildren?

It wouldn't reconcile with anything she knew about Bern. She couldn't really remember anyway. She must have misunderstood what was being said.

"Slow down a bit, you'll get the stomach cramps." Refilling her dish with cubed melon, Bern sat down again and helped himself to some fruit in turn. "Well, Salli, it's like this. It wasn't planned this way, but as it turns out— Varrick's people know you're an avalanche soldier, Meeka's sister, and a believer. Can I put it that way? A believer?"

"I know that Varrick is the Awakened One." Bern had

yet to wake. It wasn't up to her to open the curtain of his mind. He had received teaching from Varrick. The rest was up to him.

"While the rest of the establishment, I should say the Shadene Secular Authority, knows you're an avalanche soldier, did voluntary debrief, good Pilgrim stock, still on the side of public order. I'm extrapolating a bit here."

He was extrapolating quite a bit. No, he was being presumptuous; but it was Bern's business to know how people's actions were going to be interpreted by others. It was his job.

"You're saying I've got credibility." She herself did not feel inclined to grant credence to so far-fetched a claim. "Acceptable go-between, both positions. One problem, Bern. I'm not a negotiator. Never have been."

He'd thought that one through already. "That's why you take me with you, Salli. Independent confirmation of message content, but also—well, we can support each other's weak points."

She could eat the entire melon by herself. There was nothing like miracle melon when a person was thirsty. But Bern was right: she'd get a bellyache if she didn't slow down. Salli folded her hands in front of her on the kitchen table.

"What do we do next, then, Bern? I need to go see Varrick. I'd hoped to be with her before now."

He pivoted suddenly in his chair, straining his neck to look at the timepiece on the window clock behind him. "Council of war. Let's go see Varrick, see what kind of a mood she's in. The press have been nasty. If you're feeling up to it," he added hastily, settling himself back at the table as quickly as he'd moved. He liked to startle people. "Thirsty?"

Yes. Thirsty to the point of despair, to know that the Holy One was in the world and she so long away. "I'll need clothing, Bern, I'm not stepping into the street in your underwear."

That brought the red blood to his cheek. Salli was amused to see it. "I'll just go down to the corner cleaners, Salli. Don't let anyone in."

Oh, then this was a traditional household, one in which communal tasks—laundry and baking and brewing, spinning and weaving, plaiting the wall hangings as well, once upon a time—were still done at some central location outside the dwelling place. Salli had always felt that the idea was a sound one. Life as an avalanche soldier was fundamentally communal—shared dormitories, shared mess facilities, shared baths.

Salli drew the bowl of melon closer to her bosom and waved Bern off on his errand.

The clothes she wore felt so much better, now that they were clean. Salli hadn't realized how comfortable she'd gotten in Wayfarer gear; but—paradoxical as it sounded—she actually did feel she had a greater freedom of movement in the mid-shin skirts and sockfeet of a decent Fool. She still had no identification, no money, no personal possessions of any particular value. She was a Fool, right enough.

In her mind she had half imagined Varrick encamped in a great tent city outside the walls of old Pellassa, surrounded by hundreds if not thousands of true believers ready to give their lives for her at a moment's notice. She knew better, but the realization of the extent of that fantasy was still poignant.

There were no tents outside the city walls, no hordes of devotees either more or less fanatical. Varrick was in protective custody, and it was avalanche soldiers who stood guard at the control points between the entrance to the Shadene Secular Authority's administrative compound and the post's residential area where Varrick was housed.

"Is the Synod really that scared of her?" Salli asked Bern in wonder as the ground car traveled slowly over smoothly graveled lanes. Shadene Secular Authority compounds were security installations. One usually had to be an employee of the Shadene Secular Authority— or an avalanche soldier—to so much as gain admittance.

"Well." Bern looked a little pleased with himself, his enjoyment in possession of inside knowledge all the more transparent for his diffidence in sharing it. "She's outspoken, your Varrick. And she's been out speaking. The Old Ways rhetoric they're using against her, for one, is nothing short of savage."

As though that would surprise anyone. The Old Ways heterodox were savagely against anything they felt to be contrary to their rather narrow interpretation of the writings the Wayfarers had inherited by default when they'd come to Shadene. That was why Salli had never been able to take Old Ways believers seriously. They were as newly come to Shadene as the rest of the Wayfarers, with no more insight into the thought of the Holy People than was available to anyone who could read. The Holy People had been long gone by the time the Old Ways heterodox had started in with their absurd claims to tradition.

Salli thought about Bern's explanation for a moment, turning a comment over in her mind. The Shadene Secular Authority didn't extend protective custody to every teacher who had invoked the self-righteous ire of Old Ways heteros. There had to be some more to it than that: but before she had made up her mind quite how to approach the issue the ground car slowed to a stop in front of a blue-brick building that might have been a warehouse in a previous incarnation.

It would keep.

One of the avalanche soldiers at the doorway came forward at the trot to shoulder the passenger cabin's access door into its upright and locked position. Salli had to swallow back a grin. She'd been an avalanche soldier, and she remembered guard duty. It was surprisingly fun to be treated like an important ranking official by her own former peers.

Inside the archway over the great front doors the building changed its character completely from old once-warehouse to a still close silent world of padded-board walls and thickly napped carpeting. An avalanche soldier in the building's small front lobby nodded at Bern—who seemed to have been expected—and led the way, up one hall and down another and around several flights of stairs until they came to the upper stories and the wing where Varrick was apparently staying.

More guards and more salutes, and Salli noticed that the only curiosity she herself seemed to arouse was a genial knowing interest. Friendly. They didn't know who she was, then, or else Bern had told a really good—completely brazen—story to cover her desertion from her unit.

Finally they were through: the door into the inner sanctum opened in response to Bern's respectful knock, and Salli could see into Varrick's suite.

A sudden sense of panic paralyzed her at the thought of seeing Varrick.

What if?

What if she had only been exhausted and vulnerable to brainwashing, before?

What if she had been duped?

What if Varrick was no longer the Varrick Salli remembered, the Varrick for whom she would be willing to sacrifice her career, her position, her job, everything?

The woman who opened the door was someone Salli recognized, Herony, one of the people who had been in charge of running the kitchens at the Corabey encampment. Herony put her upraised fingers to her lips, enjoining silence; then she looked past Bern to Salli, and her face changed. Joy, and sorrow.

Herony beckoned them in, giving Salli a quick hug on her way past. Salli supposed it was on Meeka's behalf, and she appreciated the gesture.

Herony led Salli and Bern through the front room of the luxury apartment and out to a terrace that was fabulous with botanical specimens in pots, a hothouse roof, birds kept captive there by nets strung two stories higher yet. Running water.

Ripe fruit on the partson trees, and here it was well past the harvest and into the first snows of winter—the news had been full of cheer, the mountain resorts would all be opening early this year.

Snow levels had fallen to a mere three thousand feet, and a generous wet wind from the ocean was putting down inch after inch of good base for winter sport. The avalanche soldiers would be busy this year keeping the resorts safe and the passes clear.

As for the Holy One, however, Salli was not to face her moment of truth as she had feared; because Varrick was in meeting, being catechized. Herony settled them where she and Bern could listen, and went away.

In an informal seating, lawn furniture beneath fragrant night-blooming perlix, there was Varrick and a party of heterodox from Synod—all in business dress, and Salli only guessed them for Synod by their questions.

"You must know that there's room for a wide range of seemingly divergent thought within the churches of Shadene as they are." Nor were the questions entirely friendly, professionally unctuous though the speaker certainly was. "Why do you insist that your Teaching merits separate recognition? Can you not find a place

within an established teaching, and spare us all this un-
necessary divisiveness?"

Salli couldn't see Varrick's face from where she sat.
Varrick had her back to them. Her back was just anybody's ordinary back, but that didn't disturb Salli. Varrick's light didn't shine from behind. It was when you
could see Varrick's face that you knew you were in the
presence of Godhead.

"I don't want to create divisiveness any more than any
of you. Gentle people." The interview did not seem to
be going well. Varrick's imperfectly concealed rage and
contempt were all too eloquent in her tone of voice. "But
I have no intention of being folded meekly into someone
else's historical error. The point is that this is a departure
teaching. The point is that a separation must be made
between what has gone before, because it has been an
error which must not go uncorrected any longer."

This seemed to have been a sore point from earlier in
the conversation, because another of the examiners
jumped on the tail of Varrick's rebuttal a shade too
quickly. "The authorized Teachers of all the Wayfarer
churches agree that the signs are signs, and the age of
miracles has not passed. Even the Pilgrims agree, or else
they would not be here. And yet one person, one person
without lineage or schooling, claims by divine inspiration that every Teacher in Creation is wrong. Only she
is right. Forgive me, Teacher,"—oh, the subtle sneer of
it!—"but it stretches one's credulity."

Varrick dropped her head, as if discouraged. Salli
wanted to fly to her defense; but if these were Synod as
they seemed to be, this inquiry was part of the formal
process of Evaluation, and Varrick had to answer for
herself.

"This is my truth," Varrick said; and her voice was no
less powerfully convincing for its low hushed tone. "I
can speak no other. Mock me as you will, it is you who

will answer for it. I make no claims to superseding other paths, but before God I have true Teaching to establish and impart."

Varrick straightened her shoulders and raised her voice, fixing each of her interrogators in turn as Salli imagined with the sharp piercing glare of her burning brown eyes. "You tell me to repudiate my word because it might cause trouble between Wayfarer and Pilgrims? There is already trouble between Wayfarer and Pilgrims. You cannot halt or heal it by trying to suppress my Teaching."

It was a long speech, and Salli took it to her heart with a glad and grateful spirit; not so the examiners from Synod, who seemed merely bored.

"Very well." The woman who sat in the middle facing Varrick was apparently the senior member of the delegation. Now she shot her cuffs and smoothed some bit of something off of the upper part of her left sleeve in an almost insultingly dismissive manner. "A courier will come with a transcript of our discussion, Teacher, for your review. You'll be able to add or delete material from your responses, then we'll take the package forward. You must know that the challenge is quite, er, challenging. There has not been a new Teaching in Shadene for two hundred years, and even then there was a clear line of descent. A Teacher's endorsement. None of this urban terrorism. We'll do what we can to present you in the best possible light, of course."

Now Varrick stood up, and Salli almost felt sorry for the delegate facing her. The line of Varrick's spine was as straight as a stone's free-fall. Salli could imagine the cold fury on Varrick's face that made the delegates pale, to one degree or another, as they rose in turn to take leave.

"Of course." *And be damned to the lot of you for the blind bureaucrats that you are.* The delegation was supposed to be comprised of accredited Teachers, but there was not one Teacher in all of Shadene with a fraction of Varrick's charisma—of Varrick's personal power.

That, if nothing else, could tear the Wayfarer heterodoxies apart, Salli realized—and would, unless the Synod in sheer self-defense extended formal recognition to Varrick as an Awakened One in this generation.

And now the delegation was gone, and she and Bern would have Varrick to themselves.

Varrick turned to watch the Synod delegation leave, and saw Salli; locked eyes, and Salli felt Varrick's gaze plunge deep into her soul, and opened her mind and heart to Varrick's examination in an ecstasy of grateful humility.

There was no need to have wondered.

This was the Holy One for all ages.

"Salli." Varrick moved to embrace her gently, laying her hands on Salli's shoulders and kissing her carefully—with great deliberation—on either cheek. "It's good to see you." Varrick's tone lightened, then, and she shook a disapproving finger at Bern.

"Bern Travers, you are miscreant. I have had disappointing report of you."

Salli could have sworn that Bern blushed. "Teacher, I have only done what had to be done. And brought you Salli safe from that mess at the Synod House. —Why did you do it?"

Bern had to ask, but Salli already knew the answer. Varrick had had nothing to do with the riot at the Synod House. There had been a woman's voice, true enough, but only so people would think of Varrick. It hadn't been Varrick's voice.

Had it been, Salli could half convince herself that there would have been a mass Awakening instead of a riot at Synod House, because Varrick had the power.

Bern made to rise as Varrick came to sit down on the

couch beside him; Varrick put her hand to his shoulder to prevent him. His right shoulder, and—turning toward him—put her left hand against Bern's right side between his arm and his ribs, and held it there. Looking at Bern's shoulder, as if she were thinking about something.

"I had no hand in that, Bern, and you know that already." When Varrick took her hand away from Bern's side she was holding something in the palm of her left hand. Taking his right hand in her right hand, she turned his hand palm uppermost and dropped something into his curious grasp. Bern stared at the things in his hand: Salli didn't quite understand. He was as white in the face, all of a sudden, as a man might be who thought that he had seen a ghost.

Varrick spoke on calmly. "And all the same I must accept the blame for it. I should have been more careful with my batchelders when I still could have controlled them. Salli, I'm sorry, but your brother can no longer be absolved of crimes at Jarrod."

She was dying to see what Varrick had put in Bern's hand. Straining her neck from where she sat in a chair to Bern's left, Salli barely registered what Varrick was saying until Varrick mentioned Meeka.

"My brother is dead, Holy One." She couldn't make sense of Varrick's comment. She couldn't make sense of what Bern was showing her, the things in his hand: little things, thin as wire and no longer than the first joint of one's forefinger. Pins. Surgical pins. Surgical pins like doctors used to stack fractured ribs in series while they healed. "I saw him fall. And blood on the staves, and killing fury behind them." The bloody staves, that was.

Why had Varrick given Bern a handful of surgical pins?

Where had they come from?

Bern was no help, he simply sat there and stared at the surgical pins that he held. Varrick shook her head.

"Down, Salli, yes. But I don't think he's dead yet, he's too hardheaded, yes? I'd be sorry if he was dead, but I can't be glad of what he and the other batchelders are doing. They believe they can bring about the Awakening. They're wrong. And it's so much easier to overlook doctrinal error when nobody's getting hurt."

Varrick seemed to imply that Meeka was involved in more serious business than just disrupting the Holy Fool's appearance. Varrick hadn't seen what Salli had seen. Varrick was the Holy One; but that didn't have to mean infallible in all things. Did it? Meeka was dead. Surely.

"Holy One." Salli put her confusion over Varrick's claim aside; she had more troubling questions on her mind. "If they are acting in your name, but without your direction, why don't you repudiate the batchelders? Doesn't maintaining silence make you seem complicit, Teacher?"

Yet the Holy One had her own good and necessary and sufficient reasons for what she did. Salli didn't need to understand what those reasons were. It was enough for her to know that Varrick was the Awakened One.

"I decline to dignify the issue with a public repudiation," Varrick replied, very firmly indeed. "Because I find the very idea to be so offensive as to be beneath notice. And also there is no understanding of the manifest mercy of the Creator. Sometimes people will wake from a nightmare when nothing else can shake them loose from sleep."

Salli glanced at Bern, sharply, concerned. If she had been Bern, or anybody else representing the secular authority, Varrick's argument might well have sounded too disingenuous by half.

Bern wasn't paying attention.

Bern simply sat there looking at the pins in his hand, and the tears ran down his cheeks to soak into his neatly buttoned shirt collar without him seeming to have noticed that he was weeping.

"Bern?"

Salli couldn't quite figure him out. What had sat on him so hard, so fast, that he could not so much as react when his name was called?

"Oh."

Then Bern seemed to shake himself, as if awakening from a trance. "Oh, Holy One. It would be so easy for you to prove yourself and be done with all of this. Why? I don't understand."

"It's not supposed to be that easy," Varrick rebuked him, gently. Lovingly. "It's supposed to be the soul's awakening, and not a circus trick. And you know as well as I that a circus trick is all the unconvinced world would ever see. Or admit. Besides."

Varrick stood up once more. Putting both hands to the small of her back, she stretched, leaning backwards. She looked as lithe as an avalanche soldier herself, when Varrick stretched. "Besides. I'm the one telling people that signs and portents are hollow mockery. I mean to wake the world to the exercise of reason in the service of the Awakening. So I can't afford to associate myself with things that are too far beyond reason. Salli, are you going to be my liaison?"

Salli began to understand, but only began. And it set her brain spinning. "Yes, Holy One. Bern's lied up and down to his superiors for me. I'm almost convinced I didn't just run away from my unit myself."

Grinning, Varrick gave Salli's shoulder an affectionate shake. "You've hooked yourself a keeper, Salli, I think you should hang on to him. Nothing but good will come of it, trust me on this. Excuse me. I'm hungry."

The tension between what Varrick said, and who and what she was, had seldom been so tearing for Salli. Varrick spoke quite casually, like a cousin or an aunt or just a friend. And yet if Salli understood what Varrick was saying, she had witnessed a miracle, and one so naturally done that it had taken her this long to figure it out.

"So talk to me. Bern. Snap out of it."

Bern counted the pins in the palm of his hand carefully, once, twice. Counted them three times; then put them into the inner pocket of his worn leather jacket. "You wanted to know why I hadn't come for you in debrief, Salli, and I told you I was detained. Eight hours of surgery, and I'm to take medication faithfully to prevent any chance of infection while my ribs heal, and it's hurt to breathe ever since. Eleven pins in my ribs, Salli. It doesn't hurt to breathe anymore."

The Holy One whose coming had been promised would come with the healing touch. And Wayfarer Teachers through the ages had laid claim to the power, from time to time; some of the stories were credible. Some not. Within the past hundred and fifty years Creation had seen three Wayfarer Teachers whose claims had won them a wide following, and one had eventually stopped making claims under pain of exposure or fraud, and Shadene public opinion was still of two minds about the other two.

But not Orthodox.

Orthodox knew that the Holy One with the gift of healing would be the one, the only, the sole and unique Awakened One, not just another in a long line of Wayfarer teachers.

And Varrick was the Holy One.

Even Bern would have to realize that now.

Salli could have wept, but kissed Bern on the cheek, instead. A kiss chaste and sisterly, in token of his great distress of spirit. "Go on with you, then," she suggested. "And come for me when we need to meet. Bern. Thank you so much. For everything."

And he, he was too moved and too confused to do more than nod and go away.

Salli sat on the garden terrace by herself for quite a while before Herony came to call her in to have a cup of kelp tea.

Could it be true that she loved Bern, and he loved her?

And if the Holy One had said it, how could it not be so?

Nine

It was a very long two weeks, waiting for Synod's decision. Delegations came and went, but Varrick never wavered in her course; she was determined now, it seemed, as she had not been before, that Synod should accept the fact of her inspired Teaching. Varrick had seemed relatively indifferent to the question of whether or not she was to have official recognition, when Salli had first come to know her on Corabey. But now that Synod had failed to embrace her, Varrick's attitude had hardened. Synod would see truth now or be damned.

Salli supposed it was no wonder if the issue seemed to have become a personal one to Varrick. She was suspected of having secret ties to terrorist radicals precisely when urban terrorism—while yet fairly minor in terms of lives or livelihoods lost or threatened—represented an increasingly serious challenge to the equanimity of the city of Pellassa in particular and Shadene in general.

The threat of terrorism in the mountain resorts or at the hill shrines was one thing: there were avalanche soldiers to guard against it, and besides such acts of vandalism were usually directed against property. Not people.

But disruption of the basic infrastructure of daily life in one of the major cities of Shadene—traffic stalled out for miles because of a gaping crater in the roadway, tons of produce rotted overnight by the surreptitious introduction of a particular gaseous compound into the warehouses after hours—that was the sort of thing that could really create a headache for the common citizen, and discourage tourism as well.

One way or the other, it was a tense period; but Salli herself was more or less oblivious on a deeper emotional level to the turmoil of it. The security issues she could appreciate and understand. The influence of external events on Varrick's hardened determination she could isolate, evaluate, analyze.

The potential disruption of civil life in the state of Shadene as Wayfarers pressed the issue of enclave autonomy and expansion that Meeka's accident had originally raised, the destabilization of the Wayfarer church as factions either championed or resisted Varrick's claim to integration, the worsening of relations between Pilgrim and Wayfarer as the Wayfarer churches succumbed to internal conflict—all these things Salli saw, and sorrowed for, but nothing touched the ever-deepening well of faith and serenity within her.

Varrick was the Awakened One.

Salli, as Varrick's accepted liaison, was even closer to Varrick than she had been at Corabey. As people came to argue theology, as people left either adrift in wonder or stubbornly fixed in their own self-delusion, Salli sat at Varrick's side and let Varrick's word soak deep into her heart to be enshrined there.

This was a world-changing paradigm, a true Awakening.

What had survived of the aeronautical and aerospace scientific communities of Creation was not slow to notice that, once Varrick began to speak. Varrick received delegations nearly every day from universities all over Creation, and spoke to hopeful people of the Awakening that she brought.

She sent them all away again inspired with hope and on fire to reclaim the heritage of the scientists who had gone before—and fearful, even so, conflicted between the truth that Salli knew from personal experience would be self-evident to their souls on one hand and the past century of teaching on the other.

It was no problem for the less devout, but there were devout enough in Creation to make an issue out of whether Synod would recognize Varrick's Teaching. If Synod accepted Varrick's Teaching as good Wayfarer theology, it would encourage the members of the Orthodox church who wished to modify the Promise to permit at least air travel, if not a return to space. That could only lead to an increased apostasy rate—Pilgrims abandoning the faith of their fathers in favor of a faith that better answered to their needs.

That in turn might lead to an eventual Orthodox relaxation of the religious prohibition against atmospheric or space research—one of the real and immediate concerns throughout all of Creation. It was either that or suppress Varrick immediately and absolutely, and her Teaching with her.

It was in the context of this emotional and intellectual turmoil that Varrick had stirred up that Synod made its decision.

The signal came at the door in the afternoon, and Salli nodded to Herony—waiting with her in a small sitting room to one side of the entrance—to go answer. She had had a message from Bern telling her that the announcement was expected.

The voice she heard as Herony opened the door was not expected.

"Squad Leader Morrissey. To escort the Teacher's proxy to a meeting."

Salli leapt to her feet and rushed out into the antechamber, beside herself. Morrissey. Morrissey, and—

and—yes. Carpi and Solt, Techam, Ware, her own team, and her squad leader acting as team leader in her place. Standing there in full-dress uniform as smug as you please and full of satisfaction about the joke of it.

It might have seemed to another that there was no emotion in these carefully muted expressions, on those professionally blank faces. Salli knew better. This was her team. They were laughing, fit to snap their cross-bracings at the fun of it.

"Morrissey?" Salli demanded, half-unbelieving. She saw him with her own eyes. Of course it was Morrissey.

But the last time she had seen him he'd been angry at her—they'd all been angry at her. Debriefing. Escorting her from her suite to where Meeka had been waiting for her, and the temperature below freezing every step of the way. Walking past her own team, with the gap in the line where she should have been standing. It had been very hard: and yet here was Morrissey now, and he broke ranks and grinned at her.

"You, young lady, are in a very great deal of trouble." There was no hostility left there. No anger. Not even much resentment. Either Bern had told a great many lies, or her fellows understood and had forgiven her. Or both.

"Here the snow is the earliest it's been in years . . . and the avalanche crews are working double shifts to keep the passes clear for Holiday, and we're stuck on the nice, warm, rainy coast. Wearing these things. Doing nothing, or the functional equivalent of nothing, when we could be gelling our gollies so that tourists everywhere can come and go in warmth and comfort."

Well, Morrissey had a point. On top of his head. No, there was a sense in which the easy duty was a species of Holiday itself; and a sense in which being on escort duty rather than in the foothills was in fact an embarrassment to an avalanche soldier.

"If Synod's done the right thing, we can be back to

Tarpeter in three days." It didn't occur to Salli that she was including herself back with her unit until she heard herself use the word, we. She could have blushed: but Morrissey didn't seem to have noticed.

"Right, let's go then. Oh boy. Back to Tarpeter; I can hardly wait."

Tarpeter was her unit's primary posting. They didn't have any resorts, but there was a piece of highway that they owned for avalanche control, and several shrines—eight, Salli thought. Three of which saw fairly good business around Holiday. People did pilgrimage, visiting, some number of shrines or all of the shrines in thus-and-such a Teaching. Morrissey and the rest of the crew could be busy.

The ground car took them into city center to the administrative building where the Shadene Secular Authority was accustomed to convening Wayfarers and Pilgrims together. There were reporters at the compound gates: somebody knew that something was up. What—Salli wondered—would they be reporting, in two hours' time?

There were a lot of Security all around, though Salli didn't see any other avalanche soldiers. It wasn't a good sign. The only reason to be prepared for violence to break immediately was if Synod was going to say something it didn't think the batchelders would like.

Between the reporters and the guards—

What would happen now that Synod had made up its mind, and erred? Because the conclusion was inescapable, the verdict no longer in doubt if it had ever been. Salli was sure of it, and it made her more angry than sad. Synod hadn't been asked for anything unreasonable. Its reply to recognizing Varrick's Teaching as genuinely inspired, that was unreasonable.

Setting her thoughts in order with an effort, Salli concentrated on being in the moment. The announcement had not been made, not yet. She could display only hopeful anticipation before the fact.

Her Security escort took her up from the parking floor through a restricted lift-belt passageway to an upper floor of the administration building. The view was spectacular, even in the rain; but Morrissey and the others had to leave her at the door to the conference room.

"Steal some pastry for us," Morrissey suggested, speaking low and without moving his lips. "I like squishberry."

The joke heartened Salli; and she was grateful for it. All pastries were squishberry once they'd spent any amount of time in the thigh pocket of an avalanche soldier's duty uniform. Salli went through into the room; Bern was waiting there, and she could have laughed to see him—he was so formal and so carefully groomed. He was wearing his best uniform, with his rank on it: Colonel Bern Travers, Shadene Secular Authority.

She hadn't seen much of him over the past two weeks, and that had been all right for as far as it went. She'd been embarrassed and confused about Varrick's instruction. Fortunately for her Bern seemed as much at a loss as to how to find the right place and sit down as she was.

"Good afternoon, Miss Rangarold. Thank you for coming; this way, please."

Bern Travers, usher. Colonel Travers, and the lowest-ranking person there apart from Salli herself. Well, and the guards at the door. Salli supposed she outranked them and Bern as well by virtue of her diplomatic proxy, since she was no longer to be evaluated by the modest but highly valued rank she had once earned as an avalanche soldier.

"Wouldn't miss it, Colonel Travers." You were supposed to call him *Bern* in class, and she'd never stopped calling him Bern. He looked very much the ranking officer in his uniform. Salli looked at the decorations on his epaulettes—bridging, clearing, organizing—and found, to her surprise, that she could only see the supple skin over the sleek muscle that she'd paid entirely too much attention to the night they'd found that hot springs at Allin.

Salli blushed.

"This place is for you, Miss Rangarold. Can I get you anything?" Bern asked, deep into formal automaton mode. At least Salli could trust that he had no idea why she had blushed.

"I promised Morrissey stolen pastries. Squishberry. You know what to do." If he was going to be formal she was going to be imperious: but Bern grinned, and winked, and turned away so quickly that she wasn't quite sure that she'd seen him grin at all.

She sat down.

There were three people there in clerical robes of a sort worn by senior Orthodox ministers; five people in uniform from the Shadene Secular Authority; three people not wearing uniforms—the elected officials who commanded the Shadene Secular Authority. No Wayfarers: not yet.

Moments passed, people went in and out. Bern came back to sit with her, handing her a tray-plate with a cup of kelp tea and a pastry that looked as though it had been pressed between two rocks. "I had Sergeant Tenos sit on it," Bern explained, in response to her lifted eyebrow of inquiry.

A door opened behind one empty table, and the low chatter of conversation died away. Here were the Synod representatives; and among them the woman any avalanche soldier was expected to recognize on sight, Speaker Harish, the elected representative of the combined Wayfarer churches in Shadene.

Her eyes scanned the room as she sat down and lingered a moment on Salli's face; yet when she turned to

make a comment to the Teacher on her left it was with
an air of thinking about something else entirely, quite
removed from anything Salli might have called into her
mind.

Salli felt a surge of resentment on Varrick's behalf.

Regardless of Synod's decision, Varrick had demon-
strated her grasp of scripture and her mastery of the
theological arguments—qualities that would qualify her
to teach any given Wayfarer theology she chose. It was
belittling of Speaker Harish to decline to so much as recognize Varrick's representative.

Would Speaker Harish have treated Varrick herself
this way, had the Holy One been present? The question
was moot. The atmosphere was much too volatile for the
Shadene Secular Authority to risk a personal appearance
on Varrick's part.

She had little time to sit and seethe, however; the
Speaker cleared her throat and started talking.

"Thank you all for coming. Synod appreciates the concern expressed by the Pilgrim religious establishment
and the secular authority in what is, after all, a strictly
internal affair."

Synod did no such thing. But if they were going to
create a great deal of trouble—indirectly for orthodoxy,
directly for the Shadene Secular Authority—it was probably good politics to pretend otherwise.

"In the evening broadcast from Synod House I will
meet with Teacher Saurdish and discuss our findings
and decision on the petition of a woman called Varrick
to be recognized as a divinely guided teacher in a new
development of our doctrine, one she has described as
the Creation Rising theology."

It was difficult to understand how best to categorize
or characterize Varrick's theology. The "Get on with
Your Life" theology. The "Don't Blame It on God" theology. The "Use the God-given Capacity of Your Mind"

theology. But Speaker Harish was, as could be expected, still talking.

"This woman has become associated in the public mind with the batchelder terrorists, whether fairly or unfairly. These batchelder terrorists are known to be an unsanctioned radical offshoot of the Creation Rising theology, and so long as the woman Varrick refuses to repudiate them publicly they can be expected to defend her cause. A certain amount of civil unrest must therefore be anticipated."

Speaker Harish recited the phrases in something close to a monotone, for all the world as if she were merely rehearsing a memorized text. Perhaps she was. Perhaps Synod was concerned enough about Varrick to be mindful of being very, very careful about what it actually said about her.

"In order to establish a new line in our doctrine, three things are required of us. There must be a teacher who is divinely inspired, and evidence of divine inspiration is granted to be fundamentally subjective. Our evaluation committee cannot agree among themselves as to whether Varrick may be said to be genuinely inspired."

This Salli had not been able to understand. Varrick spoke so clearly, so true, so perfectly, so purely to the innermost core of Salli's heart and soul—how could it be that others did not see the same things?

And yet others did not wake up. Bern merely kept his distance; but for these Wayfarers, stubborn and self-willed spiritual deafness was the only explanation Salli could come up with to account for it. Such people needed to be shaken until their teeth rattled—all in the name of the soul's Awakening, of course.

Yes.

"Let us set aside the first qualification for the moment. The second requirement is for an element basic to the

Teaching that is not present, or not fundamental, to any existing Teaching."

Speaker Harish tapped one short strong finger against the crackly surface of a sheet of text. "On this point we are all agreed, the woman Varrick proposes a Teaching that contains as its primary element a claim directly contrary to all fundamental Teachings in our doctrine. Contrary to the Pilgrim articles of faith as well."

Salli knew what was coming, now. This was the crux of the challenge Varrick presented to Orthodox and Wayfarer churches alike, the first new idea in the spiritual life of Creation in more than one hundred years.

"That the claim that the age of miracles has passed, that the claim that there are no signs from God on high to witness to the Will of the divine, is contrary to all devout thought—this does not mean of itself that it is not true Teaching. We have received many persuasive petitions from all over the world, urging us to look charitably upon this—confrontational claim."

Petitions from schools and universities. Hospitals. Transportation companies. Even from progressive seminaries, all of them with one eye on the silent vigil that the sentinel satellites of centuries ago still stood in the starry heavens, waiting for pilgrims to other worlds who had yet to come. Synod had a choice as to exactly how to interpret Varrick's cornerstone Teaching: it could be seen as liberating; or it could be seen as reactionary.

"Such Teachings may be looked upon as new beginnings, or they may become innocent tools in the hands of the small criminal element that seeks to destabilize the balance of respect and segregation between Wayfarer and Pilgrim that has contributed so materially to the well-being and security of the state for many years. It is true that, once granted, this Teaching fulfills the third qualification without question: it cannot be accommo-

dated or otherwise adequately subsumed in any existing
Teaching."

They knew that Varrick was the Awakened One. How
could they not know? Even if they were to claim that
Varrick was not *the* Awakened One, but simply another
in a long line of revered teachers as an Awakened One,
how could they not recognize the obvious truth of the
Teaching that was within her?

"There are to consider in addition the transient acts
performed in the name of Varrick's Teaching by persons
claiming desire to put forward her claim to recognition."

Speaker Harish was being scrupulously fair, up to a
point. She didn't call Varrick's own motives into question; she carefully separated Varrick from "persons
claiming" to be Varrick's supporters. Speaker Harish
stood up; Salli could not take her eyes off of the
Speaker's face. She could no longer see anyone else in
the room, only barely conscious of Bern at her side. She
knew that disaster was about to descend upon the heads
of everybody here. She knew that there was nothing that
she could do to stop it.

"We have prepared a memorandum for the woman
Varrick," Speaker Harish proclaimed, handing the flat
black envelope to the sergeant at arms to be given over
into Salli's keeping. "In this memorandum we express
our appreciation for her God-centered life and her evident zeal. We document the steps we have taken to evaluate her petition. We express our regret that her petition
must be publicly rejected at this time—"

There was a stir in the room, but only a muted one.
Speaker Harish needed only the merest pause before she
could continue.

"—and explain that reasons which cannot be made
public drive this decision. Synod no more than the secular authority wishes to give any encouragement or extend any sanction to these batchelders, and we hope very

devoutly that once things are quiet—once the batchelders have gotten tired of throwing bricks and breaking glass—once the public issues are not so sore and tender, we can revisit Varrick's petition, and quite possibly make a different finding."

They could not deny the Holy One. But they didn't want to acknowledge her, so deep were they in their own Dream that they could not see the sun risen behind the mountains. The Wayfarer church repudiated the Holy One in the eyes of the world simply in order to keep the peace: a forlorn hope indeed, and oh, so weak an argument in the face of the living sun that was at Varrick's spiritual core.

Salli couldn't breathe. She struggled to catch her breath somehow, clutching the envelope that the sergeant at arms had given her; she could not make her ribs move to make space in her belly, to expand her diaphragm. She could not breathe. She could only gape openmouthed at the ceiling, gasping like a fish—mindlessly, because it took air to give voice to a gasp, and Salli could get no air.

"As far as the public announcement goes. Synod will make no judgment on whether Varrick may be a woman divinely inspired. We will reject the Teaching as contrary to good and orthodox understanding—"

Orthodox, Speaker Harish had said. But they were heterodox. How dare they use the word? And yet there were Pilgrim Orthodox present, and Pilgrims were less likely even than the Wayfarer churches to be able to understand that Varrick was the Awakened One. It all came to a conspiracy, at the end—Wayfarers, Pilgrims, the Shadene Secular Authority. Salli could see nothing except bright spots in front of her eyes, dancing like errant embers in the dusk against the backdrop of a forest that had faded into black night.

"—subject to some satisfactory demonstration on Varrick's part of her claim to inspiration."

Salli blinked rapidly, frowning. The room came back up into focus, as if painted on a backdrop cloth raised from below her line of sight. Speaker Harish was staring at her, with a peculiar look of intense concentration on her face.

"Synod in assembly joins with the representatives from the Shadene Secular Authority and our Pilgrim congregants to present this message to Varrick via her recognized representative. We do not mean to reject the teaching outright. But we cannot afford to give any encouragement to batchelder terrorists. We earnestly ask for Varrick's charitable understanding."

But they would not grant her credence. For no better reason than the vandalism of a few overenthusiastic souls they were ready to tear the entire state apart; they had no idea—

"Steady on," Bern urged low-voiced, beside her. "Keep a good grip. No gratification."

Bern was right.

To express the outrage that overflowed within her, the protest against so narrow-minded and shortsighted a decision here and now would surely seem mere wounded pride; or worse, a damaged sense of self-importance.

They were all waiting for her to say something.

"As it is my responsibility to the Holy One known to you as Varrick, as well as the responsibility of any decent citizen, to preserve the public order, I will present both public and confidential messages to Varrick my teacher as soon as you have laid them out for me."

It was her role, and her right. Her duty.

Now she needed to get back to Varrick before the rumors could explode, and see the Holy One as best prepared as possible for the firestorm that was almost sure to follow.

*   *   *

Morrissey took charge of Salli as she quit the room
with her envelope and her errand. Salli knew how to
behave on escort: she was to relax and do as she was
told, because she herself had trained with Carpi and Techam and Ware and Solt, and she knew from experience
that they were constantly aware of their situation and
any potential dangers or delays. And delay could mean
danger, when they were in the middle of a city and
needed to get out.

Packed into a ground car—they'd picked up a passenger, Bern, and it was more crowded in the passenger
compartment than it had been coming out—they crept
carefully through narrow streets and alleyways, taking
the occasional shortcut through the loading docks of one
blank-faced, block-long warehouse or another. The
streets were rapidly filling with people and vehicles,
which in turn meant grinding to a halt. Pellassa was an
old city. It had never been intended for modern vehic-
ular traffic.

There had been a gap in security somehow, a leak in
the system somewhere along the line. Salli was sure of
it, unless it was only that there was to be a riot regardless
of the decision the Speaker was about to announce. The
secular authority's traffic control was out in force on
the major streets; Salli glimpsed the traffic directors
and the emergency vehicles from time to time as the
ground car crept past through some too-narrow alley-
way or emphatically unpromising all-but-certain-to-be-
a-dead-end street.

Nor did traffic seem to clear as they escaped from city
center—fleeing as fast as they could, at the equivalent of
no more than a fast trot. Salli kept peering through the
window panel between the passenger compartment and
the cockpit, waiting for the moment when the car would
clear the gates of the secular authority's compound and

the road would clear. It seemed to take forever; traffic was moving at a maddening crawl, and—staring dully at the backlit glistening of a gray-stone pillar as they passed—Salli realized with sinking fear that they had reached the compound at last, but its security had been breached. The gates had given way, or been forced, or been abandoned as a prudent matter of facing facts as they were. There was no security within the Shadene Secular Authority's compound. But how then would they find the Holy One, if the Shadene Secular Authority could not protect her from a mob?

It all depended on which mob it was, Salli decided.

Her feelings of claustrophobic panic, of desperation to be out of this trap of traffic gave way to a profound sense of peace. Tranquillity. It all depended on which mob it was, and Varrick was the Holy One, Salli knew it.

The ground car crept on inch by painful inch over the graveled track.

Salli had an idea.

She rolled down the window and pulled herself halfway out of the car, sitting on the window well, clinging to the roof.

"Salli!" Bern's strangled yelp from the interior came with an iron grip attached to it, or attached to her ankles, rather. Crushingly secure. Salli couldn't be bothered with Bern or with the normal protocols observed by avalanche soldiers on escort. She wasn't the avalanche soldier this time. She was the personage being escorted. She could do no wrong.

She waved the envelope that she still clutched in her left hand to attract the attention of what portion of the blocking crowd had not already noticed that there was a woman hanging off the roof of the ground car.

"Hello. Ladies and gentlemen. Do you think that you could let us through, I'm to report to the Holy One. If you would be good enough to clear the track, she's waiting for us."

Abstractly, yes, such behavior was just as likely to get her torn from the car and trampled underfoot if she misjudged her mob. She hadn't. This mob was her mob; and, with a steadily growing chorus of cheers and encouragement, they cleared the track.

Salli was hysterical, an hysteria induced perhaps by that of the crowd. Bern Travers was swearing like a parson's mistress from inside the car, and she didn't even care, though she was glad that she had not long to endure it before the car reached its destination.

The track cleared of bodies in front of the ground car only to freeze solid with the anxious crowd behind them once again as soon as they had passed.

The soldiers securing the building would have turned Morrissey and Salli's team around at the foyer, but Salli gestured grandly with one hand. "My escort," she claimed, firmly, and strode on defiantly for the lifts with Bern still muttering in her wake. Bern was confusing Morrissey and the team. That was all right. Bern confused Salli often enough; it was someone else's turn.

Up in the suite where Varrick was quartered the doors along the side of the great wall had all been opened onto the terrace, and the noise from the crowd below could be heard even through the thermal barrier that glassed in the conservatory. Salli found Varrick standing in the well of an alcove, a prowlike projection from the conservatory wall. She was looking down at the seething hordes of people five stories below.

There was a broadcast apparatus there, and the conservatory's warming lights had been reoriented to serve as ad hoc spotlights. If Salli looked hard at the broadcast equipment, she could see the squat blue box of a private transmitter, its little lights blinking with mad merriment as it played dodge-the-signal-block with the unsuspecting public programming that it was set to override.

Pirate transmitters were illegal, and interfering with the free transmit of commercial programming was a crime.

So Salli avoided looking carefully at the equipment.

"What did they say to you, Salli?" Varrick asked. She looked pale in the bright lights from the conservatory reflected off the stone that lined the balcony alcove. Varrick already knew.

"They said . . ." Not the excuse, not the pretense of an analysis. All Varrick wanted was the rise and run of it. The rest was just so much road grading, and would wait.

"Synod reserves judgment on the issue of whether or not you are the Holy One. They reject your Teaching subject to a more complete, no; a more satisfactory demonstration of your claim to divine inspiration."

Salli knew she didn't have to cushion it, sneak up on it, or try to honey-coat the words. Varrick already knew. She had only asked because it was good form to do so.

Varrick turned her head and looked back over her shoulder at Salli. Her eyes were shadowed in the strong light; yet Salli felt that gaze clear to her blood and bone. As always.

"You. Salli." Yes, that was her name. Varrick was only making sure that she remembered. No, Varrick was asking for a professional opinion. "What did you think? Do they sincerely question my Teaching? Or is it just these batchelders of mine?"

The batchelder terrorists whom Varrick would not publicly repudiate, on principle. It was an odd sort of principle. But it made sense to hear it from Varrick.

"They sincerely wish you would not rock the boat. They are afraid that they must accept your claim. They'd rather not have to. It will mean a very great deal of work for everyone if we may take to the skies without fear of trespass, and challenge one of the few things that Orthodox and Wayfarer agree on."

" 'Satisfactory demonstration.' " Varrick repeated the earlier phrase, musingly. " 'Satisfactory.' I am fundamentally opposed to there being any such demonstrations. And given that, how can I compromise myself with circus tricks?"

It seemed to be a rhetorical question; Varrick asked it of black night. Salli had no answer. It certainly seemed that Synod had found a box in which to shut Varrick up: either she made a "satisfactory demonstration" or Synod declined to believe her; and if she made a "satisfactory demonstration" she violated all of her own Teaching about the foolishness of seeking for signs and omens in a world in which the numinous no longer intruded quite so directly.

"Well, no help for it but to go forward, then," Varrick said, with an air of having made up her mind to do something unpleasant. Stepping forward, Varrick moved into the circle of light; and the crowd saw her.

The noise rose to a roar of such intensity that the very foundations seemed to shake around them, and Salli knew that that could not be literally so.

Varrick put out her arms with the palms to the ground, five stories below. Making shushing gestures. Making damping signs. Slowly the crowd noise died back; then Varrick took up the broadcast input, the tiny handheld as sexy as any Salli had ever seen.

"You are very kind to have come."

The amplified voice rang out as clear and as crisp as daylight. The crowd stilled further. There were people crowded into every available bit of standing room as far as Salli could see, in the bright lights. She'd never seen so many people in one place before in her entire life.

"You will have heard of the decision of Synod. I do not look for help from the secular authority; they cannot

have been without input already. In fact I am scorned
by three: Synod, the Shadene Secular Authority, and the
Pilgrim church."

The crowd stirred with wavelike motions, as if Varrick's words were a perturbation moving across the face
of the ocean. *The Awakened One commands the elements,
and all things waken to the Word.* It wasn't a crowd made
up of people any longer. It had become a single unitary
entity, a living being in its own right, with its own sentience and its own ways of knowing.

"This then I have to say to you here, and to everyone
within the Holy Land with ears and an open heart." Varrick's voice deepened in intensity, somehow, though it
grew no louder. If anything it was more hushed; and of
all the people gathered below, throughout the entire
body of that great beast of a crowd, Salli could hear no
more than a sort of respiration. It was five stories. But
there were a lot of people down there.

Varrick spread her arms out wide, as if she could embrace them all.

"Come to me at Corabey," Varrick said, and the crowd
roared as if with a single voice. Varrick stood motionless
until the sound died away, and finished her thought.

"Come to me at Corabey, children. Holiday is coming.
On the day when the sun rises on the peak of the mountain I will speak to you there, and there *will* be an Awakening."

The crowd noise rose like the surf against the shore,
but a new sound crested the breakers and rode the wave.
A chant. *Varrick. Varrick, Varrick, Varrick, Varrick.*

Varrick dropped her arms back to her sides and
turned away. The light shadowed her face so strongly
that she seemed a death's-head to Salli, for just one moment. A gesture from Varrick, and the garden's bor-
rowed floodlights were extinguished. The voice of the
crowed had not abated: *Varrick, Varrick, Varrick, Varrick.*

"Come on," Varrick said to Salli, her voice curiously flat. As if she were depressed, or perhaps just tired. "We have work to do."

Morrissey and Salli's team stood against the open-glassed wall of the conservatory, staring, clearly impressed—if not actually stunned—by this demonstration of the power of Varrick's personality. Varrick beckoned to them, pulling Morrissey along with her with her hand to his shoulder. "These are your team? It's good to meet you all, I'm Varrick, and we've got to get back to Mount Corabey."

Varrick was tired. Her words were disjointed, her thoughts not following directly from one to the other. They would all go. Whether or not Salli's team believed that Varrick was the Holy One—and to look at them they were half-convinced already—every avalanche soldier that the Shadene secular authority could spare would be needed at Corabey, now that Varrick had made her announcement.

Salli followed Varrick into quarters, closing the conservatory doors behind them.

They left that night.

People had been sending money as well as gifts for weeks; Varrick had cash. A small fleet of bumblers—deep woods transports, three fat wheels, minimal impact technology—was arranged, and arrived between midnight and morning. The grounds were still crowded all around the building that housed the Awakened One: Salli watched the people from the foyer of the building, as one of the others checked on the delivery papers. They were people again, not a crowd or a mob. People, standing in small groups, sitting on blankets on the ground, singing amongst themselves. It was cold, and that had thinned the crowd—but not so much as Salli would have guessed.

She could empathize.

What was cold, or any other bodily discomfort, to people who knew that they were close to the sacred person of the Awakened One?

After the bumblers came the great transport tracks, two of them, and the bumblers were all checked out and fueled and loaded while Salli helped pack. She had charge of the mountain gear on Varrick's behalf, but in practice she stepped back into her subordinate role, with Morrissey there. They were a team once more, if a little awkward with each other.

Her fellows might not completely understand what she'd done and why she'd done it, but moving Varrick to Corabey in a controlled fashion was a common goal that they could all support wholeheartedly without examining their motivations too closely.

Varrick had been the guest of the Shadene secular authority for weeks.

She had had no shortage of visitors, and even the merely curious had brought offerings out of respect for the Teaching.

With less than an hour before dawn they were away. Bern had cleared the convoy with the Shadene secular authority; the last thing the secular authority wanted to do now was keep Varrick—the city had been in an uproar all night.

With Varrick gone perhaps the crowds of people in the street would finally disperse: so Varrick's convoy left the secular authority's compound for the mountains, and as they pulled out of the compound onto the highway dozens of vehicles followed them. People who had been waiting all night for a chance to follow them.

Salli had never seen so many vehicles on one road in her life, and all of them intent on following Varrick.

It was something.

But Salli had been up all night.

She saw Varrick safely into the back of the first transport before she climbed up into the back of the second transport truck. Morrissey and the others came, too, as if as a matter of course. Nobody seemed to think twice about it. The last of the crates to be loaded in the second transport truck had been the rugs and wooleries; as the transport truck pulled away they broke open the crates and spread out the rugs, and wrapped themselves in fleece and wooleries.

Bern was there, in a particularly choice spot—sort of a wide bench made out of crates and cartons, with a slightly taller crate at one end to form a raised place on which to pillow a person's head.

Salli was tired.

She crawled up onto the crate-bench with Bern and put her back to him, pulling the woolery that he was wearing over her own shoulder. Punched his shoulder a few times to see if it wouldn't fluff up somewhat more softly; laid her head down on Bern's shoulder and went to sleep with his arms around her, without thinking twice about what she was doing.

By the time the truck reached its terminus it was late afternoon, and Salli was stiff from sleeping on the crate. A flood of cold air through the doors of the truck wakened her. Yawning, she stretched, rubbing the side of her face to erase the wrinkles pressed there by a fold in the woolery she'd been sleeping in; then elbowed Bern in the belly to get him to loose the hands he had clasped around her waist, so that she could get up.

Bern lifted his head blear-eyed and looking cross about the mouth, and Salli rubbed his face, too, to raise some life into it; until the noise from outside distracted her, and she went out to see what was going on.

She recognized the trailhead: they were ten days' walk from Corabey. Ten days' walk, but with the bumblers that meant two days' travel, maximum. And she and her team were avalanche soldiers. They knew how to travel on bumblers through the forest by night.

By now orders had come from the Shadene Secular Authority, delivered by Colonel Janelric herself. The avalanche soldiers were to render all due assistance, and Captain Clemens had come to help set up crowd control on the way in.

Salli and her team set the bumbler convoy in line under Morrissey's supervision. There were twenty-eight people, all in all, and some of them had officially sanctioned experience. Several more obviously knew what to do and how best to do it without the tedious necessity of having been licensed to possess such knowledge.

Nonetheless, bumbling in the dark was more risky a proposal than bumbling by day, no matter how practiced the drivers.

But the trailhead was far from deserted, and more people seemed to be arriving moment by moment—people who had followed in convoy all day. If Varrick was to get through to Corabey in time to prepare for her winter greeting—the Awakening she had promised—they needed to be able to make the distance before the track packed solid with pilgrims.

Solid with pilgrims . . .

Had Varrick stopped to think of what she was doing, when she called her people to her at Corabey?

Three months ago it had been parties collecting carefully, quietly, coming through the woods. And now it was to be a race to get to Corabey for Varrick's midwinter blessing within six days' time.

Six days?

What day was it?

What did it matter?

She was needed with the bumbler party. And that demanded all the attention that Salli could muster.

*   *   *

They made good time to Corabey.

They passed people on the trail, and there was plenty of evidence of other recent passages before them—not always so conservative a vehicle as a bumbler, with its stripped-down frame and the weight-distributing, rough-terrain-negotiating, overinflated puffy tires that gave the vehicle its clumsy awkward gait and its eke-name. Salli noted the signs without comment. There was nothing to be done about it now but impact minimization.

A quick break for dinner at midnight that first night of travel, a quick break for a nap; then on the track again by sunrise, urged on by the awareness of the increasing numbers of people who passed their camp during the night all unawares of its inhabitants. By midday they had made it to the Linshaw Pass, and by midafternoon Salli was home at Corabey again—and yet how different it was!

There was snow.

The people who had already arrived had filled the summer booths, digging the sunken dirt floors free of snow and tenting their canvas awnings to prevent more snow from accumulating. The hot springs at the west end of the caldera smoked and steamed, the water vapor brilliant white or a ghostly blue tint against the snow; while the spring's font itself remained black and bare and glistening with moisture.

There was no telling where the caves were on the low slopes; the great prayer bell itself was half-hidden in the snow beneath the peaked roof of the shrine shed. But most of all, the people; so many—and so soon. All of them come out of respect for Varrick, all of them waiting for her Word. None of them people Salli knew.

The bumblers could be unpleasant to ride on in snow

if one forgot oneself and sped up. Carefully the convoy crept across the sunny caldera to work its way upslope to where the shrine shed stood, where the entrance to the main cave was. There were few footprints in the snow here: people had respect for the bell, and—oddly enough—for once it seemed that respect had successfully outlasted curiosity.

Unlike in Bern's case, earlier, when he had struck the bell just to hear it—

Bern was downslope in the meadows, talking with Morrissey and taking notes. Logistics, no doubt: they would need portable lavatories, tanks full of potable water, a field hospital, warming tents. A field-expedient road surface if a paving ground machine could not be located quickly, because the track up to Linshaw Pass would soon be chewed into plowed mud.

In order to preserve the larger forest it would be necessary in this instance to allow a bit of it to be destroyed, at least temporarily, and encourage people to stay on a road by providing one.

Varrick passed the prayer bell and went down into her residence cave.

Salli grabbed a road broom off the back side of the bumbler nearest her and began to sweep the snow out of the shrine shed, out of respect for the prayer bell and in order to have something to do.

She didn't like this.

People were coming.

It was cold and dry, and the surface snow was as light as down; but within a knuckle's worth of the surface the snow had been sealed over with a hard, smooth, glassy shell of ice. It made sweeping very easy indeed: the top layers of snow, at least, had no cohesion.

What made for easy sweeping also made for an avalanche—

She wasn't going to brew trouble, Salli told herself firmly. No. She wasn't.

She was going to tell Morrissey about the avalanche danger, and let the secular authority worry about it.

Ten

Sundown of solstice eve, and Salli took her broom to clear the granite-flagstone floor of the shrine shed. It was her private time, her quiet time, her time to look out over the caldera and do her best not to think about what impact so many people in one place at one time would have on the fragile subalpine meadow environment.

The pilgrim path that crossed the saddle of the Linshaw Pass was a broad black scar that she could see from clear across the caldera, glittering under the emergency lightsets and contrasting all too emphatically with the snow on either side. The more people came, the more bitterly Salli regretted Varrick's action in inviting them here—though it was possible that not even Varrick had foreseen the depth of the public's response to her gesture.

"Status report, Team Leader," Captain Jule Clemens called out to her, making her way up the shallow black-slate steps to the broad apron in front of the shrine shed. "How's your party doing? Tomorrow's the big day. Day after tomorrow—cleanup."

There was enough light left in the darkling sky to betray the wolfish gleam in Captain Clemens's black eyes as she said it. The predatory glint of the light against her cutting teeth, and Captain Clemens had very long teeth.

Long and narrow. Definitely a carnivorous grin, be-
speaking a strong instinct for prey.

"Varrick's inside. Psyched. Staying centered. It's only
the last chance some of these people will have, to hear
wisdom and gain understanding. Damn Synod anyway."

Synod meant nothing to Captain Clemens. Like the
rest of the avalanche soldiers, Captain Clemens, while
impressed with Varrick's message and delivery, remained casually Orthodox and took Salli's intensity in
stride, almost as though it was something she expected
Salli to outgrow in time.

Captain Clemens stamped her feet on the bare ground
to knock the snow off. "Well, we're ready to be out of
here. The baffles are all on-line, but I'll be happier—"

As if she hadn't noticed that Salli had been sweeping.
Salli tossed the broom at her, disgusted. It surprised the
Captain a bit, but realization apparently came quickly;
she was grinning even as she caught the broom, and
went to repairing the damage with a will, finishing her
thought seamlessly.

"—when we've got all of these people out of here. I
swear the run-out zone clears half the caldera. Well, the
big one, anyway."

Because there were as many run-out zones as there
were potential avalanches, and Captain Clemens and the
rest of the avalanche soldiers had planted baffles on each
one. Avalanche sheds, their roofs upsloped and their
rakes extending out from the side of the mountain.

They weren't intended to divert the avalanche—no
splitters here—but to slow enough of the slab or the
loose powder to put a brake on it. A solid roof would
just guide snow up and over and down, like a ski jump,
and that in turn would propagate the avalanche downslope.

Snow when it started sliding compacted like concrete

as it stopped. The raked fins of the avalanche sheds could catch and hold enough of an avalanche in motion to stop it cold in seconds flat.

"I'll be happier when you're all gone. With respect, Captain. It's not my fault. But do you think they listen?" She'd been catching merry hell from her erstwhile team since they'd got here. She appreciated it—mostly. It was their way of telling her that she was forgiven, after all, for Meeka's sake, because anyone could guess that whatever Bern had said was not quite true. She'd been the recipient of much hilarious and unappreciated advice regarding Bern, as well.

"Not coming back to us then, Salli?"

The question took Salli by surprise. She hadn't thought about it. She only thought about what Varrick needed done next. And somewhat about Bern. "Ma'am. This is awkward. I'm not sure I could. Colonel Travers, he—"

"—recognized a useful contact when he saw one, Miss Rangarold, and took appropriate action to safeguard the resource. Salli. It's different now that Varrick's gone mainstream." Examining the swept floor of the shrine shed with a sharp and critical eye, Captain Clemens nodded her head decisively, as if pronouncing it good. "All right, just think about it. You have the option. That's all I need you to understand here and now."

Salli couldn't imagine going back. And still, to be told that she could . . . "Very charitable, ma'am. Thank you." Her voice sounded too small and humble in her own ears. This wouldn't do. She had to try for a lighter tone. "Colonel Travers has said something about seventeen children, though. I can't see where I could find the time."

It was intended as a joke.

But Captain Clemens simply took it on its face as a statement of fact. "Oh, well. Don't say I didn't try. We'll have the patrols out per usual, Miss Rangarold. See you in the morning."

It should have been hysterically funny that Captain Clemens took the outrageous claim seriously; and yet the captain's bland acceptance was more disturbing, than anything else.

What did Captain Clemens know about her and Bern that Salli herself didn't know?

Salli stabbed the bristles of the broom up and down against the shrine shed's sounding-pallet floor, utterly frustrated by the unreason of it all.

Then she put all such peripheral matters out of her mind and went to talk with Varrick, to be there with the Holy One as Varrick waited for sunrise and the sermon that would form her challenge and her vindication alike before Synod.

Down the bridge of stairs at the back of the shrine shed into the cave in the mountain behind it, shivering a bit in the cold air that blew up from the black well of empty space immediately below the great bell—its sounding well.

Across the cave floor to the raised platform with the fireplace in its base, its flat surface covered with rugs and wooleries, its rear partition screened off from profane eyes with curtains that stirred gently as the air currents in the cave ebbed and flowed.

It was very dim in the cave; almost the only source of light was the fire in the furnace beneath the dais upon which Varrick had taken council earlier in the year. There were no Security posts. Corabey was secured by avalanche soldier patrols and the Shadene Secular Authority, major access routes patrolled, minor access routes closed and passage prohibited.

There were Security surrounding the shrine shed itself at all times, and that meant that nobody got through without a Security challenge, so Salli was almost alone.

Almost. There were people to tend the fire and look after late-night meals. But none of them spoke to Salli or stood in her way as she reached the short ladder at the side of the platform and climbed up to its flat top to speak to the Holy One.

Varrick lay in a tumble of rugs and wooleries, half-reclining, half-propped-up. There were the remains of her dinner on a tray. As Salli joined her Varrick waved her hand; dreamily, as if acknowledging Salli's presence without paying a very great deal of attention to the fact that Salli was there.

"Holy One." Salli had seen this happen before. Varrick sank into a deeply lethargic state after speaking; and sometimes before, when she anticipated a challenging experience. "Shall I refill the pitcher?"

Varrick also drank a very great deal of water before and after. Sometimes juice: but while she was at Corabey she evidently preferred spring water to all other beverages. The wellhead was upslope, and several hundred meters to the left of the shrine shed. It was exceptionally sweet water, and Varrick's pitcher was only a quarter full. But Varrick raised herself, unsteadily, instead of replying directly; Salli helped her settle back into a more upright seated position.

"Not just yet," Varrick said. "But thank you, Salli. Let's just talk, we won't have another chance for a while. Things are going to get busy around here. Come, make yourself comfortable, wrap yourself up."

The resonance chamber, the reverberation chamber below the prayer bell sunk deep beneath the floor level at the front end of the cave, was an overflowing well of ice-cold air; the furnace in the platform's foundation radiated welcome warmth. Together, the effects of the combined airstreams created a constant draft that kept the curtains at the back of the platform fluttering. Salli was glad to wrap herself in a woolery and nestle into the warm surface of the platform.

"We haven't talked in ages," Varrick mused, as Salli sought and found the perfect spot, dissolving in sybaritic ecstasy in the basic but deeply comforting combination of soft cushioning fabric and a warm platform-bed. "Not about the important things. Everything but. You've been angry, though, at the world, for not seeing things your way when it comes to your Holy One."

Well, yes. She had been. Why should she be surprised that Varrick knew? Varrick knew everything. "It's true, Holy One. I don't understand it. How could anyone hear the Teaching, and not know?"

From the very start she'd been able to speak to Varrick as though Varrick was a teacher of the academic type. It was part of Varrick's divine approachability; she was down-to-earth, so natural.

Now she sighed.

"And I'm glad we can talk about that before things go too much further, Salli Pilgrimsdaughter."

Salli's heart sank to hear the name. Why did Varrick rebuke her? And yet there was no rebuke in Varrick's voice as she continued.

"You were raised Pilgrim, I was raised Shadene. I am Shadene." Yes, Salli knew that she was—Wayfarer. The Holy People had come from Shadene. That the Holy One should elect to incarnate in the alien Wayfarers was a mystery of great and profound significance, the likes of which could take years to interpret. "If you were Shadene, Pilgrimsdaughter, you would not be troubled. You would know. There are so many different routes out of the dream landscape of the deluded."

Salli could see where Varrick was going with this, and it turned her previously leaden heart to ice. Varrick meant to deny her own divinity. Oh, she was much worked upon by Synod, if she could so much as consider such a thing; yet—to be fair—Varrick had never claimed more than her place as one of the Wayfarer church's teachers. Salli had always assumed . . . because Salli knew—

"You are the Holy One." Salli choked out her protest, her voice suddenly thick with tears. "You can be no other. I have touched your hand, and seen the universe, and stood within the mind of God. Holy One. Oh, I beg you, don't do this to yourself. To us."

"Now, Salli." The compassion in Varrick's voice was almost enough to break Salli's heart. "I'm sorry. I should have confronted you earlier about this. We are Shadene, Salli, it is understood. There is no one here who has mistaken me, but you."

"No." How could Varrick say such a thing? How could Varrick do this to her, after all—Meeka, and the debrief, and the avalanche soldiers, everything Salli had turned her back on, everything Salli had lost or abandoned to follow in the footsteps of the Awakened One . . . and yet Varrick had been the Awakened One masquerading as a Shadene teacher, one of many, all along.

If Varrick had lost her belief in herself under pressure from Synod, Salli could not rebuke her. She could remember nothing, nothing, nothing from all that she had seen Varrick do or heard Varrick say that could be used to prove a statement out of Varrick's own mouth that she was the Awakened One of the Orthodox rather than a Holy One of the Shadene, Wayfarer, heterodoxy.

"Salli, there are so many things . . . your brother came to us—" Varrick seemed to run out of words; then pushed herself into an upright position with an effort, as if she had made up her mind. When she spoke again it was with great determination, and with the peculiar resonance in her voice that always marked her words when Varrick was speaking the will and the way of God.

"Daughter of Pilgrims, daughter of this land. In all of

this time there has been no Teaching for you, and you alone. Is this not so?"

It was true. She had not approached Varrick to beg for a Teaching. She had been the universe. She had stood within the mind of God. She had in all this time asked nothing more of Varrick than to sit in her holy presence and put her teaching forward.

Varrick continued without waiting for a response, since they both knew the answer.

"I am not the Awakened One of the Pilgrims who call themselves Orthodox, Salli. I am only for you the clarion call. From me you can take Awakening, Salli, but that your teammates amongst the avalanche soldiers don't see things your way is not because they're blind. It's because they'll hear someone else's Teaching—but not mine."

This could not be.

She was good Orthodox.

Varrick was the Awakened One for all of history—

"I will go and get more water, Holy One."

Salli could hardly choke the words out.

She took up the almost-empty jug from its place on the tray at Varrick's side, and fled.

Outside the cave it was warm for the season, and the light of the moon on the sparkling crust of snow was muted and eerie behind the thick clouds. Snow clouds, maybe. It wasn't what she wanted to see, but Salli was too absorbed in her own fearful misery to pay so much attention to the weather.

Varrick had denied herself.

Varrick repudiated her own divinity, and yet Varrick was the Awakened One. Salli knew. She had touched Varrick's hand, and been one with the universe. She had seen Varrick put her hands to Bern's side and call surgical pins from miraculously healed ribs through unbroken skin into her hand. There was no questioning the evidence of her own heart and mind: so how could Varrick deny it?

Salli could not believe she had not seen and felt what she had seen and felt.

Varrick had the power of divinity in her touch.

But among the Orthodox only the Awakened One, the one and only Awakened One, had such power; all else was either self-delusion or the malicious joke of the world of illusion, contributing to the confusion of dreams.

There was nothing of self-delusion to the experiences Salli had had of Varrick. Salli was an avalanche soldier. She was a good Orthodox woman. She knew how to tell the difference. She had tested herself during ten days of debrief. It had not been drugs or deceit that had given her a glimpse of eternity that morning on the apron before the prayer bell at Mount Corabey.

Could it have been the inexplicable humor of the material world, the treacherous joke of the world of illusion?

The material world was Creation, and Creation was on balance good. It was sometimes difficult to interpret the course of the natural world in a manner consistent with a benevolent Creator; but what was Varrick's Teaching, if not that there were no supernatural messages to be drawn from natural events—and by implication, no supernatural sentience at work that was not one with Creation?

And if Varrick was in truth Holy and Awakened, and at the same time not the single and history-halting Holy One of the Orthodox, then—

Then the Orthodox way of seeing the world was wrong.

There were many Holy Ones, and the Awakening was something that happened bit by bit—piece by piece—in cumulative steps, over time, and within the material world. Not some post-Awakening utopia. This world, the world of Creation.

How could she reconcile her rejection of the Wayfarers with the knowledge, cell-deep in the bone and blood now, that Varrick was a divinely inspired teacher who spoke to them all from the center of the universe?

How could she reconcile her fierce burning resentment of Varrick for denying her own divinity with her ardent love for the truth that Varrick spoke when she raised her hands to teach?

She'd told Varrick that she would go and refill the water pitcher, and that meant hiking the relatively short distance upslope to the cave where the wellhead was. She needed snowshoes, weight spreaders.

There was an administration tent down at the foot of the stone stairs that led up to the apron in front of the shrine shed. Salli stumbled through the thermal barrier and sat down to strap on the nearest pair of snowshoes. She didn't look at anybody in the tent. She didn't want to. The last thing she wanted to do was to make eye contact, to have to speak to anybody. Snowshoes, a thermal hood, night lenses, and she was out into the night again.

The lights in the caldera twinkled like moonlight on dark water in the warm night air. The snow crunched crisply underfoot: a respectable layer of ice, which was good so long as it didn't snow. But it was snowing—so lightly that she could still see clear across the caldera—the faintest cluster of powder. Snow as light as a feather, as dry as a bone.

Not good.

Still, the baffles were in place. Salli climbed the slope until she could see the cave mouth where the snow had been cleared away to provide access to the wellhead; it didn't run quickly enough to provide water for the entire camp, so there were few tracks at any time coming and going. What faint tracks there might have been had been filled in with snowy dust, until Salli could see no trace of footprints on these slopes at all.

The snow was still powder, but coming in more heavily now. It wasn't a problem with night lenses, no, Salli could see where she was going. It was the principle of the thing that she didn't like. Hard crust, warming trend, layer of powder, maybe a layer of heavy wet new snow on top of that, the shape of Mount Corabey—but the baffles were in place. She was climbing above one of them now.

When baffles were in place one did what one could to keep one's line of ascent centered over one of those upswept grilles; that way if one was unfortunate enough to get caught in an avalanche it would be easier to recover the body. It was just a courtesy thing, common sense.

Crossing the slope to angle toward the wellhead, Salli raised her head and searched upslope for the position of the next baffle to show her where she was. It would be offset from the one downslope; avalanche sheds were staggered for best coverage.

There.

She could only see it dimly even through her night lenses. The thickening snowfall was an ever-shifting screen, a gently waving curtain presenting an illusion of movement even as the uncertain light from the cloud-covered moon varied and wavered.

This was annoying.

Salli dropped to one knee in the snow by force of habit, switching snow filters over the night lenses with a practical economy of movement.

That was better.

There was the avalanche shed. There, not five meters upslope, was the wellhead; but the avalanche shed was another twenty meters away. No wonder it had been easy to imagine someone moving down below the upraked ribs of the baffled roof. No one could see clearly in the snow and night at twenty-five meters.

And still Salli thought that she saw something.

It was cold on the slope, even though comparatively mild for winter. She was dressed warmly enough for a hike up to the wellhead and back, but not really dressed for a tour of the lower slope of Mount Corabey on snowshoes at night. And there had to be a perfectly natural explanation for the wavering blackness she thought she saw, moving ever and always around the leftmost foundation post.

There was nothing up here but snow, a cave, and an avalanche shed.

Anything black should have been ice-coated white days—if not weeks—ago.

She set the water jug down at the cavemouth entrance to the wellhead, and trudged up the slope with determination.

Ten meters now from the avalanche shed, and Salli saw the black shape change—elongate—straighten, and resolve itself into the figure of a man. He'd heard her coming; it was snowing, true, but there was still the crunching of her weight over the snowshoes against that ice crust, even cushioned as it increasingly was with powder. Whoever it was seemed to stare for a long moment as Salli continued closer: then waved, and crossed beneath the avalanche shed's baffled roof to the other of the shed's two primary supports.

There was something about the figure that looked familiar.

Morrissey?

Sergeant Hopskil?

Captain Clemens?

What would anybody be doing out beneath the avalanche baffles after midnight, in the preternatural silence of a snowstorm silent and deadly?

Only one way to find out. Salli hunched her head down between her shoulders and plowed through snow grown too light and powdery and dry to snowshoe over, making her way up to the avalanche shed.

Sheltering beneath one of the wide ribs, Salli caught her breath, loosening her head wrap to vent the excess heat from her exertion. She heard nothing; she saw no one. Had she imagined a figure in the snow?

No.

The shadow-figure of a man came out of the deeper darkness and hung a tactical lamp from the thin lower portion of a baffle rib. The sheltering wings of the tactical lamp kept its low red light from reflecting too brightly out across the slope, but as Salli's eyes adjusted to the relative glare she found she could see very well. Of course. That was just exactly what a tactical lamp was for.

So who was this man, out doing what in the dark, in the night, in the snow?

He turned his face toward her and grinned.

It was Meeka.

It was Meeka, and that grin was so dear and so familiar—

Flinging her arms around him, Salli stood for long moments without thought or speech, all of her world focused on embracing her brother.

Meeka.

"I saw you struck down." She was crying, and she hadn't noticed. "Meeka. I saw the blood. I was so certain you were dead."

The word was too terrible almost to say. But she could say it now, because Meeka wasn't dead. Meeka was alive, and here, whole and uncrippled. "Oh, Meeka, what happened to you? How did you—"

"Escape?" He finished the question, because Salli had run out of words. Yes, she wanted to know how he had escaped. She also wanted to know how he had stayed away, stayed out of sight, not sent word for all the days that had gone into all the weeks that had passed since the Holy Fool riot—days she had spent with mourning in her heart, if she had not had time to spend them in mourning.

How had he escaped, yes.

But also, how had he been able to let her think that he was dead?

"It was partly fortuitous and partly planned, Salli. We needed a way to drop out of sight. If the Shadene Secular Authority thought that I was dead, they'd not waste any more time looking for me. If my sister thought I was dead, it would be that much more convincing. That was the fortuitous part."

Salli struggled with her emotion, biting her lips to stifle her sobs. Wiping her face with her handkerchief, blowing her nose to clear the weight from her flooded sinuses. She could smell something, beneath the cold blue cucumber scent of newly fallen snow. She blew her nose again.

"Meeka." It was hard to accept what he was saying to her. "You used me. That was hard of you, Meeka. What could have been so important that you could put me through that? Seeing you fall. Seeing you beaten down. Seeing the blood."

"Seeing the pulped redsugar root, rather," he corrected, sounding incongruously pleased with himself. There was no regret in his voice; no concern. No indication that he could connect with her feelings at all. What had happened to him? "Worked beautifully, didn't it? It took days to wear off my skin, though. Look. My hair is still stained."

Because redsugar root stained everything it came into

contact with. Meeka stooped down so that she could look at his stained hair, and pointed at the place. Yes. Stained. The smell was strong on Meeka's body, on Meeka's clothing, and she didn't like it, whatever it was. It reminded her of the hills of rotting fish that piled up in spawning pools at the headwaters of the Matiejinn River, once the fish had mated and spawned and died. Sharp and organic, and in a sense poison.

"Yes." She could speak more calmly now. She was beginning to understand. "Stained. Well. What brings you here, then, big brother, on this night of all nights."

What was she going to do?

Meeka grinned at her again, with a pure and unsophisticated delight that suddenly seemed demonic to Salli.

"There will be an Awakening," Meeka said. "Teacher has proclaimed it. Synod will see, won't they? And with a martyred teacher we can split Shadene right down the middle. Then the cleansing can begin."

It was acid that she smelled.

Corrosive demisca, easy to make, easy to transport in its inert gel form, easy to apply. A favorite of terrorists everywhere with sufficient organization and a killing hatred of ski lifts or bridge trestles that was strong enough to stomach the loss of lives that resulted from catastrophic structural failure. Because demisca didn't crack and fracture the load-bearing composite and steel. Demisca just weakened the load-bearing elements, and then the next time the structure was stressed—

"Meeka." Salli stared at her brother's face, paralyzed with horror. "Meeka. You are out of your mind. You can't mean. It's not possible, you, you're a policeman, Meeka—not a murderer—"

"We have the word of the Teacher, baby sister." His face was fanatic, and utterly alien. He looked at her with all-consuming certainty in his eyes, and it made him so ugly that she only knew abstractly that he was her brother—she could no longer recognize him. "You don't know much about what it takes to be a batchelder. But I know more about what you've been up to than you might expect. So you can just forget about running to the Shadene Secular Authority—"

He was too close, and menacing. But the avalanche soldier in Salli was impotent, incapable of breaking through the paralysis of horror that froze the sister in her place when every instinct of the avalanche soldier was to flee by any means. To flee at any cost. Meeka was her brother. She was his sister. Meeka could never mean her harm, not even Meeka as changed as he had become—

"—to tell your lover all about those big, bad, batchelders in time to evacuate. You want to know something, Salli? It's already too late to evacuate. All that's left is for you to hope for a miracle . . ."

He hit her, sudden, fierce, and brutal.

Punched her in the stomach so hard that she staggered back under the force of the blow, and cracked the back of her snow-hooded head against the support of the avalanche shed with ferocious finality.

". . . and me to make one of my own."

She couldn't breathe.

The world was dark already; now the world went black before her eyes.

Her brother—

Meeka seized her by one arm and dragged her down the slope, through the snow, and she couldn't move a muscle to clear her face of the light powdery snow that trickled up into her nostrils and filled her open mouth and melted with a sting like fiery coals against the bare surface of her stunned and staring, open eyes.

Meeka had hit her. And she couldn't breathe.

Sallie went down into the darkness, trying to understand.

How could Meeka and this man be the same person?

She came to herself in a convulsion of coughing, as though a bit of gravel had lodged at the back of her throat and would not be dislodged. Her head ached with a fierce bright burning ache that felt like the broad width of a fiery hatchet had been buried in her brain; and it was cold.

It was black. No light. Cold, but no snow. Where was she?

The ground was dressed flat, graveled, smelling of water—

Coughing took her again, and it was long moments before Salli could master her breathing. So sore. Her throat was rasped raw with coughing, and her head—

Meeka had been there.

Meeka.

Where was she? It was dark—it was still, there were no air currents moving against her skin—

In the dead silence the sound of her own breathing rattled like coins in an old metal tin.

Gradually easing.

Slowly regulating.

Finally settling down to where she could quiet herself, hear herself think. Then she heard the noise.

It was quiet and it was subtle, but it was there. The wellhead didn't bubble very briskly this time of year. In the late summer the stream had still been fed by the last of the summermelt from high up on Corabey's slopes. This was midwinter, though, and the stream was at its lowest, the basin filling at a mere trickle to sink back through the porous rock and reenter the mountain. The stream itself finally came out into the world farther down the mountain, but its surface course was frozen solid now—there had to be a basin somewhere in the mountain, a cavernous cistern of some sort that filled with the winter's overflow and served as a hidden lake to receive the springmelt.

Cavern, mountain, stream.

She was at the wellhead.

She'd come out to refill the water pitcher for Varrick, because she'd been upset.

How long ago had that been?

How long had she been here?

And how long, oh, Holy One, did they have till morning, when Varrick would call the assembled to prayer for the Awakening that she had promised would come?

If this was the wellhead, there was a snow tunnel that would lead her back out to Mount Corabey's slopes.

Where?

She wasn't tied up. Meeka had been in a hurry, perhaps. She still had her pack, she could feel it; the weight on the one strap had cut off circulation in her left shoulder and put her arm to sleep. Feeling around her blindly in the dark, Salli couldn't find her night lenses, let alone her snow-goggles.

No help there.

Probably dropped in the snow somewhere between the avalanche shed and this cave. Meeka had dragged her in here, and gone off. That had been thoughtful of him; if he'd left her in the snow she might have taken injury from the cold.

How could he come to do such cold-blooded and cowardly murder, and still stop to take steps to guard her from frostbite?

Never mind, Salli told herself, sternly. She didn't have time to brood on personal issues of that sort. She had to get out. She had to get to her team. The Shadene Secular Authority needed to know. There were terrorists here. And the avalanche soldiers' reason for existence was to guard the general public against acts of terrorism committed by religious zealots, fanatics—of any persuasion.

She had to think.

What did the wellhead look like?

Closing her eyes—a meaningless gesture, but it helped her concentrate—Salli conjured up the image of the wellhead in her mind. There was a low lintel to the cave mouth; one ducked one's head to go in. Then there was a very short space that was narrow, so that for the space of one step a person had to draw in one's shoulders not to touch the sides—or go sidewise, for the men.

When the cave mouth opened out again there was a little rock chamber, and the wellspring itself bubbling up in a basin at floor level at the left of the back of the cave.

So, first, find the basin.

Dizzy and sick, Salli stood up, carefully conscious of the pain in her head. Feeling around with her hands till she touched a wall, Salli put both hands flat to it.

Now.

If she was at the right side of the cave, then the cave mouth was on her right, and if she followed the wall right she would find the tunnel. If she was at the left side of the cave the basin was on her right as she followed the wall, and when she tripped over the basin she would know where she was.

In either event she would find the cave mouth eventually as long as she followed the wall; it was just a question of whether she would find the basin first.

Yes.

There it was.

She rubbed her face briskly with palmsful of water to try to restore a degree of alertness to her bruised and battered brain; drank some of the water—it was so cold, but it was so good, so sweet, and so clear—and turned toward the place where the cave mouth had to be. Once she knew where to look she could see the lesser darkness amidst the greater, the place where the mouth of the snow tunnel glowed gently with a few scattered rays of reflected light from the caldera.

Stumbling in her haste, Salli sought the way out, flailing in the snow that had drifted into the tunnel to clear the passage.

What time was it?

Once out of the cave, she had to stand and determine her whereabouts yet again. The snow was coming thick and heavy and warm, the worst that could happen on top of powder that covered a hard crust of ice. The immediate problem was finding her way to help, and giving the alarm—for what good that would do.

Downhill was the obvious choice, a no-brainer. She'd lost her snowshoes, but they wouldn't have helped now anyway. Waving her arms wildly to keep her balance, Salli started downslope, her postural muscles—stiff and sore from lying on the moist cold of the wellhead cave floor—protesting at every step. She would have much preferred simply sitting down, maybe going to sleep. She probably had her emergency covers with her, in her pack; she could stay warm.

But there wasn't much light, which could mean it was late—late enough for the moon to have gone down to the west of the mountains. She had to tell people. She struggled on. The foot of the slope had been kept clear for people to assemble, but between the standing-field and the tents the avalanche soldiers had set up housekeeping. She would find a tent. All she had to do was to keep on walking downslope, and she'd find someone, or they would find her—

Her head hurt and her heart ached, and she lacked the will for the struggle. She only kept moving out of stubborn self-discipline. It was her job to give warning. No matter how long it took to find someone to warn, and it seemed to take hours, hours, hours, with the snow coming down all the time.

She fell down.

Picked herself up; started on again.

Fell again, almost too weary to care. Stood up once more, and fought her way forward.

Lost track of how many times she fell down, until finally when she fell and stood up and staggered forward it was only to fall down yet again; and after repeating the experiment two or three times Salli realized that she had run into the side of a tent.

It was almost too much.

The side of a tent; but how was she to know where the entrance to it was? And how was she going to get in if she couldn't figure out how to find the tent flap?

At the absolute end of her resources, Salli struck at the side of the tent with pathetically weak and only half-clenched fists, screaming angry demands that came out scarcely a whisper.

"Let me in. Damn it. It's cold out here. I've got to talk to Colonel Janelric. Wake up, you lot. Why isn't someone on watch? I'm freezing, call Colonel Janelric."

There was no response.

Why should there be?

She was alone in a snowstorm at the foot of Mount Corabey: and the tent was probably a warming tent, in place for tomorrow but deserted tonight.

She was going to have to find a tent with people in it.

She pushed herself away from the side of the tent, sobbing through clenched teeth in frustration; then the side of the tent opened up, a brilliant light from inside of the tent blinded her, people came rushing out toward her and grabbed her and hurried her back into the warmth and the lights inside the tent.

It was the mess tent, warm and heavy of atmosphere with cooking and the constant seething of great vats of hot soup. Hot tea. Hot cocoa. Hot everything. Salli felt herself falling across a bench, and knew a moment's panic as hands on all sides stripped away at her clothing; but it was just cold-injury management, there was nothing to worry about, hadn't she run this drill herself more than once?

Take off the gloves. Take off the boots. Strip down the outer garments, and check the blood pressure, layer the warm clothing back on if vital signs are good enough, and never stop warming those hands and feet. Salli surrendered to the flurry of activity because she realized she had no chance to get anyone's attention until they were satisfied that she was stable.

Her brain seemed to start working once again as she got warm.

"Colonel Janelric," Salli croaked. "Important. Vital. Terrorist activity. Avalanche sheds."

The tidal wave of hands and doses and mugs of tea receded, and left her half-reclining on a bench wrapped in blankets. Her feet were laced into warming boots, her hands gloved in like wise, her head buzzing slightly from the effects of the drugs she'd been given to ward off frostbite. Her nose tingled and her cheeks itched; was she going to have black ears?

She hated black ears.

Woozily, Salli focused on the nearest face: Colonel Janelric.

"I hate it when my ears get nipped," Salli explained. "Ointment. Gets in your hair."

She sounded drunk to herself. She needed tea. The colonel waited while someone helped Salli drink.

"What's your story, soldier?"

What, indeed. The Holy One denied her own divinity. Meeka had lost his sense of proportion; the batchelders meant to create a disaster. There were so many things she had to tell, but only one that made much of a difference here and now.

"Batchelder terrorists, Colonel. Found my brother Meeka. Dosing the avalanche shed foundations with demisca. The shed above the wellhead for sure, I don't know how many others."

And it was snowing.

Meeka had hit her.

Salli didn't have to explain that to Colonel Janelric, who stood up and called out to some troops behind her.

"General alert. All troops. Get up and get out, with soap-syrup, and get me a status report."

Good call, Colonel, Salli wanted to say. Soap-syrup would slow the corrosive effects of the acid, though there was no quick fix for what damage had been done. The colonel already knew that. Salli didn't need to tell her.

"What's going on?"

Salli woke with a start, and whoever was sitting next to where she lay on the mess bench protested the rude awakening.

"Colonel Travers. See what you've done. She's awake."

Solt. Bern Travers crouched down on his heels next to Salli's head; he smelled cold and wet, and faintly of soap-syrup. "I'm sorry, Salli. How are you? Go back to sleep."

Make up your mind.

". . . tapering off," the meteorologist was saying, in the background. There seemed to be quite a number of people in the mess tent, for the late hour—what time was it? "Not very encouraging. Of course if it keeps snowing, there'll be no sunrise, and everyone will just go home."

"And if it stops snowing, Varrick can have her moment of glory, and then everyone will go home. So long as we can keep people off the upper slopes, we should be able to make it work. And if the slab breaks lower, it won't run that far: the slope's too flat, after all."

Colonel Janelric. Closer, Solt was muttering to Bern.

"How's it going, Colonel?"

"No panic. That's my watchword, no panic, we can start evacuation as soon as we can get anyone to move, but nobody's moving till after sunrise. Has anyone talked to the teacher?"

Why should anyone bother Varrick with this? Salli wondered. Varrick had enough on her mind. What good would it do to upset her? She would need all of the energy she could muster to face the sunrise sermon, the single most important address of her career to date.

Solt didn't share that with Bern.

Solt simply said "I don't think Colonel Janelric sees a point to it, sir."

Quite right of Janelric.

Salli yawned, then winced as the gesture pulled at a sore muscle in her cheek.

Everything under control.

Back to sleep.

Eleven

"Hsst," Salli heard, too close to her ear for comfort. "Salli. Time to get up. Come on, we should get upslope."

Reluctantly, she opened her eyes to a near-empty mess tent. It was still warm and fragrant with the steam of all sorts of hot beverages, but there was next to nobody there—except for her, and her team, and Bern Travers, who was trying to wake her up.

What?

Groggy and still bone-weary, Salli sat up and drank from the mug that Bern offered her. Sweet kelp tea. She could feel the stimulant it contained run through her almost as she drank. "Bern, Solt, guys. What's happening?"

Techam came into her field of vision with her boots; she had to get dressed, she had fallen asleep with the warming boots on. Morrissey was here as well, in uniform, avalanche guns all 'round—except for her, of course. It didn't bear thinking on. Salli dressed herself, people talking all the while.

"All of the upper avalanche sheds have been compromised," Morrissey said, getting the worst out first. "The lower course was spared, probably because you surprised the batchelders before they were finished and ran them off."

That was tactfully spoken, "the batchelders," and not "your brother."

"Yes, while you were sleeping, the rest of us have been working, Salli," Bern taunted her. Gently. "But sunrise is in less than half an hour. People are beginning make a crowd; come on, we don't want to miss this."

One way or the other.

She was sore from head to foot, and her body didn't seem to want to respond to the commands of her brain; but with help from Morrissey and Bern Salli stumbled out of the warming tent. The cold air helped clear the last of the drug-induced cobwebs from Salli's mind; and by the time she reached a good vantage point she was walking almost normally.

Sunrise due in less than half an hour, Bern said.

The snow had stopped falling—just an hour ago, someone had told her—and Creation was glorious with it. Mount Corabey herself shone ethereally beautiful, her pristine gown of freshly fallen ice-blue satin cascading in exquisite folds from the crest of her shoulders to the hem of her garment in the caldera.

Once the snow had stopped the sky cleared.

The stars were as brilliant as stars could be between moonset and sunrise in the mountains, where there was little reflected atmospheric light to diminish their impact. Looking up into the night sky with wonder, Salli tried to imagine how beautiful the stars would be to people who were seeing them for what amounted to the first time—away from the city for perhaps the first time in their lives. Such a wonder in and of itself, was this not a species of Awakening?

Then she lowered her eyes to the caldera of Corabey, to watch the crowd gather. They'd found a good observation point, upslope to the shrine shed on their left, downslope to the caldera on their right. Salli could see the shrine shed clearly, less than fifty meters away.

With the field glasses she could see even more clearly, so she could see that someone had swept the shrine shed clear of the snow that had fallen overnight. Someone had been with the Holy One since Salli had left, obviously. Salli wondered what Varrick had done for a water jug in her absence.

The crowd that packed the standing-room and the apron in front of the prayer bell's shrine shed fell silent, suddenly. Salli lifted her glasses.

The Holy One.

Varrick stepped out of the shadow of the snowcapped roof of the shrine shed in a cloak of white furs, dignity befitting an Index Teacher in winter. Walking out to the edge of the shrine shed's foundation, Varrick stood in front of the prayer bell, and looked out over the heads of all of the people that were there.

Salli's heart relaxed within her bosom just to see Varrick's familiar figure. There was no room for emotional conflict within her breast, not with Varrick in the world—

But there was someone with her.

Varrick's face, seen through the glasses Salli used, was drawn and tense. Unhappy. There were people with her. Who were those people—where had they come from—

Batchelders.

The curtain at the back of the sleeping-platform atop the furnace, in the cave behind the shrine shed. Fluttering in the air currents, but it hadn't been just from the air currents inside the cave proper—there had to be a passageway there. Behind. Hadn't she seen Varrick dismiss one of her batchelders down that tunnel, this summer gone by?

Why hadn't she remembered that, and sent someone to see Varrick was safe?

The sky was lightening moment by moment. Turning her body to the east, watching the notch in the mountains at far Lunedin Pass, Varrick waited, along with everybody else, waited for the sun to rise like the Awakening and strike the crystal chalice of Mount Corabey's snow-covered slopes with a white light as cold and pure and brilliant as the wellspring of Creation itself.

The caldera was solid with pilgrims come to hear Varrick's Teaching, and every head turned toward the Lunedin Pass in the east.

One of the batchelders with Varrick unlimbered the prayer bell's great mallet-beam from its immobilizing swing, and began to tap the side of the prayer bell gently.

Bern shifted uneasily beside her.

"Salli. Is that who I think it is?"

Yes, it was.

It was her brother, Meeka.

But what harm could he do, ringing the prayer bell?

Varrick's face had lost all of its care, all of its worry. She lifted her arms toward the Lunedin Pass, and the eager waiting tension of her body was as if she was on the very edge of bursting into flame herself. The prayer bell chimed gently, its undertone sinking down beneath the level of conscious thought to buoy the excitement level in the crowd. All eyes were on the Holy One, and her eyes were on the Lunedin Pass, and when the first brilliant coal of the everlasting fire of life crept clear of the horizon Varrick cried out—so loud, so clear, that she could surely be heard halfway across the caldera, even without any technological means of amplification.

"Behold, she rises!"

And the song in response, very soft, very reverent for such a crowd. *Behold, she rises, like the sun. Oh, Holy One. May we also rise.*

No technological means of amplification were used, because an echo was potentially dangerous under the circumstances. And crowd noise could be potentially dangerous in an avalanche zone as well, but this crowd would only be speaking responses, and its voice would not be sufficiently well synchronized to create a sound wave of dangerous intensity.

Salli began to relax.

The sun seemed to rise quickly, on the horizon—an optical illusion, but an effective one. The golden light caught the peaked hood of Mount Corabey and ignited, blue-brilliant as white phosphorus, as clean and bright and sharp as the glittering facet of a diamond; and the light ran down the slopes of the mountain, covering Corabey with transcendent glory, deeper and deeper into the many folds of Corabey's garment as the sun cleared the eastern pass.

Varrick stood in front of the shrine shed, and the shrine shed's roof shadowed the prayer bell, but somehow—through some trick of the light—the rising sun set Varrick's white furs on fire, reflecting its splendor as if from a mirror.

The crowd fell back by a fraction in involuntary response, and some people knelt. *Oh, Holy One, let us rise to Awakening, and praise the glory of Creation forever.*

The prayer bell fell silent; and Varrick started to speak. "Listen to me, children, I bring you Teaching, and the proper purpose of Teaching is to bring enlightenment. The sun rises today as it has forever, as it will continue to rise forever, and who can look upon Mount Corabey and doubt that Creation awakens every morning, for those who have opened their eyes to see?"

It was Varrick's voice, but the holy brilliance that reflected from the white-fur cloak against Varrick's face made seeing her actual person impossible. Salli had an idea.

"Receive this in Teaching, first, that Creation is holy, and the world itself Awake. Only we sleep. Wake up now, children, wake up."

The crowd's recited response didn't distract Salli. She knew this Teaching already. *Creation is holy, and the world itself Awake.* Salli was more interested in getting a closer look at the phenomenon involving Varrick's cloak.

Lifting her glasses, Salli tried to focus on Varrick's face; but somehow her aim was off. She'd thought she was looking at Varrick, but she saw only the blindingly bright snowfield instead; and the sharp flash of light through the glasses' lenses had Salli seeing spots in front of her eyes.

Well.

That hadn't helped.

"I have said that Creation is holy, and the world itself awake." Varrick's voice sounded a little peculiar to Salli: the caldera's acoustics were affected by the snowpack, unquestionably. And by the presence of so many people.

The sound of Varrick's voice seemed to be coming from a distance, in some sense.

Or not so much Varrick's voice as simply *a* voice, clear and calm, speaking from the heart of a presence that burned in the light of the midwinter sun. "Now I say that Creation does not act with intent. Creation is, children, it does not 'do.' The only causality under the sun is the natural result of natural causes, and what does this mean?"

Salli rested her eyes on the darkness of the shrine shed's shadowed interior. How it could be dark beneath that roof, while Varrick in front of the shrine shed was spectacularly backlit by the reflection off the snow above and behind it, Salli did not know; she'd worry about it later. The dark spots were swimming in front of her eyes, but she thought she saw people moving into the shrine shed.

"Beloved, this means that events in the real world can only caution us with their causes. If the fish die, do we look to the water, or to our prayers? If grain rots on the stalk, do we look to the weather or to the church?"

Someone moving in the shrine shed, the batchelders. What were they doing? Something with the mallet that was used to strike the bell, to make it sound. If she thought about it she could remember a dimly glimpsed view of the striking-mallet's furniture, the great twisted ropes that cradled the mallet-beam, wrapped over and over above the supporting crosspiece. Rather a lot of rope.

"No, children, Creation is the natural world, and its messages are in its own tongue. Natural events have natural causes, and natural lessons. Nothing more. Nothing else. No message from God beyond that which is written already within the text of Creation, which lies open to be read by any and all."

The batchelders had lowered the mallet-beam. That was what they had been doing. It was a lot lower than it had been. Meeka—her brother—swung the hammer at the bell, gently, as if to check the point of impact. The bell spoke quietly: but its voice, its voice had dropped into the subflooring.

The rest of the batchelders vanished into the mountain, fled into the cave behind the shrine shed. Varrick didn't seem to have noticed, and her voice kept the crowd still and focused on her.

"This then is also the Teaching I have for you. Children, there are no judgments from God in the events of the world. There are no more teachings in such events than that of the natural chain of events."

The crowd. Hundreds upon hundreds, perhaps thousands of people. Gathered at the foot of Mount Corabey the morning after a heavy snowfall that had fallen on a layer of powder that overlay in turn a thick, hard crust of glassy ice. And the voice of the bell, with the mallet-beam adjusted to impact toward the bottom of the bell rather than at mid-height, was as deep as damnation, and there was a resonance chamber beneath that bell besides.

Meeka swung the mallet-beam more forcefully this time—warming up, perhaps, or building the reverberation upon itself for maximum power. Salli couldn't look. She dropped her field glasses and took half a step backwards. What was she to do?

The bell spoke again, and the snow broke suddenly across the peaked roof of the shrine shed. It was all too obvious. Salli stood paralyzed with dread, straining for a sign from her team. Couldn't they see what was going to happen? Why didn't they move? Why didn't they take action?

But beneath her anguished, silent reproaches Salli knew. They couldn't know. They couldn't guess. And she, she didn't have time to explain it. If anything was to be done to prevent a catastrophe, a disaster, the mass destruction of all of these people—she had to do it.

Varrick was Holy, whether Orthodox or Wayfarer, and Meeka was her brother. But that was personal, and nothing to do with the crowd who had come to hear Varrick's Teaching.

An avalanche soldier's duty was to protect civilian life and property; and she had to do something.

Reaching out to where Morrissey stood beside her, Salli grabbed Morrissey's avalanche gun.

"Better get down." There was no time to explain. Was it her imagination, or had the surface of the snow upon which they stood started to vibrate in sympathy with the bell as it was hammered, again, and again? "We're going to have backblast."

She couldn't shoot her brother. She couldn't shoot Meeka. There was an echo chamber beneath the prayer bell, and it functioned like a reservoir to feed the ever-louder voice of the prayer bell. It wasn't a prayer bell. It was an avalanche bell. The Holy People hadn't made them to call people to prayer, but to make the mountains safe to return for prayer.

She had to stop the resonance of the bell, and the only way she could do that before it was too late—was by destroying it.

"Salli, have you gone out of your mind? You'll kill the teacher—"

Morrissey and Solt rushed at her, tried to wrestle the gun away. Salli held on grimly, not listening. She had ears only for the sound of the bell as it deepened and broadened, rolled and echoed and increased. If she brought down the shed on top of the bell it would kill the people there without assuring that the vibration of the bell could cease. She had to kill the bell, and the bell was holy, and killing the bell would take Meeka's life— and Varrick's as well.

Varrick was the Holy One.

"Do what she says, get down!" It was Bern's voice, shouting. Some of the people in the caldera had begun to turn toward them where they stood, pointing, wondering, a panic about to happen. "She says get down, get down!"

Half-crouched in the snow, Salli propped the gun up and rested the tube on her right knee. She took aim. Varrick had turned toward her, arms raised in an embrace of sorts.

Was it benediction?

Or a plea for her life?

It didn't matter. Varrick was the Holy One.

But Meeka continued to strike the bell, the resonance continued to build, and there were hundreds upon hundreds of people assembled at the foot of Mount Corabey. Dead in an avalanche run-out zone that covered most of the caldera.

"Clear in back!" Salli called, but it came out a scream. Every second she delayed increased the danger. If she didn't act now, Varrick would die, and it would all be for nothing—

The bell spoke, ferocious, terrible, full of power.

Salli fired the gun, her teeth clenched against her own scream of anguish, half-blinded by tears.

Rocket-propelled grenade, and it would at least crack the bell, and that would stop the bell's reverberation.

And kill anyone within twenty meters, shred them with molten shrapnel and scatter the charred fragments in a red-and-black rain that would stain that white snowfield forever.

Oh, Holy One.

If only it worked—

She heard the backblast kick up the snow behind her.

The grenade tore into the shrine shed, and the roar of the explosion as the grenade hit the bell drowned out any reverberation that might have survived the impact. The sonic shock punched deep into the echo well beneath the bell and bounced back up again, blowing the roof of the shrine shed into the sky like a geyser made of wooden chips and rope shreds and not water.

The bell itself collapsed, and toppled, the gaping wound torn in its side smoking with heat in the cold air. Where the bell touched wood the wood began to burn, and all around the shrine shed there was scrap and sawdust, red meat and black cinders, and no trace of the people who had been there at all.

The report of the impact hit Corabey's slope like a fist, and the fracture in the snowpack ran west and east like a spark down a piece of detonation cord.

But low on the slope.

Low on the slope, where the angle was all wrong for an avalanche, where the avalanche sheds had not been sabotaged, where the snow slab would move—but not very far—

So the people would be safe.

But Varrick was dead.

Varrick and Meeka, and Meeka was her brother even if he'd turned terrorist, and Varrick—and Varrick—and Varrick was the Holy One, *the* Holy One, the Holy One for all ages, in Salli's heart even if nowhere else—

The stress fracture ran across the snow upslope from Salli, cracking like a whip. The people below in the caldera were screaming in shock, in fear, in horror; what did they have to scream about?

Salli threw the avalanche gun from her and collapsed on her face in the snow, heartsick in agony.

She had murdered her Holy One.

She was an avalanche soldier, and she had done her duty; but she had killed her Holy One.

The avalanche took her where she lay, and wrapped her around and around and around in thick white suffocating snow, and rushed her downslope to the foot of Mount Corabey.

She was an avalanche soldier, and she had done her duty, but she had killed her brother. And the Holy One.

The snow stopped running with rib-crushing suddenness and force.

Salli came to a halt.

There was no air. Her mouth and nose were packed with snow. She had been screaming in her anguish, and now the snow was solid as a rock in her open mouth, and unforgiving.

It was all right.

She had killed her brother. She had murdered the Holy One. She had seen no other way to save the people; but now that it was over she could die.

Oh, Holy One, Salli prayed, as the last of her oxygen ran out.

I could not have done this thing at all had I not known it was my best and only choice. And for that reason alone I can hope to be forgiven, if I've made a mistake.

* * *

It was pleasantly warm, and the bed that cradled her was wonderfully shaped to the contours of her body. She could smell the slightly burnt fragrance of clean linen sheeting that had been dried at high heat, which was a little puzzling—only hospitals did that; it was expensive. Tended to wear out bed linen.

There was a conversation going on somewhere.

"—demonstration in front of Pellassa Synod Hall today, peacefully dispersed after Speaker Harish addressed the crowd. She promised a full and open-hearted reexamination of Synod's previous assessment as to Teacher Varrick's status as genuinely holy."

Female voice, little emotion, careful enunciation. It was a newspaper, Salli decided. How could that be? Newspapers couldn't talk. Oh. Well. The news-transmit, then.

"Though the access to Mount Corabey remains strictly controlled in the aftermath of last week's startling and tragic events, several credible witnesses have registered with Synod their willingness to testify to miracles performed by acts of grace subsequent to Teacher Varrick's disappearance and presumed death."

Presumed death? No "presumed" about it. Salli could still see it, every fraction of time sliced and frozen and preserved in matrix, unchanging forever and ever. Again and again she could see it, Meeka swinging the mallet-beam with all his might, Varrick standing so close to the bell looking at her. Varrick, the Holy One, *her* Holy One for all the ages, and Salli had fired the gun.

She'd had no choice.

It had been Varrick—Varrick, and Meeka—or betray the trust that the people and state of Shadene had put in her when they had made her an avalanche soldier.

Lights out.

Salli slept.

*   *   *

It got cooler, but the coolness was welcome, she'd been hot. Sweating. Every bone in her body ached, and she wished everybody within earshot straight to hell in the irritation that came from pain. There were too many people here, whoever they were.

"—can come off in two days' time, the pins will be set by then. We'll have a closer look at the rest of the leg later. It's still attached, despite Travers's best efforts . . ."

What nonsense. Whatever it was. Salli was glad someone interrupted this insane babbling.

" 'Xten-circs, Doctor. That slab was *moving*. I'm lucky I caught her ankle in the first place."

She knew the voice and relaxed gratefully in its presence. She wasn't at all sure what it had just said: but she knew the voice.

"Damn it, Travers, you stay in bed till I say you can get up, or you leave my hospital. Right now. I swear before God I won't be disobeyed in this flagrant manner. It's bad for discipline, but more than that, it's bad for your bones, or don't you care? That avalanche tried to make a corkscrew out of you, too, or have you forgotten that already?"

Salli could tell the doctor that it would do no good to swear at Bern. It never did. For it to matter Bern would have to be sensitive, vulnerable to what other people thought of him. And he wasn't. Except with her, of course.

She was serenely confident that the doctor would be sorry he'd raised his voice to Bern Travers.

Secure and happy in that knowledge, Salli went back to sleep.

This time it was an agitated sound of footsteps that awakened her, bright lights so suddenly switched on that it was painful even with her eyes closed—as they had been for however long. Hurried whispers, hoarse undertones.

Batchelders. The last of them, thank God. No reverence for anybody in that, it's plain terrorism, no excuse. Wait till the newscasts get their hands on this, hunted jackals converge on hospital for revenge on unconscious patient in serious traumatic injury ward. Serve them right.

Meeka had joined Varrick's batchelders, and Salli hadn't realized then what that would mean. She didn't think Varrick had realized that the self-nominated batchelders would develop their own elitist interpretation of her Teaching, and take it upon themselves to make things happen according to their warped misinterpretations of her message.

But how could Varrick *not* have known?

She was the Holy One.

And had denied it, claiming instead to be merely Teacher, Holy One in the limited Wayfarer sense. Not the true Orthodox sense.

But the Wayfarers were closer to the truth than the Orthodox. It could not be otherwise: the Wayfarers were the Holy People, the people who had been the Holy People.

The bell proved it.

Not a ritual object to call people to prayer. A practical mundane civil-defense object, rather, designed to trigger any avalanches that were waiting to happen after a snowfall, so that it would be safe to return to the summer booths. Didn't the scripture say that the bell called the faithful to prayers?

The bell told the people when it was safe to return to the mountainside. One note to propagate slab avalanches; another note to propagate a powder avalanche; and once the bell had rung it was safe to return to the normal life of the camp. That was all it meant.

There had been argument for years between Pilgrim

and Wayfarer, each of them claiming to be the true indigenous people of the holy land of Shadene. The party who could claim true native status had a clear moral claim on the land itself: and now she knew it was the Wayfarers who were the true heirs to the Holy Land. Wayfarers, descended from the hills into the coastal plains over the centuries as the weather grew colder and the mountains became inhospitable.

Consistent and continued occupation over time with incremental adjustment to changes in the climate—not the discontinuity of the failure of one population well before the arrival of another.

It seemed so obvious to Salli now.

Maybe it had been obvious all along.

Maybe the only reason the Pilgrim Orthodox church had even pretended otherwise had been in order to engineer a nostalgic return to a homeland that was not—and had never been—their home.

Certainly this evidence that the Wayfarers were native Shadene, and not fisher-folk come lately after all, would strengthen the autonomy of the Shadene Secular Authority. Perhaps there would be a redistribution of power—perhaps so much as an end to the Pilgrim enclaves, dissolution of the pilgrim police, integration of Pilgrims into Wayfarer life as petitioners, not absentee landlords threatening the existence of the squatters who had found their way onto one's property while one was away.

On the other hand Varrick's Teaching was that the age of miracles had passed . . .

Salli turned her face away from the light and fell back into deep restful unconsciousness.

In the fullness of time Salli's conscious mind surfaced from its long dreaming to engage with the waking world once more, and when that happened someone was sitting at her bedside, reading.

> *Thou art my Holy One for ever and always, and to look into your eyes is to know Awakening.*

Salli recognized the passage.

It was the Dream Lover theology; and the Dream Lover was the theology she loved best among the Wayfarer heterodox, the Shadene churches. Dream Lover was almost not a theology: there were unceasing objections to it down through the ages, the sensuality of its imagery and the frankness of its language a constant challenge to people whose experiences of the divine had been rather more prosaic than ecstatic.

> *Now that my soul has once seen thee, now that I have once more awakened to your presence, my desire is to be with you forever.*

Salli favored the Dream Lover because no other Teaching came close to expressing the passion of her soul's desire to awaken into the living presence of the Creator. Courting couples in Shadene had adapted it from the beginning as a theologically acceptable—and therefore unobjectionable—framework for making love.

> *Do not deny me the blessings of the presence of the living God in my life. It is you that my heart desires, and no other.*

Blinking her eyes open, squinting in the bright lights of the hospital room, Salli strove to make sense of who she was and where she was. It was Bern reading, though; she knew that before she opened her eyes. She knew his smell. It was like apples and dry grass, with a handful of kelp thrown in.

I will hold your body sacred as the crucible of Creation as we know it. I will hold your heart sacred as my greatest treasure. Your wisdom will be guidance and gladness to me.

That didn't explain why Bern was sitting with her in hospital reading Dream Lover theology. As much as Salli wanted to confront Bern with all the questions she had in her mind, this was intriguing enough for her to be willing to let him play his scene out.

Come and share my life, and you will be sacred always in my eyes. Your children will call you blessed and your grandchildren will call you wise but I will only ever call you Holy.

"Bern," Salli said, staring at the ceiling as the room gradually came into focus. "Bern, is that you?"

Because though on one level she knew it was, on other levels of awareness Salli was utterly confused by his choice of text and the peculiar tone of voice in which he was reading it. Or reciting it.

She heard the scraping sound of a portable chair being dragged across the uncarpeted floor, and Bern's face leaned into her field of vision. It was rather alarming, Bern's face, because it was marked and livid with recently closed cuts and scrapes, and the creases beneath his eyes that gave him such an owlish look had quadrupled. And turned purple, from apparent lack of sleep.

"Salli. Glad you could make it. Marry me?"

Not only that, but Bern's face seemed huge, as close as it was. Salli reminded herself—her mind befuddled, and her thinking unclear—that though she and Bern might be the same general size, and they were, Bern was a man. His skeletal structure was noticeably heavier, and his head was big in proportion to his shoulders compared to hers. She could suggest that to him; Bern, your head's too big. Yes. That would be worth a few hours' excitement.

"What are you talking about?"

Big head, small hands, small feet. There was persistent folklore that correlated the shape and size of a man's feet with portions of the anatomy rarely seen uncovered except within the conjugal or parental relationship.

" 'Thou art to me as the Holy One,' " Bern quoted, and put his left hand across her right ankle. " 'Holy art thou to me, and to be without you is to be without joy.' " Putting his right hand on her left shoulder. Salli lifted her head to let him pass his hand behind her neck, amused. Raising her head was more effort than she had expected.

She knew what he was trying to do.

She also knew it wouldn't work.

" 'Put therefore and trust to me the comfort and health of your heart and your body, that I may have benefit from your wisdom; and I in turn will pledge to thee the very best that heart and mind can offer in our life to come.' "

He sounded so serious.

And he couldn't possibly be serious.

"You haven't said yes yet, but we can pass over that." Bern leaned back in his chair again, lifting his hand from her ankle. He tried to remove his hand from her shoulder, as well, but Salli wasn't inclined to let him. That long wrist felt just fine right where it was. "Well, now that we're married, what would you like for your gift-of-intent?"

"I'll get you a book of proper ritual, young man." If he was going to be ridiculous, she was going to be ridiculous. "That isn't the way it's done. You're supposed to put your hand under the sole of my foot. And your other hand on top of my head. Don't they teach you anything in Folkways class?"

Wait. Bern taught Folkways class. Now he shook his finger at her in an admonitory manner. "That's what I would do if I was a Pilgrim. But I have more respect for you than that, Salli. If you're Shadene, you don't dare to presume to decide where a woman will choose to walk— even away. Still less do you presume to claim infringement rights on the autonomy of her mind. I won't marry you Orthodox, Salli, it's Shadene or nothing."

This was too surreal to be believed. "Why should I marry you either way, Bern? I mean. Really."

Unfortunately, he seemed to take the question seriously. "Well. For one, I've done you a number of important favors lately. Your job. Your pension. You're getting a state livelihood, by the way, for saving all those people from the avalanche, at great personal cost."

A state livelihood. A nice solid state-funded annuity, and free lodging in quarters at Hilbrane, and several honorary posts and exemptions. "But I killed Varrick, Bern."

"In the line of duty. You're the only person who could have killed Varrick and not started a civil war. And anyway, they have yet to find any trace of the body; you'd think they would have come up with something by now."

All right. So far so good. "You were explaining why I should marry you."

Nor had he gotten tired of the absurd game yet, apparently. Bern hitched his chair a little closer with his free hand and continued.

"Then there is the fact that I may have saved your life. Twice. Once in the riot at Synod House. Once in the avalanche, you were pretty deep under, but fortunately for both of us one of my feet was sticking out."

And Bern, who had claustrophobia, Bern who could not abide small enclosed spaces, Bern had voluntarily dived into the ice-coffin of an avalanche in a desperate attempt to save her life. Salli had to admit that that was genuinely impressive. But still not a good reason to marry.

"Still. Varrick's dead, even without a body. And her Teaching, won't that die with her?" Varrick had had the true charisma. Her Teaching was her Teaching; but without Varrick to put it forward—

"Setting aside for a moment the little issue of 'dead.' I know and you know that she must be, but there will always be rumors. And the healings have already started. Corabey's sequestered, so they're all happening just south of the Linshaw Pass."

And the last thing Varrick would have wanted was to become a miracle-worker, she who had tried so hard to free the thinking of Creation from interpreting a natural disaster as divine guidance. "She'd hate that, Bern. And you haven't convinced me."

Bern shrugged, but only at the first part of Salli's remark. "Maybe not. Synod has ruled to reexamine the doctrinal correctness of a unilateral ban on technologies that leave the ground. As for the rest of it—"

Shifting his seat, now, so that he sat on the edge of the bed, where he could put his free hand to her cheek. "It's true I have a limited number of reasons to offer. I love you, Salli Rangarold Pilgrimsdaughter. And I earnestly beseech you to consent to share your life with me. Because I love you. And I can offer you comfort and security. Companionship. Children, not as though you couldn't get them elsewhere. My heart's true love, and my soul's desiring. Marry me because I love you, Salli, and make me a happy man."

Well.

In that case.

"I'll have to think about it, Bern." Because it was no good to marry a man just because he loved you. If she didn't love Bern she had no business marrying him. She was fond enough of him by now . . . she had certainly grown accustomed to his constant presence in the background, and was grateful for all his help and moral support. But that wasn't enough to marry on.

Was it?

What had Varrick told her?

And did she in fact love Bern Travers, and simply hadn't noticed it before?

"I'll have to give the matter. Serious thought." She was beginning to sink again beneath the warm blanket of whatever drugs the doctors had her on. Her body didn't hurt much. By that token Salli knew that she was doped up but good. "Let's put off. Naming the children. Till I can give you a decent answer."

She heard the shifting of sheet and blanket as Bern moved, sensed by the heat of Bern's body that he was leaning over her. There was the scrape of his moustache against her forehead; *forehead*? thought Salli, with a moment's indignation.

We've just been married, at least Wayfarer-wise, and this forehead business is the best that you can do?

"Promise me I'll be the first to know, Salli."

Fair enough.

Salli slipped her dream-ship loose of its moorings and set sail.

She dreamed a dream of Corabey again, Mount Corabey in the person of a Shadene maiden dancing in the tall green waves of the alpine prairie grass of the caldera. Barefoot, and weaving cloud patterns with the bells in her hands, her face obscured by the long brown hair that flew in every direction as she tossed her head in the rhythm of her dance. There was no music; there was just her dance.

And her skirts were jeweled with prairie flowers, her blouse rich with silver streams of snowmelt garlanded around her neck and shoulders. The figure was indistinct at first, but as Salli fell more deeply asleep—as her breathing slowed and deepened, as her heart beat more slowly and restfully, as the careworn consciousness within her brain closed down to rest—the dancing figure slowed.

The halo of dark hair around her face fell into a loose cloud around her shoulders, with the occasional wisp of a lock wetted black with sweat and plastered along her cheek or throat.

Her skirts stopped moving, falling once again into decorous folds that concealed her feet and melded seamlessly with the prairie in the caldera. Corabey drew her shawl of mist and roses up around her shoulders and sat down, working her transformation from maiden to mountain as she went.

Settling in to her place, looking out across the caldera toward the Linshaw Pass.

Now for the first time Salli saw her face, the face of the goddess, the face of Mount Corabey, the maiden from the time of the Holy People.

Varrick.

Corabey had been Varrick all along, or Varrick had been Corabey—

It didn't matter.

Varrick was in her dream. Varrick had come to her; and Varrick smiled. There was no trace of anger or resentment. Varrick smiled, full of transcendent love; and the sun of Awakening rose within Varrick's bosom to show that she was the Holy One, alive or dead.

In her sleep Salli smiled back; and then began to snore.

We hope you've enjoyed this Avon Eos book. As part of our mission to give readers the best science fiction and fantasy being written today, the following pages contain a glimpse into the fascinating worlds of a select group of Avon Eos authors.

In the following pages experience the latest in cutting-edge sf from Eric S. Nylund, Maureen F. McHugh, and Susan R. Matthews, and experience the wondrous fantasy realms of Martha Wells, Andre Norton, Dave Duncan, and Raymond E. Feist.

SIGNAL TO NOISE

Eric S. Nylund

Jack watched his office walls sputter malfunctioning mathematical symbols and release a flock of passenger pigeons; his nose was tickled with the odor of eucalyptus. Inside, the air rippled with synthetic pleasure and the taste of vanilla.

"I need to get in there," he told the government agent who blocked the doorway.

"No admittance," the agent said, "until we've completed our investigation on the break-in."

Puzzles, illegalities, and dilemmas stuck to Jack—from which he then, usually, extracted himself. That gave him the dual reputation of a troubleshooter and a troublemaker. But the only thing he was dead sure about today was the "troublemaking and sticking" part of that assessment.

The agent stepped in front of Jack, obscuring what the others were doing in there. National Security Office agents: goons with big guns bulging under their bulletproof suits. And no arguing with them.

Today's trouble was the stuff you saw coming, but couldn't do a thing about. Like standing in front of a tidal wave.

Jack hoped his office *had* been broken into, that this wasn't an NSO fishing trip. There were secrets in the bubble circuitry of his office that had to stay hidden.

Things that could make his troubles multiply.

"I'll wait until you're done then."

The agent glanced at his notepad and a face materialized: Jack's with his sandy hair pulled into a ponytail and his hazel eyes bloodshot. "You have an immediate interview with Mr. DeMitri. Bell Communications Center, sublevel three."

Jack's stomach curdled. "Interview" was a polite word that meant they'd use invasive probes and mnemonic shadows to pry open his mind. Jack had worked with DeMitri and the NSO before. He knew all their nasty tricks.

"Thanks," Jack lied, turned from the illusions in his office, and walked down the hallway.

From the fourth floor of the mathematics building, he took the arched bridge path that linked to the island's outer seawall. Not the most direct route, but he needed time to figure a way out of this jam.

Cold night air and salt spray whipped around him. Electromagnetic pollution filtered through the hardware in his skull: a hundred conversations on the cell networks, and a patchwork of thermal images from the West-AgCo satellite overhead.

Past the surf and across the San Joaquin Sea, the horizon glowed with fluorescent light. Jack regretted that he'd stepped on other people to get where he was. Maybe that's why trouble always came looking for him. Because he had it coming. Or because he was soft enough to let little things get to him. Like guilt.

Not that there was any other way to escape the mainland. Everyone there competed for lousy jobs and stabbed each other in the back, sometimes literally, to get ahead. He had clawed his way out with an education—then cheated his way into Santa Sierra's Académe of Pure and Applied Sciences.

But it wasn't perfect here, either. There were cutthroat

maneuvers for grants, and Jack had bent the law working both for corporations *and* the government. All of which had helped his financial position, but hadn't improved his conscience.

He had to get tenure so he could relax and pursue his own projects. There had to be more to life than chasing money and grabbing power.

Now those dreams were on hold.

His office had been ransacked, and the NSO had got too curious, too fast, for his liking. Had they been keeping an eye on him all along?

He took the stairs off the seawall and descended into a red-tiled courtyard.

In the center of the square stood Coit Tower. The structure was sixty meters of fluted concrete that had been hoisted off the ocean floor. It had survived the San Francisco quake in the early twenty-first century, then lay underwater for fifty years—yet was still in one piece.

Jack hoped he was as tough.

The whitewashed turret was lit from beneath with halogen light, harsh and brilliant against the night sky. Undeniably real.

Jack preferred the illusions of his office; sometimes reality was too much for him to stomach.

No way out of this interview sprang to mind, and he had stalled as long as he could. The crystal-and-steel geodesic dome of the Bell Communications Center was across the courtyard. Jack marched into the building, took the elevator to sublevel three, and entered the concert amphitheater.

On the stage between gathered velvet curtains, the NSO had set up their bubble.

Normal bubbles simulated reality. Inside, a web of inductive signals and asynchronous quantum imagers tapped the operator's neuralware. It allowed access to a world of data, it teased hunches from your subconscious, and solidified your guesses into theories. They made you think faster. Maybe think better.

But this wasn't a normal bubble. And it was never meant to help Jack think. It was designed for tricks.

THE DEATH OF THE NECROMANCER

Martha Wells

She was in the old wing of the house now. The long hall became a bridge over cold silent rooms thirty feet down and the heavy stone walls were covered by tapestry or thin veneers of exotic wood instead of lathe and plaster. There were banners and weapons from long-ago wars, still stained with rust and blood, and ancient family portraits dark with the accumulation of years of smoke and dust. Other halls branched off, some leading to even older sections of the house, others to odd little cul-de-sacs lit by windows with an unexpected view of the street or the surrounding buildings. Music and voices from the ballroom grew further and further away, as if she was at the bottom of a great cavern, hearing echoes from the living surface.

She chose the third staircase she passed, knowing the servants would still be busy toward the front of the house. She caught up her skirts—black gauze with dull gold striped over black satin and ideal for melding into shadows—and quietly ascended. She gained the third floor without trouble but going up to the fourth passed a footman on his way down. He stepped to the wall to let her have the railing, his head bowed in respect and an effort not to see who she was, ghosting about Mondollot House and obviously on her way to an indiscreet meeting. He would remember her later, but there was no help for it.

The hall at the landing was high and narrower than the others, barely ten feet across. There were more twists and turns to find her way through, stairways that only went up half a floor, and dead ends, but she had committed a map of the house to memory in preparation for this and so far it seemed accurate.

Madeline found the door she wanted and carefully tested the handle. It was unlocked. She frowned. One of Nicholas Valiarde's rules was that if one was handed good fortune one should first stop to ask the price, because there usually was a price. She eased the door open, saw the room beyond lit only by reflected moonlight from undraped windows. With a cautious glance up and down the corridor, she pushed it open enough to see the whole room. Book-filled cases, chimney piece of carved marble with a caryatid-supported mantle, tapestry-back chairs, pier glasses, and old sideboard heavy with family plate. A deal table supporting a metal strongbox. *Now we'll see*, she thought. She took a candle from the holder on the nearest table, lit it from the gas sconce in the hall, then slipped inside and closed the door behind her.

The undraped windows worried her. This side of the house faced Ducal Court Street and anyone below could see the room was occupied. Madeline hoped none of the Duchess's more alert servants stepped outside for a pipe or a breath of air and happened to look up. She went to the table and upended her reticule next to the solid square shape of the strongbox. Selecting the items she needed out of the litter of scent vials, jewelry she had decided not to wear, and a faded string of Aderassi luck-beads, she set aside snippers of chicory and thistle, a toadstone, and a paper screw containing salt.

Their sorcerer-advisor had said that the ward that protected Mondollot House from intrusion was an old and

powerful one. Destroying it would take much effort and
be a waste of a good spell. Circumventing it temporarily
would be easier and far less likely to attract notice, since
wards were invisible to anyone except a sorcerer using
gascoign powder in his eyes or the new Aether-Glasses
invented by the Parscian wizard Negretti. The toadstone
itself held the necessary spell, dormant and harmless,
and in its current state invisible to the familiar who
guarded the main doors. The salt sprinkled on it would
act as a catalyst and the special properties of the herbs
would fuel it. Once all were placed in the influence of
the ward's key object, the ward would withdraw to the
very top of the house. When the potency of the salt wore
off, it would simply slip back into place, probably before
their night's work had been discovered. Madeline took
her lock picks out of their silken case and turned to the
strongbox.

There was no lock. She felt the scratches on the hasp
and knew there had been a lock here recently, a heavy
one, but it was nowhere to be seen. *Damn. I have a not-
so-good feeling about this.* She lifted the flat metal lid.

Inside should be the object that tied the incorporeal
ward to the corporeal bulk of Mondollot House. Careful
spying and a few bribes had led them to expect not a
stone as was more common, but a ceramic object, perhaps a ball, of great delicacy and age.

On a velvet cushion in the bottom of the strongbox
were the crushed remnants of something once delicate
and beautiful as well as powerful, nothing left now but
fine white powder and fragments of cerulean blue. Madeline gave vent to an unladylike curse and slammed
the lid down. *Some bastard's been here before us.*

SCENT OF MAGIC

Andre Norton

That scent which made Willadene's flesh prickle was strong. But for a moment she had to blink to adjust her sight to the very dim light within the shop. The lamp which always burned all night at the other end of the room was the only glimmer here now, except for the sliver of daylight stretching out from the half-open door.

Willadene's sandaled foot nearly nudged a huddled shape on the floor—Halwice? Her hands flew to her lips, but she did not utter that scream which filled her throat. Why, she could not tell, but that it was necessary to be quiet now was like an order laid upon her.

Her eyes were drawn beyond that huddled body to a chair which did not belong in the shop at all but had been pulled from the inner room. In that sat the Herb-mistress, unmoving and silent. Dead—?

Willadene's hands were shaking, but somehow she pulled herself around that other body on the floor toward where one of the strong lamps, used when one was mixing powders, sat. Luckily the strike light was also there, and after two attempts she managed to set spark to the wick.

With the lamp still in hands which quivered, the girl swung around to face that silent presence in the chair. Eyes stared back at her, demanding eyes. No, Halwice lived but something held her in thrall and helpless.

There were herbs which could do that in forbidden mixture, but Halwice never dealt with such.

Those eyes—Willadene somehow found a voice which was only a whisper.

"What—?" she began.

The eyes were urgent as if sight could write a message on the very air between them. They moved—from the girl to the half-open door and then back with an urgency Willadene knew she must answer. But how—Did Halwice want her to summon help?

"Can you"—she was reaching now for the only solution she could think of—"answer? Close your eyes once—"

Instantly the lids dropped and then rose again. Willadene drew a deep breath, almost of relief. By so much, then, she knew they could still communicate.

"Do I go for Doctor Raymonda?" He was the nearest of the medical practitioners who depended upon Halwice for their drugs.

The eyelids snapped down, arose, and fell again.

"No?" Willadene tried to hold the lamp steady. She had near forgotten the body on the floor.

She stared so intensely as if she could force the answer she needed out of the Herbmistress. Now she noted that the other's gaze had swept beyond her and was on the floor. Once more the silent woman blinked twice with almost the authority of an order. Willadene made a guess.

"Close the door?" That quick, single affirmative blink was her answer. She carefully edged about the body to do just that. Halwice did not want help from outside— but what evil had happened here? And was the silent form on the floor responsible for the Herbmistress's present plight?

With the door shut some instinct made the girl also, one-handedly as she held the lamp high, slide the bolt bar across it, turning again to find Halwice's gaze fierce and intent on her. The Herbmistress blinked. Yes, she had been right—Halwice wanted no one else here.

Then that gaze turned floorward, as far as nature would let the eyes move, to fasten on the body. Willadene carefully set the lamp down beside the inert stranger and then knelt.

It was a man lying facedown. His clothing was traveler's leather and wool as if he were just in from some traders' caravan. Halwice dealt often with traders, spices, and strange roots; even crushed clays of one sort or another arrived regularly here. But what had happened—?

Willadene's years of shifting iron pots and pans and dealing with Jacoba's oversize aids to cooking had made her stronger than her small, thin body looked. She was able to roll the stranger over.

Under her hand his flesh was cool, and she could see no wound or hurt. It was as if he had been struck down instantly by one of those weird powers which were a part of stories told to children.

THE GILDED CHAIN

A Tale of the King's Blades

Dave Duncan

Durendal closed the heavy door silently and went to stand beside Prime, carefully not looking at the other chair.

"You sent for us, Grand Master?" Harvest's voice warbled slightly, although he was rigid as a pike, staring straight at the bookshelves.

"I did, Prime. His Majesty has need of a Blade. Are you ready to serve?"

Harvest spoke at last, almost inaudibly. "I am ready, Grand Master."

Soon Durendal would be saying those words. And who would be sitting in the second chair?

Who was there now? He had not looked. The edge of his eye hinted it was seeing a youngish man, too young to be the King himself.

"My lord," Grand Master said, "I have the honor to present Prime Candidate Harvest, who will serve you as your Blade."

As the two young men turned to him, the anonymous noble drawled, "The other one looks much more impressive. Do I have a choice?"

"You do not!" barked Grand Master, color pouring into his craggy face. "The King himself takes whoever is Prime."

"Oh, so sorry! Didn't mean to twist your dewlaps,

Grand Master." He smiled vacuously. He was a weedy, soft-faced man in his early twenties, a courtier to the core, resplendent in crimson and vermilion silks trimmed with fur and gold chain. If the white cloak was truly ermine, it must be worth a fortune. His fairish beard came to a needle point and his mustache was a work of art. A fop. Who?

"Prime, this is the Marquis of Nutting, your future ward."

"Ward?" The Marquis sniggered. "You make me sound like a debutante, Grand Master. *Ward* indeed!"

Harvest bowed, his face ashen as he contemplated a lifetime guarding ... whom? Not the King himself, not his heir, not a prince of the blood, not an ambassador traveling in exotic lands, not an important landowner out on the marches, not a senior minister, nor even—at worst—the head of one of the great conjuring orders. Here was no ward worth dying for, just a court dandy, a parasite. Trash.

Seniors spent more time studying politics than anything else except fencing. Wasn't the Marquis of Nutting the brother of the Countess Mornicade, the King's latest mistress? If so, then six months ago he had been the Honorable Tab Nillway, a younger son of a penniless baronet, and his only claim to importance was that he had been expelled from the same womb as one of the greatest beauties of the age. No report reaching Ironhall had ever hinted that he might have talent or ability.

"I am deeply honored to be assigned to your lordship," Harvest said hoarsely, but the spirits did not strike him dead for perjury.

Grand Master's displeasure was now explained. One of his precious charges was being thrown away to no purpose. Nutting was not important enough to have enemies, even at court. No man of honor would lower his standards enough to call out an upstart pimp—certainly not one who had a Blade prepared to die for him. But Grand Master had no choice. The King's will was paramount.

"We shall hold the binding tomorrow midnight, Prime," the old man snapped. "Make the arrangements, Second."

"Yes, Grand Master."

"Tomorrow?" protested the Marquis querulously. "There's a ball at court tomorrow. Can't we just run through the rigmarole quickly now and be done with it?"

Grand Master's face was already dangerously inflamed, and that remark made the veins swell even more. "Not unless you wish to kill a man, my lord. You have to learn your part in the ritual. Both you and Prime must be purified by ritual and fasting."

Nutting curled his lip. "Fasting? How barbaric!"

"Binding is a major conjuration. You will be in some danger yourself."

If the plan was to frighten the court parasite into withdrawing, it failed miserably. He merely muttered, "Oh, I'm sure you exaggerate."

Grand Master gave the two candidates a curt nod of dismissal. They bowed in unison and left.

KRONDOR

The Betrayal

Raymond E. Feist

The fire crackled.

Owyn Belefote sat alone in the night before the flames, wallowing in his personal misery. The youngest son of the Baron of Timons, he was a long way from home and wishing he was even farther away. His youthful features were set in a portrait of dejection.

The night was cold and the food scant, especially after having just left the abundance of his aunt's home in Yabon City. He had been hosted by relatives ignorant of his falling-out with his father, people who had reacquainted him over a week's visit with what he had forgotten about his home life: the companionship of brothers and sisters, the warmth of a night spent before the fire, conversation with his mother, and even the arguments with his father.

"Father," Owyn muttered. It had been less than two years since the young man had defied his father and made his way to Stardock, the island of magicians located in the southern reaches of the Kingdom. His father had forbidden him his choice, to study magic, demanding Owyn should at least become a cleric of one of the more socially acceptable orders of priests. After all, they did magic as well, his father had insisted.

Owyn sighed and gathered his cloak around him. He had been so certain he would someday return home to visit his family, revealing himself as a great magician, perhaps a confidant of the legendary Pug, who had created the Academy at Stardock. Instead he found himself ill suited for the study required. He also had no love for the burgeoning politics of the place, with factions of students rallying around this teacher or that, attempting to turn the study of magic into another religion. He now knew he was, at best, a mediocre magician and would never amount to more, and no matter how much he wished to study magic, he lacked sufficient talent.

After slightly more than one year of study, Owyn had left Stardock, conceding to himself that he had made a mistake. Admitting such to his father would prove a far more daunting task—which was why he had decided to visit family in the distant province of Yabon before mustering the courage to return to the East and confront his sire.

A rustle in the bushes caused Owyn to clutch a heavy wooden staff and jump to his feet. He had little skill with weapons, having neglected that portion of his education as a child, but had developed enough skill with his quarterstaff to defend himself.

"Who's there?" he demanded.

From out of the gloom came a voice, saying, "Hello, the camp. We're coming in."

Owyn relaxed slightly, as bandits would be unlikely to warn him they were coming. Also, he was obviously not worth attacking, as he looked little more than a ragged beggar these days. Still, it never hurt to be wary.

Two figures appeared out of the gloom, one roughly Owyn's height, the other a head taller. Both were covered in heavy cloaks, the smaller of the two limping obviously.

The limping man looked over his shoulder, as if being followed, then asked, "Who are you?"

Owyn said, "Me? Who are you?"

The smaller man pulled back his hood, and said, "Locklear, I'm a squire to Prince Arutha."

Owyn nodded, "Sir, I'm Owyn, son of Baron Belefote."

"From Timons, yes, I know who your father is," said Locklear, squatting before the fire, opening his hands to warm them. He glanced up at Owyn. "You're a long way from home, aren't you?"

"I was visiting my aunt in Yabon," said the blond youth. "I'm now on my way home."

"Long journey," said the muffled figure.

"I'll work my way down to Krondor, then see if I can travel with a caravan or someone else to Salador. From there I'll catch a boat to Timons."

"Well, we could do worse than stick together until we reach LaMut," said Locklear, sitting down heavily on the ground. His cloak fell open, and Owyn saw blood on the young man's clothing.

"You're hurt," he said.

"Just a bit," admitted Locklear.

"What happened?"

"We were jumped a few miles north of here," said Locklear.

Owyn started rummaging through his travel bag. "I have something in here for wounds," he said. "Strip off your tunic."

Locklear removed his cloak and tunic, while Owyn took bandages and powder from his bag. "My aunt insisted I take this just in case. I thought it an old lady's foolishness, but apparently it wasn't."

Locklear endured the boy's ministrations as he washed the wound, obviously a sword cut to the ribs, and winced when the powder was sprinkled upon it.

Then as he bandaged the squire's ribs, Owyn said, "Your friend doesn't talk much, does he?"

"I am not his friend," answered Gorath. He held out his manacles for inspection. "I am his prisoner."

MISSION CHILD

Maureen F. McHugh

"Listen," Aslak said, touching my arm.

I didn't hear it at first, then I did. It was a skimmer.

It was far away. Skimmers didn't land at night. They didn't even come at night. It had come to my message, I guessed.

Aslak got up and we ran out to the edge of the field behind the schoolhouse. Dogs started barking.

Finally we saw lights from the skimmer, strange green and red stars. They moved against the sky as if they had been shaken loose.

The lights came toward us for a long time. They got bigger and brighter, more than any star. It seemed as if they stopped, but the lights kept getting brighter. I finally decided that they were coming straight toward us.

Then we could see the skimmer in its own lights.

I shouted, and Aslak shouted, too, but the skimmer didn't seem to hear us. But then it turned and slowly curved around, the sound of it going farther away and then just hanging in the air. It got to where it had been before and came back. This time it came even lower and it dropped red lights. One. Two. Three.

Then a third time it came around and I wondered what it would do now. But this time it landed, the sound of it so loud that I could feel as well as hear it. It was a different skimmer than the one we always saw. It was bigger, with a belly like it was pregnant. It was white and red. It settled easily on the snow. Its engines, pointed down, melted snow underneath them.

And then it sat. Lights blinked. The red lights on the ground flickered. The dogs barked.

The door opened and a man called out to watch something but I didn't understand. My English is pretty good, one of the best in school, but I couldn't understand him.

Finally a man jumped down, and then two more men and two women.

I couldn't understand what anyone was saying in English. They asked me questions, but I just kept shaking my head. I was tired and now, finally, I wanted to cry.

"You called us. Did you call us?" one man said over and over until I understood.

I nodded.

"How?"

"Wanji give me . . . in my head . . ." I had no idea how to explain. I pointed to my ear. "Ayudesh is, is bad."

"Ask if he will die," Aslak said.

"Um, the teacher," I said, "um, it is bad?"

The woman nodded. She said something, but I didn't understand. "Smoke," she said. "Do you understand? Smoke?"

"Smoke," I said. "Yes." To Aslak I said, "He had a lot of smoke in him."

Aslak shook his head.

The men went to the skimmer and came back with a litter. They put it next to Ayudesh and lifted him on, but then they stood up and nearly fell, trying to carry him. They tried to walk, but I couldn't stand watching, so I took the handles from the man by Ayudesh's feet, and Aslak, nodding, took the ones at the head. We carried Ayudesh to the skimmer.

We walked right up to the door of the skimmer, and I could look in. It was big inside. Hollow. It was dark in the back. I had thought it would be all lights inside and I was disappointed. There were things hanging on the walls, but mostly it was empty. One of the offworld men jumped up into the skimmer, and then he was not clumsy at all. He pulled the teacher and the litter into the back of the skimmer.

One of the men brought us something hot and bitter and sweet to drink. The drink was in blue plastic cups, the same color as the jackets that they all wore except for one man whose jacket was red with blue writing. Pretty things. I made myself drink mine. Anything this black and bitter must have been medicine. Aslak just held his.

"Where is everyone else?" the red-jacket man asked slowly.

"Dead," I said.

"Everyone?" he said.

"Yes," I said.

AVALANCHE SOLDIER

Susan R. Matthews

It lacked several minutes yet before actual sunbreak, early as the sun rose in the summer. Salli eased her shoulder into a braced position against the papery bark of the highpalm tree that sheltered her and tapped the focus on the field glasses that she wore, frowning down in concentration at the small Wayfarer's camp below. They would have to come out of the dormitory to reach the washhouse, and they'd have to do it soon. Morning prayers was one of the things that heterodox and orthodox—Wayfarer and Pilgrims—had in common, and no faithful child of Revelation would think of opening his mouth to praise the Awakening with the taint of sleep still upon him.

The door to the long low sleeping house swung open. Salli tensed. *Come on, Meeka,* she whispered to herself, her breath so still it didn't so much as stir the layered mat of fallen palm fronds on which she lay. *I know you're in there. Come out. I have things I want to say to you.*

The camp below was an artifact from olden days, two hundred years old by the thatching of the steeply sloped roofs with their overhanging eaves. Not a Pilgrim camp by any means. No, this was a Shadene camp built by the interlopers that had occupied the holy land in the years after the Pilgrims had fled—centuries ago. A leftover, an anachronism, part of the heritage of Shadene and its long history of welcoming Pilgrims from all over the world to the Revelation Mountains, where the Awakening had begun. Where heterodoxy flourished, and had stolen Meeka away from her. And before the Awakened One she had a thing or two to tell him about that—just as soon as she could find him by himself, and get him away from these people . . .

Older people first. Three men and two women, heading off in different directions. The men's washhouse was little more than an open shed, though there wasn't anything for her to see from her vantage point halfway up the slope to the hillcrest. The women's washhouse was more fully enclosed. That was where the hotsprings would be, then.

Where was Meeka?

The sun would clear the east ridge within moments, and yet no man of Meeka's size or shape had left the sleeping house. In fact the younger people were hurrying out to wash, now, and there were no adults whatever between old folks and the young, so what was going on here?

Then even as Salli realized that she knew the answer, she heard the little friction of fabric moving against fabric behind her. Felt rather than heard the footfall in the heavy mat of fallen palm fronds that cushioned her prone body like a feather-bed. Well, of course there weren't any of the camp's men there below. They were out here already, on the hillside.

Looking for her.

"Good morning Pilgrim, and it's a beautiful morning. Even if it is only a Dream."

She heard the voice behind her: careful and wary. But a little amused. Yes, they had her, no question about it. She could have kicked the cushioning greenfall into a flurry in frustration. But she was at the disadvantage; she had to be circumspect.

"How much more beautiful the Day we Wake." And

what did she have to worry about, really? Nothing. These were Wayfarers, true, or if they weren't she was very much mistaken. But there were rules of civility. She had meant to get Meeka by himself, without betraying her presence; but she had every right to come here on the errand that had brought her. "Say, I imagine you're wondering what this is all about."

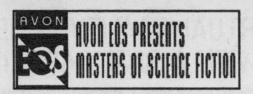

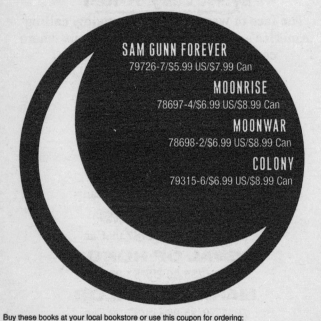

Ray Bradbury

SOMETHING WICKED THIS WAY COMES
72940-7/$6.50 US/$8.50 Can

QUICKER THAN THE EYE
78959-0/$5.99 US/$7.99 Can

DRIVING BLIND
78960-4/$6.50 US/$8.50 Can

A MEDICINE FOR MELANCHOLY
AND OTHER STORIES
73086-3/$10.00 US/$14.50 Can

I SING THE BODY ELECTRIC!
AND OTHER STORIES
78962-0/$10.00 US/$14.50 Can